Mic Drop

Passionate Beats trilogy, book 3

Arell Rivers

MIC DROP

Book 3 in the **Passionate Beats** trilogy in the Untamed Coaster series

ARELL RIVERS

Copyright ©2025 Tarnished Halo Publishing LLC

Published by Tarnished Halo Publishing LLC

2025 Edition

ISBN (digital): 979-8-9869346-7-9

ISBN (print): 979-8-9869346-8-6

Arell's Team

Editing:

Plot Coach Theresa Leigh, The FairyPlot-Mother

Developmental Editor Trenda Lundin, It's Your Story Content Editing

Editor Nancy Smay, Evident Ink

Proofreading: Roxanne Bluin

Cover design: Dar Albert, Wicked Smart Designs

Dedication

For Taylor Delong.
You put the Passionate into these Beats.

The Final Turn: Will "I Do" Twist into "Goodbye"?

Bennett Hardy, Battling for Forever

I can't live without Jenna, no matter how hard I try to return to my old life. Driven by emotion that defies reason, I track her down, desperate to understand what went wrong. When I find her, she's a shadow of herself, her heart fractured by a discovery that left her in freefall. I won't let her face this alone. I'm here, offering not just love, but a sanctuary.

Yet it feels like the whole world is closing in, poised to spin us both out of control.

Jenna Westfield, Surrendering to Grief

Bennett is my anchor, the one who saw through my walls and made me believe in a love I never thought possible. But grief is a ravenous monster, devouring everything in its path. I'm pushing him away, testing the limits of his devotion, even as I crumble inside. Then, the past explodes, a twisted echo of old betrayals threatening to destroy the fragile peace we've built.

I'm trapped in a helix of despair, the final loop threatening to shatter us forever.

Chapter 1

Bennett

The water pulses from above and I scrub harder. Why did Jenna get all defensive about using Untamed Coaster's PR team? I was only being helpful.

My right leg bends as I wash it, careful not to aggravate the muscle pull. Again. How dare Lissa lie like a two-bit bimbo on national TV? There was no baby—not from me, anyway. Considering my background, no little Bennetts will roam this earth. Ever.

Those stupid hosts, Logan and Francis, suck. They certainly didn't do any research into Lissa's story. I duck under the shower head and let the water wash over my body.

It's not refreshing.

I close my eyelids and hear echoes of sexy moans from Jenna. The way she loved exploring Graceland on our private tour. The freaking plaid miniskirt that drove me insane. The gray in her eyes that promised *more*.

I remember sharing showers with her. How adventurous she is, willing to try anything. Glancing down, my cock remembers too. My back takes the spray.

She'll forgive me for offering professional support for her clinics. She has to.

Only a stubborn woman, like the one I've fallen in love with, would refuse the help of a professional PR team. Fine, she built At Your Service PT from scratch, but she's facing a shitstorm outside her wheelhouse. No single person can bend the media to their will by sheer force alone. Damn woman has more control issues than Elvis's manager Colonel Tom Parker is rumored to have had.

Water sluices over my body, and this time I lean into the pseudo-massage. Jenna will either accept my help or not, but somehow she'll come out on top. I hope she sees the wisdom in working with UC's team, though, who have experience in handling media backlash. As for Lissa, she needs to disappear.

Looking back, I can still hear Lissa repeating the mantra that she was saving herself for marriage. As high school juniors, we'd kiss and I'd feel her up, only to be shot down by her "convictions." I was in my gawky stage, not yet full-grown or filled out. Certainly not hitting the gym like I do now. Pre-contacts, glasses were my constant companion. In addition to her. A gorgeous blonde bombshell attached to my hip. I thought things couldn't get any better.

Until Curtiss swooped in and invited her to the *senior* prom, before I even was able to ask her to the junior prom. Some best friend he turned out to be.

Dumped and alone, I'd barely had time to process their betrayal before Dad died. Leaving me twenty-four-seven with the woman who birthed only me—and to her everlasting despair, not my twin.

Twisting, I turn off the shower. Enough with this memory lane. I need to correct Lissa's bullshit and get my life back on track. Featuring Jenna. She better not still be annoyed with me. The fact she hasn't joined me in here isn't a good sign.

I grab a white towel and wrap it around my waist. With any luck, Jenna'll help me dry off. At the mirror, I examine my scruff, which can wait another day to be trimmed. With a quick finger combing of my hair and a pat to the UC pendant Jenna gave me all those years ago, I open the bathroom door ready to grovel for her forgiveness. Making her come a couple of times should do the trick.

My jaw drops when I see her packing her suitcase. "Where are you going?"

"Home! I never should have left!"

Jenna grabs a handful of clothes and tosses them into her suitcase.

My breathing accelerates. She can't be leaving over my suggestion she use UC's PR team. I shake my head to clear the wild notion. I position myself in front of her luggage.

"You have to believe me. If Lissa was pregnant, it wasn't by me. We never had sex."

She walks toward the bathroom, muttering, "Believe what you will."

Believe what I will? What am I supposed to believe? She's packing her things as if she's leaving me. No, not only me, but the entire tour. This makes no sense. First Mom, then Lissa. I can't survive another woman leaving me in the dust.

I stomp behind her and rephrase. "What are you doing?"

In response, she cradles her cosmetics and toiletries against her chest but doesn't say anything. I rake my fingers through my wet hair. "Talk to me. What's happening?"

She adjusts the bottles. "You're always so distracting."

Is that a good thing or not? "This isn't making any sense."

"The world doesn't!" She skirts around me and dumps everything into her suitcase.

Given her crappy packing job, she can't be going far. No one in their right mind would pack a suitcase for a trip like this. My hands raise to the air. "Stop!"

My growl garners the first appropriate response all day—she stands still. I temper my tone. "Talk to me. Tell me what's going on."

Her chest rises and falls in a staccato rhythm. "Nothing." She pauses a beat. "Everything." A longer beat. "All of it."

As she reaches for more shirts, I place my hand on top of her forearm and lower my voice. "Jenna."

Beneath me, she goes stiff. "I won't let you waylay me again."

Again? "What are you talking about?"

"I can't." She yanks her arm free of my grip, dumping the rest of her clothes into the luggage.

All I can do is watch her leave me. I couldn't stop Dad from leaving us way back when, and that was permanent. I couldn't stop Lissa from throwing me over for Curtiss. I have to keep the woman I love with me now.

"I need you with me."

"Bennett, I have to go home." She tries to zip up one side of the suitcase, but it doesn't close.

"I don't understand what's going on." My hands land on my hips.

"I have to leave," she cries. Throwing her entire body onto the top of the suitcase, she struggles to zip it shut.

"You don't have to go. I already told you—and the world, might I add—I didn't get Lissa pregnant." I pull her up and grab her by the shoulders. "After the way I was raised, do you think I want to have kids?"

Glazed eyes widen. "I suppose not."

Too late, I realize my mistake. "Except with you. I could relax my stance if you were the mother."

"Don't bother."

What the fuck are we doing? I let her go. "Stop this. What is going on?"

Her head snaps toward me. "It's too much."

I wasn't too much for her an hour ago. She was defending me on the talk show. Spitting mad at Lissa. She's loved being on tour with me, hasn't she? "I'm the same man I was this morning when you woke up. Naked, in my arms, might I remind you."

She shudders. "A mistake."

"What do you mean? We're not a mistake. I love you. You love me."

"You make me forget everyone and everything I hold dear." She bends and puts the suitcase on the floor, telescoping the handle.

"This makes no sense. We can do anything together."

"Not this."

"Talk to me. What happened?"

"Your mother," she begins. "No. My mother—"

I wait for her to continue, but she doesn't. "What about them?"

Her eyes fill with tears. From pain? Frustration? Oh God, is she sorry she slept with me?

"Ma tried to call several times, but you distracted me."

Her defeated tone, more than her words, bore into my soul. "I never told you not to talk with her." She can't be dumping me. Like Lissa did for a better prospect. Has another band member been sniffing around Jenna under my nose? Tris has been rather chummy.

"I let you." A big fat tear rolls down her cheek.

I refuse to believe she's faking her tears. Her orgasms were real too. "Are you leaving me?"

She sobs. "I have no choice."

I pull her into my body. "You do. You always have options." I kiss her crown, my hands skimming up and down her arms. Hers remain at her sides, while my torso gets wet from her tears. "Talk to me."

"I have to return home. Ma needs me."

Her *mother* needs her? She's literally leaving me high and dry on the tour to run back to her mother? "She's a grown-ass woman—"

Eyes rounded, Jenna steps backward. "I need to be there for her." Dragging her luggage behind her, she marches toward the door.

"What am I missing?"

Tears streaming down her face, she repeats her nonsensical words. "Nothing. Everything." She inhales. "It doesn't matter."

"It matters to me."

She sets her chin. "I can't. I just can't." Her chin trembles.

None of this makes any sense, least of which is the fact yet another woman—whom I told I loved—is leaving me. The callus around my heart, which had all but disappeared when I let Jenna into it, reforms twice as hard. Two can play this game. My hands form fists.

"Fine! Go home to your mommy!"

She sucks in her breath and scurries out of my hotel room.

Out of my life.

It's as if she took all the air in the room with her. My legs fail me, and I sink onto the bed, my hand stroking my right thigh. Where she had massaged and iced and kissed. I pull away from the offending area.

How could I allow another woman to worm her way into my heart? Didn't I learn my lesson ages ago from Lissa? From Mom before her?

My chest expands in shallow, rapid breaths.

Well, I don't need her. I've done pretty damn fine without any encumbrances for the past decade, so why was I thinking of adding one now?

I bet if I go down to the bar and snap my fingers, I'd have three women vying for my attention. I could bring all three to this room and make them scream in pleasure. Jenna doesn't own my sexual prowess.

I should do just that. Prove to her how little she means to me. The guys in the band will be happy to see me back in action, as they always hooked up without any trouble when I was on the scene. They'll probably throw a party to welcome me back into the groupie set.

Why would Jenna want to go back to her mother anyway? What was she spouting about me preventing her from paying attention to what mattered? I never told her not to keep up with her mother—or friends, for that matter.

I stand and dress for the bar, taking special time to get my hair styled. My tight shirt is guaranteed to turn heads. I bet my extra scruff will add another chick to my arm.

Placing rings on all my fingers, an errant idea takes hold. What if Jenna's there? With Tris? I shove a bracelet over my wrist. No. Fucking. Way. She better not be there, with Tris or any of my bandmates. Not if they want to keep their heads attached to their bodies.

Anger coursing through my bloodstream, I finish and check out my reflection in the hotel's full-length mirror. I'm ready to prowl.

Four long strides take me toward the door. On the fifth, my groin muscle emits a protest so loud I'm sure the rest of the hotel could hear it. I crumple down, massaging the injured thigh. Perhaps I should listen to my body and stay in tonight? If Jenna's there, Luke will text me.

Right?

My eyes slam shut. I need to take care of this injury on my own, since my physical therapist has gone AWOL. I know the drill. Who needs her anyway?

I'm better off without her.

Chapter 2

Jenna

Not even bothering to open the app for a car service, I race out of Bennett's hotel room and slip into the waiting elevator. For once, I'm all alone, which gives my tears permission to stream down my cheeks unchecked.

Ma matters more than any other living human being on earth. She needs me more than the clinics, more than his groin pull, more than any fallout from Lissa's television interview.

And he was pretty high-handed about my using UC's PR team to mop up the mess Michelle's making at my clinics. He doesn't seem to think I'm capable of handling it without help. My tears slow. I'll show him.

I need to get home to Ma and set her up with the best doctors. Not that Kara and her husband aren't fabulous, but they're not oncology specialists. Who Ma needs. I stifle a sob.

The elevator doors open and I cross the lobby. I'll purchase a plane ticket while I'm on my way to the airport, price be damned.

"Jenna!"

Who could that be? Probably some reporter looking for a new

angle on the fake story they're promoting. I don't want to talk with anyone. I keep moving.

Footsteps resound over the foyer's granite floor. "Jenna, wait!" A masculine hand grabs my forearm. "What's going on? Are you all right?"

I spin on my heel. Tristan's concerned brown eyes spear into me. Emotions beg to be let out, and I'm unable to stem the tide. The next thing I know, the new keyboardist's arms envelop me while I cry it out. He whispers comforting platitudes into my ear while stroking my back. The fact it's Darren's replacement giving me comfort and not UC's lead singer just makes me cry more.

When I'm somewhat under control, I remove myself from his person. "Sorry, Tristan." For ruining his shirt, for being a drama queen, for using him when I really want to be with Bennett. "I need to leave."

His more than five-o'clock shadow becomes convex as he sucks in his cheeks. "I can't let you leave like this."

I straighten. "I'm fine. I can handle this."

"What's wrong?"

Ma's dying from cancer. Bile rises and all I manage to say is, "Airport."

"If that's what you want, I'll get you a taxi." Numbly, I nod and follow him rolling my suitcase to the sidewalk. The bellhop flags me down a taxi and puts my luggage into the trunk. Tristan bends down and looks deep into my eyes. "Whatever Bennett did, I'm sure running away isn't the answer."

I don't have the strength to set him straight. Given that I probably won't see him again, ever, I don't bother to correct his wrong assumption. "I just need to get home."

He opens the door and I slip into the seat. "You have my number, right?"

I don't have a clue. To get rid of him, I lift my cell.

"Use it." The door closes.

The only conversation I have with the driver is to confirm I'm going to the airport. While he drives, I purchase my one-way ticket to NYC, adding a five grand helicopter ride out to the Hamptons. At this point, my only concern is getting home to Ma as soon as possible. I'll deal with the credit card bills later. Looking up, I tell the driver my airline and bang my head against the headrest. I'll be home in a few short hours.

Keeping my nose down, I manage to get on the plane without anyone noticing *the* Black Widow in their midst. For once I don't quibble about the extra cost, simply pay for Wi-Fi and spend the entire flight researching the best doctors and protocols and medicines for pancreatic cancer. None of the results give a positive prognosis. Ma will have to prove the entire field wrong.

At the airport, I retrieve my suitcase and follow the signs to the helicopter to the Hamptons. Exhausted, I arrive at the waiting room when my stomach protests its lack of food. If Bennett were here, he'd ask a roadie to get us some burgers.

Burgers.

Now all I want is a burger.

A café is located across the way, which I bet sells what I want. Seeing as there's another hour before the helicopter departs, I cross the lounge area and place my order. My mouth opens to take my first bite when someone approaches me.

"Excuse me, are you traveling to the Hamptons?"

My long-awaited burger is lowered to the plate. "Yes. Ticket counter's over there." I point across the way.

The woman carrying a couple of leather suitcases nods. "Thank you. Are you excited to return home?"

What an odd question. I give a cryptic response, "It's where I need to be."

The traveler says, "Seems like your clinics would agree."

What now?

I don't have time to reply when she adds, "I mean, having black widow spiders all over would be a deterrent to anyone needing physical therapy, isn't it? Have you completed your mission and broken up the best band on the planet? Untamed Coaster was getting everything together, but you had to go and ruin it for all of us, didn't you?"

Leaping to my feet, I abandon my meal and leave the awful woman standing next to my table. The café, which I thought was quaint with its seating open to the terminal, has nowhere to hide, not even a bathroom.

Add hungry to my long list of wretched emotions.

Thankfully, the woman with the leather bags doesn't come to the helicopter check in. With dragging feet, I wait to board, keeping as low of a profile as possible. Luck is with me because no one else approaches, and the ride is uneventful.

Yet another taxi takes me to Ma's dark house. I'm sure she's asleep—after all, only rock stars and vampires are up at this time of the morning. Leaving my luggage, I proceed to the back and lift up the birdhouse to retrieve the spare key.

Within minutes, I'm inside and absorbing the familiar smells. Now that I'm here, I find myself unable to rush to her side and get the details. Instead, I stop in front of framed photos from when I was a child on the beach. Building a snowman. Walking across the stage getting my physical therapy degree. Kara's in other pictures, including the ones from her own graduation from med school plus her wedding and with her kids. Everyone's smiling and happy. It's too soon for Ma to leave us.

Too soon.

Armed with wonderful childhood memories—and forbidding any more recent ones to surface—I decide to check in on Ma. Make sure she's sleeping. Then I can pass out in the guest bedroom.

I walk to the far end of the house, to her bedroom. The door's ajar, so I push it open to get a better look into the room. Ma appears comfortable, her face relaxed in sleep. Maybe a quick kiss on the forehead won't be amiss? I'm confident I won't wake her, since she's always slept like the dead.

My feet pause at the awful turn of phrase.

I continue my silent trip to her bed. I whisper, "I'm here, Ma. Sleep well." I kiss her, my heart thudding in my chest.

Gray eyes open and she struggles backward on the bed.

In the most soothing voice I can muster, I say, "Sorry, Ma, didn't mean to wake you."

"Jenna?"

"It's me."

Her hand lands on top of the left side of her chest. "You nearly gave me a heart attack!"

Does she also have heart issues? Kara didn't mention any. "Should I get you cardiac medicine?"

She frowns. "What? No."

I exhale the breath fighting to come out. "Good."

Ma rearranges the pillows behind her and pats the side of the bed. "Aren't you having the time of your life with Bennett, touring with Untamed Coaster?"

How much should I share with her? She's probably not too caught up with gossip, considering her health issues. "It was fun. It's over. I'm here now."

"What do you mean 'it's over'? Last I heard, you were visiting Graceland."

My stomach falls to the floor. "I did." I clear my throat. "It was amazing to see where Elvis lived." And died. I don't add that part.

"Sweet Pea. Why are you here?"

Anyone who thinks I'm stubborn has yet to meet my mother. "It's late. Well, it's early and I'm tired. Why don't we talk in the morning?" When I can deal with the truth about what Kara told me without bursting into tears.

For once, I catch a break as Ma yawns. "You're probably right. I am tired, and I'll need all my wits about me to get to the bottom of this."

I can't stop myself and give her another kiss. Then I help her become horizontal and tuck her in, like she used to do for me. "Sleep well, Ma. I'll see you in the morning." Only a few hours away.

Slinking out of her bedroom, I wheel my suitcase to the guest bedroom. I'm able to do nothing more than take off my shoes before passing out.

The smell of bacon tickles my nose. I toss my head on the pillow, but the delightful odor lingers. One eye opens, then the other. I inhale, letting the delicious smell waft over me. Ma's making breakfast.

I sit up, taking stock of the clothes that have been on my body for the past what? Twenty-nine hours? More? Better take a shower before devouring the promised breakfast of champions.

Opening my suitcase, another odor bombards me. Like I'm outside in the woods. Bennett. I stare into my luggage, trying to figure out how his scent took it over. One of his T-shirts smiles up at me. The one I wore to bed after he had it on his body. I rip it out of the luggage and ball it up, ready to toss it into the trash.

And freeze. Despite everything, I still love him. I miss him, and the way he held me tight.

After everything that went down, what must he think of me?

The last words he hurled at me make a repeat performance. "Go home to your mommy!" I never was able to bring myself to utter the words that Kara texted me, so he had no idea how hurtful he was being. Ma needs me more than he does. After all, he has the vaunted PR team that will tear Lissa from limb to limb.

Tucking the T-shirt into a drawer, I gather up the assorted bottles of toiletries, which thankfully didn't break during transit, and enter the bathroom. A half hour later, I emerge a new woman. Now with clean teeth and wearing clean clothes over my showered body, I put on some lip gloss and spritz perfume. There. Ready to fight the demons attacking Ma.

In the kitchen, an enormous breakfast awaits. "Who were you cooking for? The entire army?" I swipe a slice of bacon and crunch on it as I pour some hot water for tea and check out the selections. "Mango Passionfruit?"

"Try it. You'll like it."

I do as I'm told and dunk the bag into my mug. "Since when did you start drinking herbal teas?" No sooner are the words out of my mouth than I know the answer. The doctor had to have told her to switch from coffee to tea.

She sighs. "The doctor suggested it. I actually enjoy this one."

"We need to talk about this."

She dunks her teabag. "Kara?"

"Yeah. But you should've told me, not her. When did you find out?"

She passes me a bowl containing scrambled eggs. A plate of pancakes. Maple syrup. I take each dish from her and add a vast assortment to my plate, considering I didn't eat yesterday.

When she doesn't respond, I try again. "Come on, Ma. How long have you known about the cancer?" I nearly choke, but manage to keep it together.

She points her fork toward me, which had been hovering above her eggs. "I had a suspicion that things were off for a while. I finally went to my regular doctor and he referred me."

I swallow a bite of pancake. No one makes them better. "Which was when?"

"The week before you left with UC."

"Ma. Why didn't you tell me then? I could have stayed home with you. It really wasn't necessary for me to go."

"You were so excited for the tour, there was no way I was going to spoil it for you. I had misgivings about Bennett, as you know. Is he treating you right?"

I shovel the scrambled eggs into my mouth. After washing them down with tea—which is delicious, by the way—I decide to tell her the truth. Maybe my honesty will spur hers?

"Bennett is a nice guy, Ma. He was wonderful, looking after me. He's going through a lot now, though. Have you seen any of the tabloids or entertainment shows?"

She blows on her own tea. "Can't say I have."

I launch into an abbreviated version of Lissa's story about the supposed baby. "Then there's the media calling me 'Black Widow,' saying I'm determined to break up the band."

She shrugs. "Well, all that sounds like total rubbish."

Her unwavering belief in me warms me from the inside. "It is. However, plenty of fans believe the media hype, so the PR team for UC has been in overdrive addressing both prongs."

"I can only imagine." She breaks a piece of bacon and deposits one half on my plate while chewing on the other.

I swallow my eggs. "There's more. Apparently, the clinics have gained a graffiti artist, who spray-paints spiders on the walls and sidewalks. Court's been taking care of them, and we even put out a press release, but they keep returning. We think it's Michelle."

She rolls her eyes. "That girl needs to get a life. What are you going to do about her?"

"I'm not sure yet." I replace my mug on the table. "But that's not the reason I flew home, Ma. Kara told me. What doctors are you seeing? What medicines are you on? When is your surgery?"

"Jenna, I'm in good hands. Kara's taken me to her friends out here who all interned in the City, so it's like I'm going all the way out there for treatment. They've fast-tracked me."

"The cutting-edge doctors are in the City. We both know that."

"The ones I'm seeing here are just fine."

I keep my voice steady and repeat, "So when's your surgery?"

"I'm not having any."

My eyebrows furrow. From my research, surgery is often suggested. "Didn't the doctors recommend it?"

"No, they didn't."

I sit back in my chair. Her words don't compute. "I don't understand. Doctors need to cut the cancer out of your body. You'll need chemo, which doesn't have to be such an awful ordeal anymore. I read an article about—"

Ma places her fork on the table. "No. You don't understand. The cancer's too far gone, Sweet Pea. It's in my lymph nodes and my lungs. They simply can't take all of the affected areas out, so surgery's not an option."

I can't comprehend what she's telling me. "Don't say that. There have been so many advancements in medicine over the past few years. The doctors surely can get it out of you."

"Jenna." I stare at my breakfast plate, the large amount of food sitting like a lump in my stomach. "Look at me."

My gaze meets hers. I'm afraid my eyes are a lot more watery than hers.

"I am following doctor's orders."

I leap to my feet. "Ma! There has to be something you can do." I search the kitchen for what, I don't know. "There's plenty of treatment options I'm sure you haven't considered. I can take you to this specialist in midtown who has had success with patients like you."

"I've been to him."

"Or what about the one I read about on the Upper West Side, who has been experimenting with a combination of Eastern and Western medicines."

"Kara took me there."

"How about a woman on the Upper East Side, who—"

"Jenna, honey, I've seen all I need to see. Kara's taken me to her friends. Everyone says the same thing—that they don't have any alternatives left to try. I'm tired of it all. I want to stay in my house, surrounded by my things and the people I love." Her hand covers mine.

How have I never noticed how frail it seems?

With care, I place mine over hers.

"I can't give up," I admit. "You must not have tried every single possibility out there."

"I have, Sweet Pea."

I don't care what she tells me. I won't stop until I find someone able to make her healthy again. She's not going to end up like my grandmother.

And Darren.
She can't.

Chapter 3

Bennett

I can do this. I've done it thousands of times.

I don ripped jeans, toss a blue T-shirt over my head, and add all my hardware: rings and bracelets. The mirror tells me I look as good as ever. Even my scruff is once again the perfect length. My hands twitch to remove the necklace with the UC pendant on it, but the band promised each other we'd never take them off. Doesn't matter who gave them to us originally. I lower my arms.

Luke meets me in the hallway, craning his neck around me. "Where's Jenna?"

The hazards of keeping to myself all yesterday—the need to tell everyone what's going on since they didn't witness it. In this case, it's a good thing. Wouldn't want them to see the God-awful way things ended between us. My throat tightens.

"Gone." My voice is gruff to my own ears.

"Huh? What do you mean, 'gone'?"

"What I said. Like Elvis, she left the building." I take a couple of strides. "I dumped her." Not exactly, but close enough.

I realize Luke's not at my side and turn around. He's wearing a puzzled expression. "You broke up with her?"

My hands land on my hips. "That's the polite way of putting it."

"Why?"

"Why what? People break up all the time. Lots of different reasons. Money, sex, values. Take your pick." I continue toward the elevators.

"You two seemed like the real deal. She was sticking up for you with the whole Lissa ordeal."

Maybe I should seize on this as an easy out? Sounds better than saying she was homesick. I shake my head. Nah. Not going to lie to cover up her screwball tendencies. Better they come out now than if more time passes.

"She missed her mother. She went home. End of." I stab the call button for the elevator. The doors open and without checking to see if our manager's at my side, I storm inside.

Luke presses the button for the garage, where we're meeting the rest of the band. I stand with my arms crossed, daring him to ask anything further. Utilizing self-preservation skills, he does not.

The door pings at our floor. "I think you should tell the guys."

"On it." I stalk to the waiting limo, and am the last band member to climb in. As soon as my ass hits the leather seat, I'm handed a bottle of beer. After taking a much-needed sip, I announce, "Jenna's gone."

My work colleagues stare at me with varying degrees of surprise. All except 007, who has the biggest smile stretched across his face. "Finally!" He extends his fist toward me to bump, which I force myself to do. "She doesn't belong with UC. Glad you kicked her to the curb."

My lips tick upward. "Thanks man. Sorry to make you all spew the shit defending her in Louisville. Thinking we don't mention it again, and the hype will die down."

Coop shifts in his seat. "We defended her to the world, Bennett, because she was cool. Why did you dump her?"

Thankful he thinks I broke up with her, I reply, "Turns out she was crazy. I didn't see it before, although I should have picked up on it when we went out to celebrate her birthday with her mother. Yesterday, she was crying about missing her mother, so I cut her loose."

Coop's head bobs. "Wow."

Río blurts, "Darren thought the chick was sweet. So did I. I can't believe she turned out to be a psycho." He leans across the bench seat to whack my shoulder. "You'll bounce back. Plenty of other fish in the sea."

"Yeah." I tip my chin toward our drummer. After tonight's show, I'll choose a couple of blondes to take the edge off. Let Jenna stay home with mommy. I'm better off without her.

I chance a look at our new keyboardist, who doesn't look surprised at all by my announcement. Perhaps my assessment of their relationship was spot on? I stare him down and he stares right back. When I can't take it any longer, I snarl, "What's your problem, *Tristan?*"

"Me?" His gaze darts throughout the limo. "She seemed broken up when I helped her into a taxi, that's all."

Like I guessed, she ran to the little prick when she left my room. I pitch forward, fists at the ready, but unable to get proper leverage against *Tristan* in the limo. "How long were you shacking up with her?" Coop places his arm against my chest.

Tristan slinks back against the seat. "I wasn't, dude. I was only an ear."

"Yeah, well, she can use your *ear* anytime she wants. Mine is off limits to her." Coop removes his arm when it becomes clear I won't start a fight in the confines of the limo.

Stepping into the breach, 007 holds up his bottle. "To the Black Widow. May she never darken our threshold again!" A second later, everyone—except Tristan—toasts.

The beer trips down my throat in starts and fits. I manage to swallow and keep it down, which I consider a win. Why doesn't it taste like victory? I sent her packing. Rather, she was packing, and I told her to leave. Same diff.

The limo stops in front of the stadium. I let the rest of the band get out before maneuvering out of the vehicle, aware enough not to do anything to strain my groin muscle. After all, I didn't have any physical therapy today. I can keep it in check all by myself.

The rest of the band is nearing the back entrance when my feet hit the pavement. Unlucky for me, Tristan waits by the door.

"Not going to discuss this with you," I snap.

"Fine by me. Don't talk. Listen. Whatever went down between the two of you devastated her, and I have the wet shirt to prove it. The woman was crying so hard on me, I felt like a human Kleenex."

I ignore the pang in my chest.

I ignore the longing in my heart.

I ignore the yearning in my soul.

Instead, I say, "It's what happens when your crazy is exposed."

I walk around him, toward the band entrance, taking no heed of his murmured, "I don't think she was the crazy one."

By the time I reach the stage, my lead singer mask is more impenetrable than ever. I run through the sound check like the pro I am, interacting with the band as required. All except Tris, who can play his keyboards on the side all night without a mic or spotlight for all I care.

Luke must've taken pity on us, as this has to be the quickest sound check ever. I follow the rest of the band off the stage. "Great job, guys," our manager says. "I made a dinner reservation. Limo should be here in thirty."

We mumble our thanks. While food is the last thing on my mind, I will need fuel to get through the concert tonight. If the prick *Tristan* is there, I'll make sure to sit far away. Maybe put him at another table. With the crew. Or send him out to greet crazy fans.

One of our crew stops moving some stage items as I approach. "Hey, Bennett, Got a minute?"

"Of course, Jeb." I always have time for the crew and roadies, as they keep our show running. "What's up?"

The huge, tatted man pushes his long sleeves up. "I've been

looking everywhere for Jenna. The exercises she gave me have been great. I did as she told me and shared them with the rest of the crew, and we're all feeling better."

Bully for them. "That's good."

When I don't elaborate, he presses, "I was hoping to ask her if she could do a group session with all of us. That way, she can correct our form if someone's doing something wrong."

I rub the back of my neck. "Listen, I'm happy she was helping you, but she went back home." Not a lie.

He persists, "When will she be back?"

My control snaps. "She's not coming back. I sent her packing, all right?" I stalk in the opposite direction, fighting an urge to punch a wall. Jeb. Or *Tristan*. He would do. Why do I have to keep telling this story over and over? I open my mouth to yell that she's gone, but shut it just as fast. I'm the cool, collected, cocky lead singer of Untamed Coaster, not the hot-headed band member. I'll leave that honor for Río. I fight for a semblance of indifference.

Our stylist approaches me, pierced eyebrow bouncing. "Where are you hiding Jenna? I want to dress her for the concert tonight. I picked up something in town that will look amazing on her—"

"For fuck's sake," I growl, at the end of my rope. "I broke up with the crazy bitch. Let it go!" My arms fly around my head as I leave Nese and slam into the hallway.

I need to get a hold of my emotions. Blowing up at our crew isn't the answer, I know. Until I can force memories of the bitch out of my head, I have to rein it in. I walk in circles around the cement hallway until my breathing resembles normal. I can do this. Alone. The way it's always been.

My phone rings in my back pocket, blaring "Cleanin' Out My Closet." The ringtone doesn't register as I answer it. Even a telemarketer would be a welcome distraction. "Hello?"

"Nice of you to answer my call. Are you finished with the *friend* who answered your phone before?"

Mom. Shit. Anyone but her would be welcome. Guess I only

have myself to blame for answering my stupid phone. "What are you talking about?"

"I called you yesterday when I saw Lissa on TV. A girl picked up and said you were taking a shower. I knew she was the Black Widow."

Mom's use of the nickname strikes me as wrong. "Jenna's not out to ruin UC, nor did she kill Darren. If anything, she tried to help him through his injury and addiction." *Why am I sticking up for the physical therapist who just left me?*

"I set her straight, don't you worry. Told her about how lovesick you were for Lissa in high school after she dumped you for Curtiss. Then how you disappeared right after your father did."

My eyes close. I don't need this shit. "Mom, that's not how things went down." Well, it may be from her point of view, but I don't have what it takes to deal with her now. "You know I got the offer to join UC and couldn't turn it down."

"It's exactly how I remember it. You spent how many hours with the Lissa girl, fawning all over her? Have to hand it to her, though, she stuck it out longer than I thought possible. Rather, she strung you along as long as she could. Ditching you for Curtiss was her crowning achievement."

"Stop." Lissa and I were in love. We kissed at school, for everyone to see. She wasn't leading me on. She couldn't have been.

The way Jenna did.

I reprimand myself. Jenna didn't lead me on, she only needed her mommy more than me. Which is better or worse?

Mom continues as if I didn't say anything. "Yet, there was a baby, Bennett. Why didn't you tell me?"

"Mom. If Lissa got pregnant, it wasn't mine."

"Are you sure? Lissa seemed pretty confident on the show."

"I'm positive." Not going to admit to *my mother* I was a virgin until I joined UC, though. "No way on earth could I have been the baby's father. If there even was a baby."

"Well, this is a good thing. Lord knows you weren't ready to be a father back then." She waits a beat. "Or now."

On this score, I couldn't agree more. "You're right."

"You'll never be fit to raise another human being."

Just like she wasn't. I keep this factoid to myself. "I don't want kids."

"This is the first smart thing I've heard come out of your mouth."

"On this we agree." Needing to take this conversation in a different direction, I ask, "How's Ramona?"

"She's a gem. Today she took me to the farmers' market and helped me buy an adorable pink tablecloth."

I breathe a sigh of relief. Whenever she praises Ramona is a good day in my book. Not going to fight this fortunate turn of events. "Sounds nice. Where did you put it?"

"On the table behind the sofa, right when you walk in. I've rearranged the furniture since you were here." She pauses. "I forget how it looked when you last stopped by, but I like it now."

For today. Until another manic mood strikes her. "I bet it's great."

"It is. The pink reminds me of your sister, you know."

Here we go again. Reminding myself of her doctor's suggestion not to engage her about my twin's death in utero again, I pivot. "What are you having for dinner? I'm going out for—" I break off. I have no idea where Luke booked us for dinner. "I think Mexican."

"Have a margarita for me."

Thinking I need to meet up with the band for the unidentified dinner, I nudge her toward a close. "Well, I should be going."

"Of course you have to go. It's what you do best."

Geez, let it be. "Mom, I only meant our manager arranged for us to go out to dinner and I have to get in the limo."

"*Oh, la la.* Get in the limo. Aren't you all fancy pants now? While your poor, old mother lives in a cheap place in the middle of nowhere New Jersey. Bet you'd like me to end up like your sister and father, so you don't have to talk with me ever again."

Just like that, she turns on a dime into the raving lunatic I know so well. But knowing how she acts and not rising to the bait are two different things. With how I left it between Jenna and me, my reserves for handling her bullshit have been depleted. I manage, "That's not true."

She cackles. "I forgot to add in your little band friend to the list. Darren, right? You leave a wake of death and destruction wherever you go, and I refuse to be another body you cast aside, do you hear me?"

"Loud and clear!" I whip my phone across the hall, watching as it breaks into pieces. At least I don't have to talk with her anymore.

I'm still seething when Luke joins me in the hall. "What happened here?" His chin points to my broken phone.

Blood rushes through my veins. "Take your pick. My mother. Jenna. Tristan."

The manager's eyebrows rise with each name. He latches onto the last one. "What did Tris do to you?"

"Jenna."

"You're not making any sense."

"She leaned on him. He let her. They deserve each other."

"At the risk of garnering even more anger from you, might I remind you that you sent her away?"

"Yeah. But she wasn't supposed to fall right into his arms. Maybe the media has it right and she is a black widow, seeking to break up UC. She killed Darren, played with me, and has moved on to the new keyboardist. Makes perfect sense."

Luke cracks his knuckles. "Are you going to tell me what part of that bullshit you actually believe?"

"What? Darren's dead. I cast her out because she was moaning about missing her mother. She went right to Tristan. All true."

Luke's coffee eyes meet mine. He holds up his index finger. "You know Darren overdosed when Jenna wasn't even in the same state."

"Fine. But she was the last person to talk with him."

He shrugs. "As for two and three"—he holds up two more fingers

—"only you and she know what happened. Don't think I believe for one second the crap you spewed out there."

"Yeah." I cross my arms across my chest. "Prove it."

"I can't. Not yet. Although I did have a long talk with Tris."

My voice drops an octave. "Whatever the traitor said, I'm sure it was all lies."

"I don't know, B. He sounded pretty sincere to me. About how Jenna was crying so hard he had to hold her upright. How he helped her get a taxi. She was destroyed." He pauses. "By you."

My head shakes. "She did this to us. She kept crying about how much she missed her mother. I simply granted her wish." After my conversation with my own mother, the thought sticks in my throat.

"It's probably better she's going home. She has a shit-ton of things to deal with, thanks to the graffiti at her clinics."

"See? I did her a favor."

"Likewise. UC has more than a dump truck filled with bullshit thanks to Lissa. She's now been booked on CNN."

"Fuck!" I spin on my heel, pulling back to beat the shit out of the wall. The cement wall.

Luke grabs my cocked arm. "Stop. We need you intact, not with a sling as well as your pulled muscle."

"I need to break something," I pant.

"Fine. Let's go to the roadies' bus. Rumor has it they have a punching bag."

He drags my body toward the exit, where a bunch of our buses are parked. The next thing I know, I have boxing gloves on and I'm punching a bag so fast it almost comes off its hook. Twenty minutes in, and I collapse onto a questionable looking sofa.

"Drink this."

Luke passes me a bottle of water, which I down like the broken man I am. The bag did nothing to get her out of my system.

"Feel better?"

"Not in the slightest."

Chapter 4

Jenna

With excitement bouncing from every pore, I say, "I pulled in a favor to see this doctor at off-hours, Ma. He's a specialist with an amazing track record."

Ma's gray eyes look tired. "I'm only going because you're here. I've been to all the doctors, who all say the same thing. After this, no more. I won't live my life going from one appointment to another."

"You'll only need this one. Have your records sent to this office." I give her the contact information. "I'm sure you'll have a new outlook after we meet with him tonight." I can't believe I was able to get him to agree to meet us at six o'clock. I think he likes working with challenging cases, though it's hard to admit Ma's case is "challenging."

She forwards her medical records and reclines in her chair. "Would you mind making me some tea, Sweet Pea? Then I want you to go to your clinics and sort out all of the ruckus Michelle's been raising."

I make us both cups of herbal tea. In the living room, we drink and discuss all sorts of meaningless topics, from the royal family's latest scandal to the upcoming summer season in the Hamptons. She takes special interest in hearing about the new park overlooking the water.

After an hour, her eyelids droop and she falls asleep. I take her mug and bring it, together with mine, to the kitchen and put them into the dishwasher. Since we still have hours before her appointment, I decide to take her advice and go to the clinic, making sure to leave her a note so she knows where I am.

Court rushes to my side and gives me a big hug when I enter the building via the back entrance. No need to tip off the media of my whereabouts. She catches me up on the business, which has fallen off quite a bit, approaching the eight percent mark. My entire body plummets.

"Court, we have to get these numbers back where they were. I'm afraid I might lose the funding for the third clinic if they stay at this level." Not to mention funding for the fourth one was contingent upon my completing Bennett's therapy, which is off the table now.

"I know. I'm sure it's only a blip, thanks to the graffiti." She sighs. "I had the sidewalks cleaned and everything seems to be fine now."

"How's our contest going?" She fills me in on the details. Quite a few people have already entered, but not as many as we had hoped. We have to do something bigger to fix this sinking ship. Why is every part of my life in freefall?

CNN plays a segment featuring Lissa, and my heart leaps to my throat. With a calm I don't feel, I hit the power button.

Court asks, "How did Bennett take your coming home?"

"He told me to come." Not repeating his exact words.

"That's good. I'm glad he's supporting you."

A sob catches in my throat. Court is my best friend, and I need to share. The floodgates open. "Not exactly. Bennett wouldn't let me explain, thinking I was mad at him for suggesting we use UC's PR team to handle Michelle."

"What? Why would you turn that offer down?"

"We don't need them." I fix my already perfect ponytail. "We got this contest going. You've cleaned up. We'll be fine."

"There's fine and then there's moving forward. I'm sure the PR team could give us some good pointers."

"I can't be beholden to him or the band for my livelihood."

She squares some papers on her desk. "I don't want to say this, but it's not only your livelihood we're talking about here. You have several physical therapists working for you. Felipe, Greyson, Sylvia, and Austin are all managers, or soon will be. And me. We're in this together. If a top-notch and *free* PR team could give us new ideas, I think we should listen to them."

She makes sense. "I hear you, Court. I really do. But I think the situation's changed now. Bennett's no longer at my side. Besides, the PR team has his debacle to worry about." I point to the TV. "We'll muddle through. We always do." I muster up more bravado than I feel.

Court stands and walks over to me, reaching down to give me a hug. "You're right. I was only trying to lighten your load. Are you sure things have truly ended with Bennett? He was good for you."

She makes it sound so final. I guess it is. Ma is more important to me than living the high life with a rock star on tour. "We both knew it wouldn't last. I'm not cut out for his life. More importantly, he can't understand mine." I suck in air. "Ma's dying, Court."

"What?" She rushes to pull me into a warm hug. "Talk to me."

Between tears, I tell her about the diagnosis and how she's handling things. My best friend doesn't try to sugarcoat it for me, rather lets me cry it out.

"Why don't you take a walk on the boardwalk and clear your head?"

"Do I look that messed up?"

She gives me a pained smile. "Fresh air will help."

"Maybe you're right," I grumble. Slipping into the back elevator to go down, I take a quiet route to the ocean and breathe in the salty air.

My number one priority has to be getting Ma back to full health. I can't even focus on my clinics until this goal is achieved. Court has the graffiti well in hand—so long as Michelle doesn't pull anything else, we should weather this storm. I can't focus on Bennett's PR disaster as well. His team can clean his mess up.

An image of Lissa pops into my mind. With her perky boobs, girl-next-door baby blues, and long, bleached blonde hair. How could I compete with the likes of her anyway? Seems like love means one thing to me, and another to rock stars.

I sit on a bench and watch the waves roll in. The weather is perfect for spring, meaning it's too cold to enjoy the beach, which serves me fine. In the summer, this place is packed with sun worshippers. Today, I have it all to myself.

My mind drifts to the days when it was only Ma and me. Kara already was out of the house and starting her career, so Ma and I would come here and walk on the boardwalk. Stop for some ice cream shakes. Try on silly hats. How can we never make these memories again?

"It's gorgeous here," a masculine voice says from behind me.

"Yeah," I reply, without much enthusiasm.

The guy walks in front of me and I instantly recognize the youthful dimple on his cheek. "I thought it was you," Austin says as he sits.

"I wasn't hiding. I'm in town for a bunch of things, including cleaning up after the graffiti."

He bumps my shoulder with his own. "The spiders were drawn poorly. At first, I thought they were squashed beetles."

I can't help myself, and I giggle. The first time since I can remember when. "Thanks. I needed that."

"Sorry you had to come back from your big tour."

"It wasn't my tour or anything," I correct him. "I was giving Bennett physical therapy, and he's in a good place now." At least as it relates to his injury.

Austin nods. "We were handling things out here, you know. You didn't have to come back."

I sigh. Should I tell him the truth? Why not? Bennett thought I was being a child, so screw him. "This isn't my main reason for coming home. My mother's sick."

"Oh no." He touches my hand. "Anything I can do?"

Unless he has a miracle cure for pancreatic cancer, the answer has to be no. "I appreciate the offer, but I'm here now. I got her an appointment with a specialist."

"That's good. I'm sure things will be fine in no time."

I wish I could don his boyish optimism. All such positivity died with my grandmother ages ago. Leaning into his orbit, I reply, "I hope so."

We watch the waves, enjoying the ocean air and quiet. Which is shattered when Michelle screams, "I thought it was you. Pretty brave of you to show your face around here, given all the negative publicity."

I stand. Austin leaps up next to me. For once, I appreciate his height and good looks. See, Michelle. I always have handsome men around me, while you're alone. I set my chin. "Seems like someone has a graffiti fetish."

Her right shoulder lifts, then lowers. "I have no idea what you're talking about. I was referencing the number of patients running out of your doors."

My lips purse. If she has something to do with our cancellation rate as well, I'm going to murder her in her sleep. A picture of Ma asleep in her recliner surfaces, so I settle for outing her to the public.

"Michelle, this isn't high school anymore. You're playing with real people's lives. Stop it."

"What?" Her threaded brows rise. "I'm only doing my job. When my doctors recommend therapy, I give out recommendations. If patients call back, concerned about negative publicity, I steer them to inconspicuous clinics. I think you're the one who needs to stop living in the past."

Austin wraps his arm around me. "Jenna and I were about to take a walk." He dips his head toward Michelle. "Ma'am."

I tamp down a full-blown laugh at his treatment of my high

school tormentor-turned-adult nemesis. We walk away from her. Under my breath, I mutter, "Ma'am?"

"It's the best I could do on short notice. She's a bitch."

No arguing there. "Thank you. I appreciate the assist." We walk past an antique clock on the sidewalk and the time seeps into my brain. "I have to go. Ma has an appointment and I need to take her."

"I wish you all the best." He hugs me.

Despite my best efforts, I can't help comparing him to Bennett. While Austin is cute, Bennett's all man. Austin's arms are cuddly, while Bennett's convey love and protectiveness. Until they didn't. I step back. "See you at the clinic."

"I look forward to it."

I rush to my car and return to Ma's house, all the while banishing any thoughts of Bennett. Austin too. I don't need a man to fix my problems.

Inside the house, Ma greets me wearing a pair of jeans and a long-sleeved blouse. If I didn't know anything different, I would think she's getting ready to go to the women's club instead of an oncologist.

"You look great," I comment. "Give me a few minutes to change out of my scrubs and we can head out."

"I'm only doing this for you," she reminds me.

"What matters is you're going." I slip into the guest bedroom and change into a skirt. Might as well look like a professional.

At five minutes before the hour, we park and make our way into the waiting room. At least the paparazzi haven't figured out I'm home. Yet.

The receptionist packs up her stuff for the day and gives us a puzzled glance. "We have a late appointment with the doctor," I explain. "We'll make ourselves comfortable." She nods and leaves the office as the clock strikes six.

Ten minutes later, the doctor pops his head into the waiting room. "Jenna. Mrs. Westfield. I'm sorry to keep you waiting."

"Not a problem," I reply for both of us. "We appreciate your taking the time to look over my mother's case."

He nods and ushers us into his office. After we're seated, he begins, "Jenna, I have to admit I was surprised to receive your call. I am glad you reached out, though." He shuffles some papers on his desk.

"Mrs. Westfield, I—"

"Please, call me Faith."

"Faith." He moves the stapler. "I reviewed the paperwork you sent over, with your latest blood tests. You've been very thorough."

"My daughter." Ma shoots me a quick glance. "My other daughter is an anesthesiologist in the City. She's been taking me to doctor appointments and overseeing most of my treatment. Jenna arrived last night and wanted to step in and help."

"I understand."

Needing more than this chitchat, I butt in. "Tell me, what did you see in her paperwork?"

"Nothing the other doctors haven't already seen. Tell me, Faith, how long were you having symptoms before you saw a specialist?"

"A little while."

I turn my head toward Ma. "How long?"

She shifts in her seat. "I've been noticing things were slightly off for a couple of years, I guess. I thought it was nothing."

"Years?"

"I wasn't keeping track."

The doctor says, "I appreciate that early symptoms can be hard to discern from heartburn or random pains that come and go. How is your current pain level?"

Ma glances between us. "I'm managing with medication."

"That's good."

I address the doctor. "What's your plan of attack here? What can be done to help my mother beat this?"

The doctor pushes away from the desk. "At this stage, all I can offer is palliative care. I'm sure that's what you've heard from other doctors."

My mother shakes her head. "Yes, that's what they told me."

This can't be. I need more time with her.

Ma addresses the doctor. "I appreciate your time and the attention you put into my case. Thanks again." She sweeps out of the office.

I stare at the doctor. "I can't believe this. There has to be something you can do."

He puts his glasses onto the top of his desk. "Jenna. I know this is difficult to hear, but you know as well as I do there are limits on what medicine can do. I suggest you spend as much quality time with your mother as possible. I'm sorry I don't have better news."

Tears well. I can't lose her too. I've had too much loss. First my grandmother, then Darren. Ma can't be next. Shaking my head, I race out of the office and find Ma waiting for me by the external door. She places her hand on the doorknob. "Take me home, Jenna. We'll talk there."

Because I can't force a word out of my mouth, I do as I'm told. Once we're settled in her house again, she begins. "Sweet Pea, none of this is new to me. In my book, quality over quantity rules. Let's make this time special."

"Ma, I don't want you to give up."

"Don't you see? I'm not giving up anything. I have you and Kara, plus her husband and kids. I'm alert and alive and able to still laugh at your antics. We can enjoy whatever time I have left as normal as possible. Sound good?"

"How does Kara feel?"

"She's on board now. She was taking me all over for this and that opinion, and everyone came back with the same diagnosis. Doctors aren't gods."

"But I want you with me." A tear streaks down my cheek. For

someone who hasn't cried in decades, I seem to be making up for it now.

"I always will be. Right here." She pats her heart, which I mimic.

My sniffling turns into full-blown sobbing as she wraps me in her embrace. How will I ever survive without her love and support?

"I've been blessed. I have two wonderful girls and have lived a fantastic life. You both are well on your way to making your own marks in this world. What more could I ask for?"

"Kara's making her mark. So's her husband."

"As are you, in case you've forgotten about the two physical therapy clinics you've opened."

Into her shoulder, I mumble, "Working on three."

She chuckles. "I stand corrected."

We remain in an embrace until my crying slows and finally stops. I lean back. "We're going to have the best time ever."

She smiles, and it reaches her gray eyes this time. "There's my girl." She yawns. "I'm going to take a nap. Will you be all right?"

"I will." She kisses my cheek and makes her way into the bedroom.

Opening my messenger app, I text Kara and fill her in on today's adventure with Ma. No need to bother her about Michelle. The gnat can do whatever it is she wants, Ma's more important.

I sit in the living room, unable to concentrate on anything despite trying to go through my emails. Deciding a hit of social media is all I can tolerate, I open an app and flip through stupid videos.

Until one from "The Biggest UC Fan Ever" catches my attention. I don't mean to watch the clip from the concert. How Bennett seems larger than life onstage, in his black leather pants singing his heart out with his brothers, all the while denying their friend status. I refuse to be drawn into his green eyes, which somehow appear more expressive than ever—radiating cocky lead singer, sexy man, and pain. I bet no one else sees the pain simmering below the surface. I do.

I guess that makes us even. I'm dealing with more than my own pain.

Closing out of social media, I open my text app once again and click on my nickname for Bennett, Rock Star. The name makes me smile a bit, remembering happier times. Were we going through Graceland only a week ago?

I still love him. Guilt over how I left things between us bubbles to the surface, and the need to tell him what's going on overwhelms. I pull up his contact, Rock Star, and start typing:

> I'm so sorry I ran out on you. I had just gotten the news from Kara that Ma's sick. Really sick. As in the doctors don't have any treatment plan available for her.

Tears stream down my cheeks again. As I swipe them away, I reconsider contacting Bennett. What can he do? He can't fix Ma. What else matters?

On an inhaled sob, I delete the text. Bennett can't help this situation. No one can.

Chapter 5

Bennett

Somehow, I manage to get through tonight's performance. I'm not sure how, but Coop picked up on how I was faking it. Luke was well aware, given my session with the roadies' punching bag.

Coop didn't know anything about that, though. All he and the rest of the guys knew was Luke and I skipped dinner. At least he didn't press me for more than I was willing to give, which wasn't much.

Backstage, I strip off my shirt and take the clean one from Nese, who still is waiting for an answer about Jenna's whereabouts. I hate the fact I went from dumping her—before she dumped me, I can finally admit to myself—to missing the shit out of her.

I need Jenna at my side.

"You're on fire out there, Bennett," Nese notes. "Almost like you're trying to exorcise someone from your world."

I must not have been so clever. She fusses with my shirt. "It's been fucking awful."

"He speaks." She tugs on the hem of my shirt. "What happened?"

I can't bring myself to tell her the lie I've been telling the rest of the guys. Still, the truth isn't in my orbit either. Instead, I settle for a half-truth. I'm still unsure exactly what happened. "It wasn't pretty."

She nods. "What are you going to do about it?"

"I don't know." That's the truth.

"All right, guys. Your audience awaits your encore. Go give them what they want!" Luke riles us up. Or tries to, in my case. "Remember, there's a meet and greet before the club tonight."

A collective groan goes up from the band. Meet and greets are fine, but the more we do, the less enjoyable they are.

Luke gives us the evil eye. "No complaining. Besides, first round's on me."

The rest of the band cheers and we head back on stage to claps and screams from the crowd. We perform the last three songs like we always do, garnering the proper response from the audience. When I introduce the band, including Tris, the reception is as overwhelming as it ever is. But my heart isn't in it.

It's in the Hamptons with the woman who took it with her.

I walk off the stage, ever mindful of my thigh. Thankfully, it's the one thing that hasn't been giving me problems all day. Maybe I can call Jenna and ask her for more exercises? Or jump on Jeb's bandwagon and see if she can help them out? Perhaps even get her to come back on tour and incorporate the crew into her sessions?

What am I doing? She's through with me. She wanted to be home with her mother. Last I checked, I'm nowhere close to having a vagina. Although, I'm sort of being a pussy.

I change out of the leather pants and put on a pair of designer jeans. I also swap my wet T-shirt for a tour tee from The Light Rail and am ready to go. In the greenroom, I make idle chatter with the lighting and sound guys.

Tristan is the next to join us. Was I unfair to him before? Maybe. Maybe not. If I were an adult, I'd talk it out with him . . . but I've never been accused of being an adult. Ask Mom. Lissa.

Jenna.

It's the last name on the list who forces my feet in the keyboardist's direction. "Hey." I clamp my hand around his shoulder, which tenses. "Relax. I'm not going to bite your head off." I consider my options. "Not now, anyway."

"Good to know." His gaze darts around the room, but no one's paying us any special attention.

"I think I'm ready to hear what went down between you and Jenna." My body stiffens. If he so much as kissed her on the cheek, I'm going to lose it.

"Nothing untoward, I promise. She was in the lobby, dragging her luggage. She was in a bad way. When I approached her, she burst into tears. I held her while she cried her eyes out. She didn't tell me what happened, but I'd have to be a blind idiot not to know you two had a massive fight."

"That's the thing, man. We did, but we didn't."

He tilts his head. "Come again?"

"We exchanged a few heated comments, but I didn't think too much of them and took a shower. When I got out, she was shoving her clothes into her bag and couldn't get away from me fast enough. Kept mumbling about her mother, about needing to go home. And somehow it was all my fault."

He scratches his chest. "Something sounds off to me. If you two didn't fight—"

"We didn't."

"Then maybe something else intervened? Have you checked to see if the paparazzi has written anything else about her?"

His question brings me up short. "Not that I'm aware of, but who knows?"

He pulls out his phone, but a quick search doesn't reveal anything new. "All I see is the regular stuff about her being a Black Widow. Oh, maybe this is something. There's been graffiti at her clinics."

The tiny spark of hope extinguishes. I explain, "Someone's spray painting spiders on her buildings and sidewalks. She thinks she knows who's doing it."

He says, "She should use UC's PR team."

"No shit." I fist bump our keyboardist. "That's what I suggested when she took my head off."

He smiles. I chuckle.

"Have you tried to reach out to her?"

I rear back. "No." I hold up my empty hands. "With what phone?"

"What happened to it?"

My head drops. "It met a concrete wall. Didn't fare too well."

"Oh boy." He hands me his cell. "Want to call her from mine?"

I shake my head. "No. I'm not ready for that. Thanks, though."

"Any time."

Coop and 007 join us, chatting about the upcoming meet and greet. When Río finally joins us, Tris observes, "Nice of you to make it."

He runs his palm over his hair. "Hey, it takes time to look this good."

We slap each other on the back and make our way to the fan event. Which goes about as expected. Some people were interested in meeting us and learning about our process. Others wanted to hear about the tour. Most of the women, though, only want to hook up with a rock star. The rest of the guys oblige them, while I turn down each and every one. Including the two blondes I had specifically requested from Elias.

The head of security took my decision a lot better than the women. "Next time you place an order, should I check in with you an hour later, boss?"

"I'm not feeling them now." He nods but I call him back. "Hey, can you get me a replacement cell phone? With all my contacts and shit on it? My old one had an accident."

Elias doesn't question me. With a nod, the former Marine carries out both duties—dumping the chicks and figuring out how to replace my phone.

If Jenna was as torn up as Tris says, what made her lose it?

Nothing new has hit the internet. I try to remember what she was saying as she packed, but all I recall is a bunch of gibberish about how I made her miss her mother's calls. I might have suggested she call her back when we weren't busy, either with physical therapy or otherwise, but I never prevented her from talking with her mother.

There's one unavoidable truth. Something bad happened.

When the last fan has left the building, I follow the band into the limo and we go to the club. I'm not into the scene tonight. My mind's in Aroostook.

Luke passes me a Manhattan. "Here you go, B."

"Thanks." I sip the drink, noting a special flavor. "Hey, I recognize this whisky. Is it from Moray Distillery?"

"You have a good palate."

"Damn straight." I take another swallow. "I need to catch up with Callum." We played at his family distillery's grand opening in America a year or so back. His now-wife was the brains behind the rockumentary that revived our career after Darren's death. He's a great guy.

Luke says, "I heard the distillery is winning all sorts of awards."

"That's great."

"So. About Jenna. Are you ready to talk about what went down with her?"

My shoulders lower. I knew he wouldn't let it go. "I wish I knew. I was talking with Tris about it earlier, and we both think something is really off."

Luke raises his hand. "Hold up. You and *Tris* were talking? No one needed to break you two apart?"

"Keep up or take notes." I slap him on the back. "Yes, we were talking because, you know, we're adults and shit."

"Of course you are."

My brows come together in a fake scowl. "We are. Anyway, we were discussing how Jenna left the hotel and none of it makes any sense."

"I agree with you there. What do you want me to do? Send someone out to her house? Check up on her at the clinics?"

My head shakes. I can't outsource this recon.

"How about we post some positive stuff about her therapy?"

"Wrong track, Luke. When's our next concert?"

"Tomorrow night in New Orleans."

"That's enough time." This could work. It better.

"B, what are you cooking up?"

"I need to get to her. Talk with her. Find out what's really going on."

A grin breaks his face. "Never thought I'd see the day, but the great and mighty lead singer of UC has finally met his match."

I don't refute him. Why? He's right. "I need her in my life, Luke. I can't go on like this."

"I can get the jet fueled and ready for you in an hour. But you have to promise me you'll be in NOLA in time for the sound check at six tomorrow. Got it?"

"It's enough time with my girl to figure out what's happening and set her straight. She needs to be in my life as much as I need to be in hers. We'll figure things out and make the concert—together." I rub my palms together.

"I like your positivity. Let me get the jet ready for you."

He pulls out his phone while I search for Elias. Our head of security stands by an exit door, his eyes on all the band members at once. Impressive. "Hi," I approach him.

"Hello. Your phone should be here in about an hour."

"Thanks. Change of plans, though. Can you have it delivered to the jet? I'm taking a quick trip and will need it with me." I remember Jenna chastising me for asking the impossible. "Only if it's doable, of course."

"You got it. I'll meet you at the jet with your new phone. May I ask where you're going?"

"To get my girl."

An hour later, the limo drops me off at the private landing strip. The UC jet is fueled and ready to head out, despite it being almost three a.m. I hand my luggage to the flight crew and watch as a black SUV approaches.

The vehicle stops, and Elias emerges holding a cell phone in his hand. He holds it up as he approaches. "As promised. All your contacts are in here, as are your photos and videos."

I don't ask how he managed to get all this done in such a short period of time. Or at all. "You're a genius."

"Don't you forget that come bonus time."

I laugh and shake his hand. With a wave to security, I climb the stairs to UC's jet and we take off for the couple hour flight to the Hamptons. Because we're on a private jet, we'll be able to land at a private airstrip near Aroostook, and I'll grab a car service from there to Secluded Rest.

Once again, I'm grateful I didn't cancel the purchase when things went south with Jenna. I text King to let him know I'll be crashing there, happy to still have the code. I'm also more than thrilled Elias is on my team. I'd hate to ever go against that guy.

As soon as I get onboard, I take my seat and am fast asleep. "Mr. Hardy. Sir." My shoulder bounces. "Bennett, I need you to raise your seat."

I blink, reading the flight attendant's name tag, Ashley. My wits gather as I realize I'm going to clear the air with Jenna soon. I right my seat for landing.

When I enter the foyer at Secluded Rest, I'm struck with how empty it feels. Because I'm the only one here. It only becomes alive when Jenna's here with me. I take the stairs carefully, so as not to aggravate my pulled muscle, preparing to crash for another few hours. While I can't wait to meet up with the woman who has taken up residence in my heart, I can't do anything to scare her farther away—meeting her in the wee hours of the morning isn't a good look. Jenna's as necessary to my life as air. I need her to understand this.

She has to come back with me. I won't take no for an answer.

Before I pass out, I receive a text from King letting me know it's all right for me to use Secluded Rest. Damn good thing, considering I'm already making myself at home here.

A few hours later my phone's alarm goes off. Rousing, I turn on the television and flip the channels, landing on the local news. A story about the graffiti at Jenna's clinics runs, mentioning her as the Black Widow. They add in the whole Lissa sideshow. As an extra bonus, some industrious reporter cornered Darren's mother, who refused to comment. Thankfully.

This has to stop.

The only saving grace is they didn't show anything about Jenna's whereabouts, so they don't know she's in Aroostook. If I have my way —which I always do—she won't be here long.

After a quick shower, I put on fresh clothes and call for a car service to take me to Jenna's house. We pass a florist shop, and I make a quick detour. Back in the car with a bouquet of calla lilies on my lap, we continue to her house.

It's dark, but it's still early. No lights are on and her driveway is empty. If she's not here, where can she be?

I ask the driver, "Can you wait here?"

"It's your dime."

Holding the bouquet, I walk up to her front door and ring the bell. When no one answers, I bang on the front door but get the same result. She's clearly not here.

I drag myself back to the car and give the driver her mother's address, happy she gave it to me earlier. Considering Jenna was so intent on seeing her when she left me, perhaps that's where she is now.

This time, when we stop, the house is bustling with activity. Two cars are parked in the driveway, including her Lexus SUV. "Found you."

Now to convince her she needs to be at my side.

Chapter 6

Jenna

Ma's moving a bit slowly this morning. Instead of eggs and bacon, I make us toast, which we share at the kitchen table. She drops her piece onto the plate and I jump to help her.

"I got it." Frowning, she waves me away.

I return to my seat. "I was only trying to help," I grumble.

"I'm fine." To prove her point, she takes a big bite and starts coughing.

I want to smooth her back and tell her things will be all right, but we both know it's a lie. Instead, I sit in my seat, my appetite disappearing with every wheeze. She finally calms.

"Jenna, I'll be okay. I don't need you hovering. I love you, but I hate how smothering you are."

"I don't mean to be," I protest. She won't let me find her doctors, inject myself into her treatment plan, or even make life easier for her in the kitchen. I want to scream but manage to maintain my composure.

"How about taking a walk? It looks nice outside."

Is this her way of telling me to get lost? I consider her ask.

Perhaps a break from each other is what we both need. After wiping my mouth with a napkin, I push my chair away from the table. "Good idea. The weather's nice enough. I'll be back soon." I kiss the top of her head, trying not to notice her thinning hair. How has Kara dealt with her while I've been away?

I go to my room and grab a cardigan. The weather's nice but there's still a breeze. I slip out the front door and notice a car parked at the end of the walk. Who can this be? I close the door and prepare to fight whomever is going to intrude on our quiet day. My chin lifts.

A tall man unfolds himself from the vehicle. I suck in all the air. It can't be.

When green eyes come into focus, I exhale. I can't believe he's here. Not with the way we left things. My body wars between wanting to run into his strong arms and flee inside. Where Ma and her bad mood awaits.

While I dither, a flower-laden Bennett sends the car away and marches up the front walk. I note his gate is steady, without any noticeable problems with his groin injury. At least that's a plus.

I bite my lip. What should I do? The closer he gets to me, the more I want to bolt. The next moment, I'm running across the yard.

Why is he here? Does he want to torment me more? Taunt me for being a "momma's girl?" I stifle a sob at the situation. This isn't fair.

My feet clomp over the wet grass, but I don't care. Behind me, Bennett yells my name. I don't stop moving. I can't.

On the sidewalk, I make a right turn away from town. I don't want anyone to witness this reunion, if that's what you could call it. I enter the park and duck into a wooded area. Once there, I stop. This is as close to privacy as I can find. I focus on returning my breathing to normal.

In the distance, a couple of people walk their dogs, but no one is nearby. Good. Keeping my back to the main road, I feel the instant Bennett invades my quiet solitude. I manage to hold back my sobs. The last thing I want to do is cry in front of him. Again.

"Jenna."

His tenor voice makes women all over the world toss their panties onstage. Mine are firmly in place. I don't turn around. "What are you doing here?" I wrap my arms around my midsection.

"I don't like how we left things."

Makes two of us. "Yeah, well, I think we said everything that needed to be said."

"I disagree." He walks around and stands in front of me. I have to tip my head backward a long way to stare into his eyes.

"Aren't you supposed to be at a concert?"

He appears sheepish. "Tonight."

"Where?"

"New Orleans."

Hours away from here. He must've taken the band's jet. I refuse to be impressed or swayed by his actions. All he had to do was talk with Luke and *presto!* the jet would be available. It's not like he had to go out of his way.

My gaze drops to his thigh. "How's the injury?"

"Needs physical therapy. Know anyone you could recommend?"

Not going to fall for his playfulness. Not when I have much bigger issues on my plate. I sigh. "Why are you here?"

He shakes the calla lilies he's holding. "Because when you know in your bones that the only woman you've ever loved left you without telling you the truth about what's going on, you do the only sensible thing and chase her around the country to find out why."

When he says stuff like this, I can't maintain my anger. I blink several times.

"Tell me, Jenna. I want to help."

Smart man didn't say he wants to fix it. Because he can't. No one can. Not my sister the doctor. Not her doctor husband, or any of their friends. No one can make things right. The pain starts in my gut, demanding an outlet.

"Is it about the Black Widow nickname? We've got the UC PR team on it."

I shake my head.

"Is it about Michelle and all the graffiti at the clinics?"

My head continues to shake.

"You can't be mad about Lissa's lies? That's what they are, you know that, right? Lies."

"No." My pain bubbles up and escapes in sobs. I ugly cry in front of him. Again.

He doesn't hesitate. He wraps me in his arms, flowers at my back. "Shhh, Sweetheart."

I can't stop myself. I hug him to me, burrowing into his strength. He sways with me, whispering sweet nothings into my ear.

When the tears have dried for now, I pull myself together and step away from his warm and inviting body. He deserves to know the truth. "Bennett, Ma's sick."

His face registers shock, then resignation. "I'll get her the best doctors. Switzerland has a world-renowned healthcare system. I can get her out there by tomorrow."

"She's already seen the best doctors around here. There's nothing they can do." My sentence ends on another sob, but I keep myself in check this time.

"What does she have?"

I take a deep breath. "Stage four pancreatic cancer."

"Oh, Jenna." He pulls me to him again, holding tight. "I'm so sorry. Tell me, what can I do?"

With my forehead plastered against his hard chest, I pour out Ma's situation to him. More tears soak his front, but he doesn't flinch.

"Sweetheart." He brushes his palm against my cheek.

"I can't lose her." When did I become such a watering pot?

Using his thumbs, he swipes the tears away from my eyes. "Have you run out of doctors around here?"

"Yes."

"How about this. I'll have Luke arrange for a Zoom meeting with a world-renowned doctor. We can attend the meeting alone. Your mother need not know."

"I do have access to all her medical records. She gave them to me before our last appointment."

"That's good," he praises me.

I lay my cheek against him, letting his slow and steady heartbeat calm my thoughts. We stand like this for a long while. "Sweetheart, if you want me to arrange this meeting, I better text Luke. Will you be okay if I let you go?"

Am I so fragile he thinks I can't stand on my own two feet? "I got this." I shuffle backward, shocked when my balance isn't normal. Must be the uneven ground.

He presents me with the flower bouquet. "This is for you. I thought of you when I saw them, thinking they would complement your gorgeous gray eyes."

I accept the gorgeous white calla lilies. "Thanks."

"May I kiss you."

This man, the cocky lead singer of a world-famous rock band, is asking for permission to kiss me? I love him so much. That never will change. "Yes."

He holds up a phone. "I better text Luke first. Once my lips touch yours, there's no telling how long they'll linger."

"Better hurry."

"With the text, not the other," he quips. I watch his talented fingers dance over his screen.

"New phone?"

"Yeah. My old one had a problem." He glances up when the text is sent.

"What happened?"

"It hit a concrete wall."

Oh. OH. I don't have time to ask him if I was the cause for the flying cell before he wraps me in his arms.

"This is what I've needed ever since you walked out of my hotel room."

I can't talk because his lips cover mine in a delicious reunion. He molds my mouth to his, our tongues tangling like star-crossed lovers.

My fingers rake through his hair as he pulls me tighter against his hardening body. I keep hold of the flowers by sheer will. All I want to do is explore his body.

The ping of an incoming text is the only thing that could drive us apart. Bennett checks. "Luke came through. He's setting up a video call for us this afternoon. He'll get back to me with the exact time."

"Thanks." I need to tell him that my feelings for him never changed. Despite being mad at him for distracting me from talking with Ma while I've been away, the truth is it doesn't matter. Her cancer was here since I've been in Aroostook opening up my clinics. None of us noticed her symptoms. We're all at fault. He was an easy scapegoat.

"Bennett," I begin. "I need you to know something. When I left your hotel, Kara had just told me about Ma's diagnosis. I thought this was new, but it turns out she's been ignoring symptoms for a long time. Years, even. I was scared and mad and wanted to lash out. I'm sorry I took my feelings out on you."

"Sweetheart, I understand now. I was confused, thinking you were upset about my suggesting you let UC's PR team help out with the media surrounding the clinics. I couldn't bring myself to believe you were mad about the whole Lissa debacle, because you've been with me about that from the beginning."

"Well, not back in high school," I point out. Then I remember the call from his own mother. "I forgot. Your mother called when you were in the shower at the hotel. She said some nasty things to me about Lissa and the whole Black Widow thing."

"She's the reason I had to get a new phone."

I give him what I'm sure is a sorry excuse for a grin. "Makes sense."

"Why on earth did you pick up my phone? I don't answer half of her calls."

I shrug. "I thought I could talk with her, woman to woman. Tell her what an awesome son she has."

"You think I'm awesome?"

The way he twists my words only endears me to him more. I lay the bouquet down on a bench. With both arms now free, I wrap them around his waist. "I guess you could say you're an anomaly."

He kisses me, then pulls back. "Because I'm a rock star with a heart?"

"Well, true." I kiss him with a bit more passion than is permissible in public, but I figure the dog walkers can mind their own business. "More so because you're a wonderful man who turned into a rock star in spite of your mother."

"I'll take it."

Our talk about his mother makes my heart hurt for my own. I hug him, grateful he's in my life. "I guess we should be getting back to Ma. She's not having a very good morning, though, so be warned. She's a bit grumpy."

"Grumpy I can handle. Have you seen the guys I tour with?"

He has a point. Yet, Bennett now has to win Ma's approval when all of her focus should be on staying healthy. I hope it isn't a big mistake to bring Bennett home.

"C'mon Sweetheart. I need to be on the jet by midafternoon to get to New Orleans for tonight's concert. It seems like I'm going to be flying alone." His lips turn downward.

I guess my touring days are now officially over.

Chapter 7

Bennett

When we return to Faith's house, I steel myself to see not the woman I met a few weeks ago, but rather her shell. Jenna plucks one stem from the bouquet and returns the rest to me. "I'm going to check on Ma." Twirling the flower, Jenna enters the kitchen and stops. "Hi, Ma. We have a visitor."

I straighten, making sure the bouquet is arranged as nicely as when I bought it.

"Bennett's here."

I plaster a smile as I turn toward the kitchen. Faith stands next to Jenna, almost exactly how I remember her. She's maybe lost a few pounds, but still looks pretty vibrant to my untrained eye. My smile morphs into a real one, and I lumber across the room to kiss her hand. "So happy to see you again, Faith. These are for you." I hold out the calla lilies, mentally thanking her daughter for her thoughtful gesture with the flowers.

"Oh, thank you, young man. Can I get you some tea?"

I glance at Jenna, who shrugs. "Sure. Sounds good."

Jenna pipes up. "I'll make it. Why don't you two get comfortable in the living room?"

Her mother smells my proffered flowers and smiles, causing the rather hovering Jenna to rush over. "Here, let me put them in a vase for you." Jenna lifts the bouquet to her nose and inhales, her face reflecting pure bliss. Like mother, like daughter.

Faith nods, but I can tell Jenna's smothering is getting to her. I approach her and bow. Crooking my elbow toward her, I ask, "May I escort you into the living room?"

Jenna's mother places her hand on my forearm. "You may."

Together we leave Jenna in the kitchen. Her mother's relatively steady on her feet, which has to be a good sign. We sit while Jenna prepares the tea.

"Thank you for coming all the way out here, Bennett," Faith begins. "Jenna's not been herself with how things ended between you two."

"It was a stupid misunderstanding," I reply. "We've got it all sorted now." I pause. "I love your daughter."

She tips her head. "Glad to hear that."

"Me too," Jenna says, leaning against the doorframe.

I'm not embarrassed of my feelings. In fact, I would announce my love for this woman from the top of the Empire State Building if that were allowed. Perhaps Luke can get the words lit up on it?

Nah. Jenna doesn't need such over-the-top displays. This, right here, is more than enough for her. And me.

I direct my gaze toward the woman who owns me, body and soul. "I never stopped."

She runs her palm over her arm. "Me neither."

This conversation needs to happen when we don't have an audience. Preferably naked. For now, I settle with, "Glad that's settled." The whistle for the kettle goes off and Jenna scurries into the kitchen.

Faith leans forward. "Do you promise to take good care of my Sweet Pea?"

"I do."

"Will you not rush to any judgments where she's concerned?

Make her spell out what's going on inside her thick skull?" She taps her head.

My lips twitch at her mother's description. "I'll pull the truth out of her if need be." I pause a beat. "Anyway, it's a gorgeous skull."

Her hand flips. "Looks fade. What's inside Jenna is pure devotion for those she loves. Do you think you're worthy of such a fierce commitment?"

"Yes, and only because that's what she's getting from me. I've shared things with her I never tell another person. She knows all my warts—hell, she's dealing with the whole Lissa situation better than I am. I want to make sure she's protected and knows she's loved. I want to hold her when she cries."

Her mother interjects, "Which she's going to do sooner rather than later, I fear."

Shocked to feel a wetness behind my eyeballs, I blink. "About that. Are you sure there's nothing that can be done?"

"If there's anything I've learned from my time on this earth, it's that quality triumphs quantity any day of the week and twice on Sundays. Would I prefer to stay and watch Jenna's clinics become huge successes? Share in Kara's very full life? Of course. But that's not the hand I've been dealt. I'm all right with that."

"I could take you to Europe—see what the doctors there have to say."

Her head shakes. "I've seen the best here and they all say the same thing." She pats her thigh. "Do you blame me for not wanting to seek out more medical opinions?"

I try to put myself in her shoes. My body sinks into the chair as holding up my weight becomes harder. "I don't. Like you, I would want to spend as many healthy days with Jenna as I could. Not become a burden wasting time traveling to other doctors for no different results."

My response tapers as reality hits. Jenna's fighting against the inevitable.

Faith's blonde head nods, displaying the thinning of her hair. "You get it."

"I do," I repeat my earlier vow but in a very different context.

The need to do something to make her final weeks brighter overwhelms me, but what could it be? I want Faith to be comfortable, but it seems as if she has everything she needs here. What could I give her that she doesn't already have? My mind searches for a different outlet, one that will provide her peace. Her daughter putters in the kitchen, obviously buying us time to talk.

It hits me.

The one thing a devoted mother—which leaves my own out—wants for her children. For them to be settled and happy. I can do that for them both.

My hands lower to my knees. "Faith, I know we've only met a few times, but it feels as if I've known you forever the way Jenna talks about you."

"Jenna has shared some things about you to me as well."

I swallow. Am I really about to ask this? I've never believed for even a nanosecond I would be in this position. "I would like to ask you a question."

"Go ahead."

Does she know what's on my mind? She seems so even keeled. How can she be, when I'm careening out of control? I glance at her, her gray gaze trained on me. Better spit it out now.

"Would you give your permission for me to ask your daughter to marry me? I'm not sure when, but I need to know you'll be happy with this decision." I consider my selling attributes as if they were UC merch. My palm covers my heart. "I have a steady job, a good paycheck, and the biggest plus of all—I love her, and she loves me." What more can I add?

"You travel all the time, and her work is here."

"Good point." How can I make her understand the depth of my feelings? "I can quit the band. Or she can come with us and help out when there are any injuries." I remember Jeb's waxing poetic about how she's handling the crew's back problems. "There's a need for physical therapy on tour. Or we can be together whenever we possibly can. Any which way, we'll make it work." I clear my throat. "I'll make it work."

"You two haven't known each other long."

"We've known each other for years if you count the time when she was with Darren." Not the best idea to mention a former, dead boyfriend when asking for the woman's hand in marriage from her dying mother. "I know for a fact she's it for me. I love her. I'll do anything to make her happy. I promise."

"Have you discussed this with your own mother?"

My head shakes. "No. We're not close. In truth, she's not a caring or loving individual, like you are." I stare at my knees.

Her mother regards me from her chair. I try not to fidget under her scrutiny. When my last nerve is pulled tight, she says, "I would be honored to welcome you into the family, Bennett. You've proven yourself honorable. You love my daughter. What more could I ask of you?"

My entire body goes lax when I receive her blessing. Somehow, she probably was the easier Westfield to crack. "Thank you, Faith. I'll endeavor to live up to your trust in me every single day."

"Of that I have no doubt."

Jenna breaks the mood by bringing a tray into the living room, giving her mother a mug before passing one to me. I sip the calming hot beverage, allowing the tea to soothe my fractured nerves. I need to figure out how to ask Jenna to marry me. Before then, though, I need to help her come to grips with her mother's situation.

The two chatter about the weather and a new store opening up on Main Street, while I ponder what I can do to help the woman I love come to terms with an awful but inevitable result. I'm pulled from my musings by the ping of a text. The Swiss doctor will be meeting with us in an hour. Now to remove Jenna from her mother's house so we can take this meeting in private. And I can try to help her come to grips with the end result.

A few minutes later, I finish my tea. "Ladies, I'm beyond thrilled I got to spend this afternoon with you both. Unfortunately, duty calls, and I need to get ready to fly to my next gig."

"Such a short visit," Faith notes.

"I would do anything for your daughter." Standing, we share an unspoken pact regarding her monumental agreement to let me have Jenna's hand. I bring my empty mug into the kitchen, placing it in the dishwasher.

A giggle floats from behind me. "If only your fans could see you now. The great and mighty Bennett Hardy filling a lowly dishwasher."

The door clicks shut as I hip check it, then spin to lean my ass against the door. "They'd probably enjoy me kissing the living daylights out of my girlfriend against it more." I open my arms, into which she steps.

"I would too." She kisses my lips, but ends our contact way too soon. "Ma's waiting to say goodbye."

I play with her hair. "Come with me to Secluded Rest. Luke arranged the Zoom meeting with a Swiss doctor shortly."

"Oh."

I tug her in close. "Stick with me, Sweetheart. I'll make sure you get everything you need." Even if it's not what she wants.

We return to the living room. "Ma," Jenna begins. "Will you be all right if I go with Bennett to his house? He needs to grab his gear before getting on the plane to his next big concert." She smiles at me. "He is a world-famous rock star, you know."

"I might have heard rumors," Faith quips. I'm finding it hard to believe this vibrant woman is sick. Maybe the new doctor will tell us we have the wrong diagnosis. "You two should go. I'll be fine here. Plus, Kara's going to stop by when she gets off work later."

I approach her chair and kiss her forehead. Her skin feels a bit less resilient under my lips. "I'll be back as soon as I can."

Her hand grabs mine and tugs me toward her. "Keep her safe."

"I will." I stand to my full height and watch as Jenna kisses her mother.

We walk out of the house and Jenna exhales. "I can't believe what's happening. She seems so healthy. Don't you think she looks good?"

I don't want to give her false hope. Yet, I can't find it in myself to crush her. "Let's see what the Swiss doctor has to say, all right?"

"Yeah."

"So, I don't have a car. Do you feel comfortable driving, or do you want me to get a car service?"

"Hmmm. Maybe I should rethink this situation. You don't have a car, your work isn't located here, and you have a crazy ex out to get you. What's in it for me?"

I wiggle my eyebrows. "Me."

Her shoulders lower. "Guess that'll have to do." She tosses me the keys. "You can drive."

I help her into the car, then lean into her space. "Kiss for the road?"

"What am I going to do with you?" Her lips cover mine.

After we break apart, my hand covers the top of the window. "I messed up. I should've copped a feel."

Her arms cross over her chest. "Get in, Rock Star."

Chuckling, I round the car to the driver's side. At least I was able to get her to smile. What a contrast in hours.

We make the trip to Secluded Rest listening to the radio. When the Ukrainian anthem for children Cole Manchester wrote comes on, I sing along.

"I love hearing you sing."

"Come on tour with me. You'll hear me sing all the time."

She reaches over and shuts off the radio. "You do have a good voice. I'm always blown away by it."

So many people throughout the years have complimented my instrument, but her soft praise means more than all of them combined. "Appreciate it, Sweetheart."

"Will you give me a private concert?"

She knows I don't do this. Mom's hurtful words about my five-year-old voice are seared into my soul, so I'm not about to start. Even for Jenna. "How about I serenade you at our next concert? Make all the ladies jealous."

"Some of the men, too."

"Yeah, well, what can I say?" I appreciate her letting me off the hook. Despite what some people say, I've never felt comfortable being the sole point of attention. Give me a band as back up, and I'm golden. I simply don't do *a capella*. The few bars to the television show to prove my identity don't count.

At the gate, I give them my name and we're allowed to enter. Turning, an excellent idea pops into my head. "Hey, why don't you and your mother move in here? The paperwork is almost ready for me to sign, and the owners don't care if I'm here. There's a security gate. It might make you feel safer."

"Ma loves her home. I tried to get her to move in with me—Kara, too—but she's stubborn. She's not moving anywhere."

I tap the steering wheel. "Then how about you? You're dealing with a crazy graffiti artist. Is everyone leaving your home alone?"

Big gray eyes turn toward me. "I went right to Ma's and we've been so busy with doctor appointments, I haven't been to my house."

I move my hand on top of hers. "Don't worry. I stopped by your house this morning before going to your mother's. Nothing looked awry."

She blows out air through her mouth. "Thanks."

The situation with her mother is weighing so heavy on her that she hasn't even checked on her house. I extend my arm onto her headrest. "I'll always have your back."

We pull into the driveway and enter the house. Although there's no food, the rest of the house is move-in ready. I turn on the tap. "Water?"

"Such a big spender."

I'll take that as a "yes." We sit at the kitchen island, and I open the laptop, clicking on the link Luke sent me. "Remember, I'm right here next to you."

She swallows. "If I forgot to say it before, thanks for arranging this. I don't even want to know what Luke had to do to get this meeting."

Around the rim of the glass, I smile. "You probably don't. I'll give him a bonus in his next paycheck." Seems like I'm giving a lot of them away lately. All for good reasons.

Soon, the Zoom meeting is joined by the foreign doctor, who reviews Faith's charts and scans with Jenna. I stay off camera, considering I don't have legal permission to look at the medical records. The doctor asks several questions, for which Jenna has ready answers.

"Given all you have told me and the records I reviewed before we got on here, I'm afraid my diagnosis is the same as the others. Surgery isn't an option for a cancer that's metastasized to this degree. You really want to keep her comfortable."

"I understand." Jenna's face has morphed into a study in sadness. "None of the other doctors will answer this question. How long?"

My breath halts.

On screen, the doctor flips through some pages. "Based on everything I see, and what you've told me, I'd say she has a few months. Maybe three. At the most."

I exhale and bow my head. My Jenna doesn't deserve this.

Chapter 8

Jenna

A few months.

Three months maximum.

Months.

Ma will only be here with us for eight to twelve weeks.

My head shakes. No. No. No. This isn't happening.

I don't register the doctor asking if I have any more questions. It is of no import when Bennett leans over and disconnects the meeting. This is wrong. Wrong!

"Sweetheart."

Ma has to stay with me. I need her guidance. Who else would support my crazy decision to open ten physical therapy clinics in five years?

"Jenna."

She's been my rock since day one. With my grandmother when I was a child. When Darren died, who picked up the pieces? Ma, that's who. Despite her faking it with Bennett at first, she always adored Darren.

Hands move me physically from my chair. "Look at me."

Concerned green eyes stare at me. I blink.

"Tug on your left ear if you can hear me."

My chin bounces. What did he say? I concentrate and my left hand reaches for my earlobe. I pull once.

"Whew. I was worried there for a moment. Did you know Carol Burnett tugged on her left ear at the end of every one of her shows as a hello to her grandmother and to let her know she loved her?"

His words sink in. "No, I didn't know that."

He reaches over and tugs on my left ear. "I always loved that story."

"It's sweet," I admit.

"Now that you're talking again, how are you feeling?"

"Awful. This doctor confirmed what all the others have been saying. But he was the first one to give me a time frame." I scour his face for answers. "Weeks?"

"Oh, Sweetheart. I am so sorry."

He envelops me in his warm hug, and I allow his warmth to seep into my weary bones. "What am I going to do without her? I need more time."

His hands slide to my shoulders as he pulls back. "I talked with your mother when you were in the kitchen. Among other things, she told me she wants to end her time on this earth happy. Not going to doctors all the time." He pauses. "She's exercising her free will, Jenna."

My head shakes. "I don't like it."

"I know. But it's different from how Darren ended his life, with a mistake. Your mother *wants* to go out this way." He kisses my forehead. "You need to let her."

I step back. "I don't want to," I wail. "First my grandmother died when I stopped visiting. Then Darren overdosed. I can't believe Ma doesn't have any other options."

"You have to love your mother enough to let her make her own decisions."

I have to what? *Love* my mother enough? Who's he to talk about loving their mother? What does he know about how I can take care of her?

The need to lash out is overpowering. "Like you do to your own shrew of a mother?"

Like a cartoon quotation bubble, my harsh statement hangs in the air. His mouth goes into a straight line. If hot air could come out of his ears, I bet it would.

Good. Now he knows what it feels like.

Without saying anything else, Bennett shoves away from the quartz island and storms down the stairs. I don't hear another sound from him.

I stare at the computer as if I could open it and get a real treatment plan. Why do all the doctors say the same thing?

Shame washes over me at how I treated Bennett. He was only trying to help me come to terms with what's going on. He wasn't telling me what to do.

That's the issue, isn't it? I want to be the one calling the shots. My own need for control overrides everything and every*one* else. Including Ma.

I have to love her enough to respect her wishes.

Bennett's right. She gets to make choices for her life. I can't make them for her. Doesn't mean I have to like with them, though.

I slam my fist on the counter. Dammit. Why? I leap from the chair, needing to expend my pent-up energy. My feet take me to the doorway that leads downstairs but I turn away. Bennett deserves a break from me. Hell, *I* need a break from me.

Going in the opposite direction, I end up in the oversized family room. We could fit Ma's entire house in only this single room. I bounce between the fireplace and furniture, wearing a path into the plush throw rug. Everything about this house screams money, but not in an in-your-face way. "Comfortable opulence" is what Angie and King called it. Fits Secluded Rest to a T.

This place suits Bennett.

Exhausted, I collapse onto the luxurious sofa, my gaze zeroing in on the television remote. For want of something to do, I turn on the TV. Of course, Lissa smiles back at me.

Despite not wanting to, I force myself to watch the segment. On an empirical level, she's a beautiful woman. Her blonde hair is long and luxurious. Her blue eyes sparkle. Her skin is the perfect golden brown. Her boobs stand at attention. *She's all fake.*

The reporter asks her about her relationship with Bennett. For the first time, I sit up and pay close attention to her reply. When I've been with Bennett when she's on a show, he's exploded within seconds, and I never truly heard her side of the story.

She gleams at the interviewer, her white teeth on full display. "We meant everything to each other in high school, you know. We were inseparable."

Until you dumped him for his best friend to go to the senior prom.

"I felt like I was the queen of the school, as you can well imagine. Bennett and I were so in love. He used to bring me a flower every day before class." She giggles. "Seems trite now, but back then, it meant the world to me. Plus, all the other girls were jealous."

"You two were the couple everyone in the school envied," the reporter adds.

"Definitely. Everyone tried to get the details about our intimate relationship, as you can imagine." She bites her lower lip. *She's good.* "We refused to kiss and tell. What we had going on was our business, no one else's."

The reporter nods. "Good on you. So what happened when it came time for the junior prom?"

"I remember it like it was yesterday. I was so excited to be on his arm, get all the photos taken. I was sure we'd be named the King and Queen of the prom. It was going to be a glorious event. But—"

She draws out the preposition.

With a sigh, she says, "It wasn't to be. We weren't in good financial shape back then, and I couldn't get enough money together to buy a dress. At that time, Bennett couldn't loan me any either, so we ended up not going." Her fake eyelashes flutter. "It wasn't a total loss, though," she purrs.

The interviewer prompts, "Don't leave us hanging. What happened?"

"Well, it's been such a long time that I don't think Bennett would mind me telling you." She leans forward. *Get on with it!* "Bennett and I had our own prom, if you catch my meaning."

Liar! Unable to remain seated, I pace around the coffee table.

"We had the most amazing time, just the two of us. I wore a pretty sundress and he wore khakis with a button-down shirt and a red tie. Not appropriate prom attire, but we didn't care. We played music and danced. He even sang a song he had written for me."

"*A capella?*" the reporter interrupts.

"Yes. He had a great voice, even back then."

Is this why he won't sing for me without the band?

The reporter appears intrigued. "Have we heard this song? Is it on any of Untamed Coaster's albums?"

Lissa's bowtoxed lips curve upward. "Oh no. He's kept it only between us. It's our special song."

Bitch.

"Lucky you," observes the reporter. "Then what happened?"

"Well, after a magical night where I gave him my virginity and he gave me his, we kept up our more physical relationship. Teenage hormones are impossible to keep in check."

The host allows a pregnant pause before asking in a quieter voice, "How did your relationship end?"

Duck lips turn downward. "It's a sad story. His father died and he got invited to join Untamed Coaster within weeks. I encouraged him to go and make a name for himself. He promised he'd come back for me. We were so in love back then." She sighs. "I guess life had other things in mind." Her hand strokes her flat stomach.

"Did you tell him you were pregnant?"

She crosses her shapely legs. "I tried to reach him when I earned two pink stripes. He must have lost his phone or something, because my messages never were returned. I didn't know the rest of the guys in the band, except I had met Darren once."

I stand still. She's seriously bringing him into this story she's concocted?

Lissa tucks her hair behind her ear. "I did text Darren, who promised me he'd pass along my message. I waited and waited, but Bennett never did call." Her eyes cast downward.

In a gentle tone, the reporter asks, "Then you lost the baby?"

Her head bounces. Lissa sniffles and takes a tissue from the box sitting next to her. "I didn't understand what was happening. All of a sudden, I had these massive cramps," her arms cradle her stomach. "There was blood, too. So much blood. The doctors at the ER said there was nothing they could do to save the baby." She cries into her tissue. Not like my ugly cries, more like the dainty tears of a practiced actress.

"I am so sorry for your loss." Lissa waves her tissue. The reporter continues, "Why now? Why are you coming forward now?"

Exactly. Good question, for once.

Lissa blows her nose one final time. "Now I'm an influencer. I get paid to wear clothes, go to places to be photographed. My story needs to be told so other young girls won't have to go through what I did."

More like you see dollar signs, bitch.

The reporter puts her hand on Lissa's knee. "I'm so sorry you had to go through all this, especially by yourself. If you had the chance to speak with Bennett right this second, what would you say?"

My feet stop moving. I stare at the television. *She had her opportunity right here in Aroostook, and never mentioned this fake story.*

Lissa dabs her face. "As you know, we did reconnect recently in the Hamptons. It was magical." Her fake eyelashes flutter. "But, we didn't have time to really *talk*, if you get my drift. If he were here now, I would tell him I'm sorry I lost our baby. I would forgive him for running away. Mostly, I would ask him why he never came back for me. That's what hurts the most." She cries. Again.

My eyes roll.

Unlike me, the reporter eats up her lies. "We'll see what we can do to make this happen for you. You, and the rest of the world, deserve his apology. No man should ever treat a woman like this, especially one he professes to love." The interviewer turns to the camera. "If you're out there, Bennett Hardy, we'd love to hear your side of the story. That is, if you're man enough to tell it. We'll be right back."

Music plays as the cameras show a tight shot of Lissa, still crying.

This is bad. Really bad. Lissa's painted Bennett as some sort of monster who threw over his high school girlfriend for the promise of fame and groupies. Bennett has to make a statement. Does he have proof he's not the father?

A text arrives on my phone, and I check it.

COURT

A reporter by the name of Jeremy Davis of the Record News just called. He wants an interview with you about all the Black Widow stuff. I told him I'd pass his request along. What do you want to do?

He's the reporter who wrote a glowing review about Bennett before *Untamed Coaster Unleashed* was released. Maybe I can use this article to combat Lissa? After all, part of my horrible nickname references my dating Darren, and now Bennett. If I play my cards right, I can use this opportunity to my advantage. Even though I can't control Ma's decision, maybe I can make a difference here?

Tell him I'm game.

This has to work. I deserve a win.

Chapter 9

Bennett

I watch my avatar die, yet again, in Asteroids Deluxe. Paying less than half attention to the game, everything whizzes by me. Another kill shot. Game over. I play another. And another. "Benjamin Howell" isn't in danger of setting new records today.

Jenna took a cheap shot at my relationship with my mother. Yes, it does suck. Her lashing out at me stung. Rather than calling her out —because she's hurting over her own mother's situation—I left. More heated words between us aren't the answer.

Faith's words about not rushing to judgment with her daughter ring true. Jenna's angry, but that doesn't mean malicious. She only wants her mother to be healthy. Frustrated she can't make this come true.

How am I going to make her see reason? No matter how much she wants to, Jenna can't control everything. Like how the graffiti artist is going unchecked around here—like how Michelle hasn't been caught. If we could bend the world to our whims, things would be . . . utter chaos. I need to make Jenna see this.

I have no idea how much time has passed, but footsteps coming down the stairs catch my attention. In the game, loser music plays. Whatever. Not my focus.

The object of my true focus stops next to me.

I want to reach out and pull her to my body, but I resist. We need to talk about what she said. And why she said it.

Old me would've tossed her words into her face and found a replacement bed warmer in under five seconds. But I'm not that guy anymore. Not when I have someone as precious as Jenna in my life. If only I could make her see things the way I do. The way her mother does.

My mouth clamps shut. Her words cut, yet she came down here. She has to be the one to make the first move. I don't have long to wait.

"How'd you do?" Her chin motions toward the arcade game.

Might as well be truthful. "Sucked ass."

She clasps her hands in front of her waist. "Sorry."

"Are you really?"

"I am if I was the cause of your poor performance." Her hands squeeze together.

We're getting closer. I need to let her know how much she hurt me. I've never gotten close enough to another living being to allow their comments to make a dent in my armor. Goes to show how deep Jenna is under my skin. All the way to my soul.

"Not going to lie, your zinger hit its mark." I rake my fingers through my hair. "But I know you slammed me because you're mad at yourself for not being able to dictate your mother's health."

Silence.

She doesn't try to argue with me.

She doesn't defend herself.

She doesn't say anything.

Was I too harsh? She needs to understand this truth so she can move forward. Coddling her isn't the answer, no matter how much I want to pull her into my body and absorb all her pain.

The pain to come.

She takes a step forward and faces me. "You're absolutely right,

Bennett. The person I'm mad at is my mother for not seeking medical intervention sooner. Not you. You didn't deserve what I said."

"Thank you, Sweetheart." I can't resist any longer and drag her into my arms. With my nose buried in her hair, I add, "You're wrong, though. Your mother is fighting very hard in the only way she knows how. She's fighting to be with you, fully with you, for as long as she can." I kiss her lips, salty from her tears.

Jenna comes undone in my arms. I let her cry out her pain, holding her trembling body to mine. When her breathing returns to normal, she says, "I hate this. I hate the gods that gave her cancer. I hate everything about her situation." In my arms, she shakes. "But you're right. She gets to live out her life the way she wants."

"I'll be here for you as much as possible. If I can't be here in person, I'm only a phone call away. You're not alone. You'll never be alone."

She hugs me tight, "I love you."

Her sweet words sink into my bones. "Love you too." Because I got her mother's blessing, I ask, "Will you marry me?"

In my arms, Jenna goes rigid. She pulls back. "What did you say?"

"I know there are a million reasons why now is probably the worst possible time for me to ask this, but I love you so much. I want the world to stop calling you Black Widow." I take a breath. "I want your mother to be at our wedding."

Her mouth flies open.

Now I've made this decision, I barrel forward. "I'm sorry I don't have a ring. But I'll get you one. You can pick out the prettiest one at Tiffany's."

Her head bounces. "I don't know what to say."

I whisper, "Do this for us. For your mother." My hands cup her cheeks. "Say yes." I kiss her. "Marry me." My tongue joins the kiss. "Let me be your partner for today and tomorrow and forever."

"Bennett, I have so many other things to concentrate on—my mother, my businesses. Oh, and this new interview with the *Record*

News. I can't bother my mother to help me plan our wedding." She steps backward. "Ma! I can't imagine how she'll react to this."

I grin. "She already gave me her blessing."

She blinks several times. "What?"

"Told me she'd be honored to have me as her son."

Her head shakes. "After we went out to dinner, Ma was singing a different tune."

My eyebrows rise. "Really? I thought she loved me back then."

"She was being polite." She tucks her hair behind her ear, which springs from its confines almost a second later.

"Well, I talked with her today and she was all too happy to dump you in my lap," I tease. Her face still registers disbelief, so I add, "Once she confirmed I loved you, of course."

"You want to marry me? After how awful I was to you?"

"I've been an ass too. We're even."

"My head is swimming." She swipes her forehead as if to prove her point. "You really want to get married? When?"

"Whenever you want. We can do it next week so your mother can be with us. Or next month. Or we can wait for a year. I don't care so long as you agree to be mine."

Her hands connect behind my neck. "I came down here to apologize for being awful to you, and you proposed?"

"Seems that way."

She straightens. "I also came here to tell you about the interview I just watched on TV. It was Lissa. She told quite the tale about how you sang a song to her *a capella* during your fake junior prom. The one you and she took on your own because neither of you could afford to buy the proper attire. Where you took each other's virginity."

"First of all, I never sing without music since Mom put her hand over my mouth when I was rehearsing a song for Father's Day, saying my voice could make my sister roll over in her grave. I was five." I huff. "As to Lissa, she was still a virgin when I got out of town, at least by me. So was I until a nice groupie relieved me of the nuisance."

Her face scrunches up. "A groupie?"

"Hey. I was a seventeen-year-old with a bunch of chicks hanging off me because of the band. I also had been dumped by my high school girlfriend, lost my dad, and didn't want anything to do with starting up something serious again. Groupies came in handy."

"I bet."

A wolfish grin takes over my face. "Will you be my groupie-wife?"

"A what? No!"

"Fine. Then how about simply my wife?" She hasn't answered my very important question yet.

Her gray gaze roams over my face. "Yes."

I capture her lips in a kiss, trying to take away some of the pain of her mother's situation as well as celebrating our love. Talk about living in divergent universes. After too short of a time, I break away. I need to get to the airstrip soon, meaning there's no time to get revved up.

Something she said before clicks. "Did you mention something about the *Record News*?"

Her fingers spring over her swollen lips. "Huh? Oh, yes. Court texted that this reporter, Jeremy Davis, wants to meet with me about the whole Black Widow ridiculousness."

"He's a good guy. Are you going to do it?"

"I think I might."

I kiss her once more. "At the risk of pushing my nose where it isn't wanted, the UC PR team is at your disposal." I hold my breath, hoping for a better reply than the last time I suggested this.

She plays with her hair again. "Aren't they going to have their hands full with Lissa's story?"

"They can multitask."

"You won't think any less of me if I take you up on your offer?"

Relieved she's actually weighing my offer this time, I rush to reply, "No way. I'd think you're even smarter by considering help. With your mother, you have a full plate."

"Maybe I'll reach out to them."

I know how much this has to cost her. I'm kissing her as my phone alarm goes off. "Jenna, I would stay here if I could. Please know this. I have to get to the UC show in New Orleans, where I'll ask the PR team to get in touch with you. Spend as much time with your mother as you can." We kiss again. "And don't forget to let me know what happens with Jeremy Davis."

"Thank you, Bennett. I can't imagine my life without you in it."

"You will never have to."

After I lock up, I walk her to her car and make sure she's all right to drive. After one last lingering kiss, she leaves and I duck into the car service, which takes me to UC's private jet. I've never been this grateful to have a jet at my disposal.

"Hello again, Mr. Hardy. We'll get you to New Orleans in no time. Our pilot told me we shouldn't have any turbulence, so sit down and enjoy the flight. What can I bring you to drink?"

I confirm my recollection of her name with her nametag. "Thanks, Ashley. Please call me Bennett. I'd love a Manhattan, if you can make one?"

"Of course. We'll get underway shortly, and I'll bring it right over."

Following Ashley's advice, I sit in the leather chair and buckle my seatbelt for takeoff. My mind bounces through all of the events of today. One thing is for sure—this was the most productive trip I've ever taken.

Once we're airborne, Ashley brings my drink and I retreat into my thoughts. About Faith, and how she's accepting her fate, however awful it is. About Jenna, and how she's letting go of the things she can't control. Plus, accepting the expertise of UC's PR team.

I pull out the new cell and text Luke about having the PR team help Jenna. Gotta love traveling by private jet, where telephone restrictions don't exist.

In the silence, it hits me full force. I'm going to be a husband. More to the point, Jenna's husband. I somehow managed to get this amazing woman to fall in love with me. By saying yes, she's agreed to stay with me forever. Something no one else has ever done for me.

My phone pings with an incoming text.

> **JENNA**
> I love you with my whole heart. I cannot wait to be your wife.

What we have is forever. I let this truth sink into my soul. Yes. We're the forever I've never had.

> Right back at you.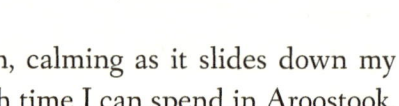

I take another sip of my Manhattan, calming as it slides down my throat. I need to figure out how much time I can spend in Aroostook, especially with her mother's condition. The ping of another text interrupts my planning.

> **LUKE**
> Of course, although they're busy with the whole new Lissa interview. Have you seen it? Any ideas about how to combat what she said?

> I didn't see it. Jenna told me about it, though.

> Here, I'll send you the link.

. . .

Once it arrives, I watch Lissa spew even more lies. Fuck. What on earth did I ever see in her? Although now she's much more plastic than in high school. She always was concerned with her appearance, making sure to have the latest haircuts and doing her makeup to align with the latest trend.

She was smart enough not to put out that we actually went to the prom together. Saying we did something private means there were no photos. Damnit.

What if she gets her high school friends to corroborate her lies? I was such a loner back then, the only friend I had was Curtiss. The double-timer who stole Lissa from me to go to the senior prom. Love how she didn't mention that *fact* in her interview.

There must be a way to refute her story. Five minutes later I'm still stewing when I get another text from Luke.

> A Curtiss Fanone reached out to me via socials. I was about to set him loose but he said he can refute what Lissa's saying. Do you know this guy? How do you want me to respond?

I unclick the seatbelt and walk to the other side of the aircraft. What should I do? I itch to reach out to Jenna, but she has enough to deal with. Curtiss told Luke he knows Lissa's lying? Should I trust him? It's not like I have more options. Or any.

> Did he give you his number?

A second later, Luke texts it to me. I stare at the digits for a long while, debating what I should do next. Aside from my mother, he's the only other person I can think of who knew the truth back then. Mom's never going to help me. Can I trust he will? Probably not, but who knows?

On an inhale, I sit and FaceTime the number. Might as well get the visual as well as the voice. Curtiss picks up, squinting into the camera. "Hello? Bennett, is that you?"

His voice is deeper than I remember, but he was only eighteen the last time we spoke. He's lost most of his previously full, blond head of hair. From what the camera picks up, he's no longer the same fit guy he was back in high school, either. He now wears the glasses I ditched to become a rock star.

"Hey. Yes, it's me. Heard you wanted to talk?"

"Damn. You've aged well. I've seen your videos and concert clips, of course, but you look a bit different from high school."

No use lying. "So do you."

He lets out a nervous laugh. "Yeah, well, I left tennis behind years ago." He rubs his balding head. "Together with most of my hair."

How should I respond to this? I decide to get him to talk about Lissa. "So, my manager told me you wanted to discuss Lissa." Can't help it. Her name comes out like a curse.

He changes the camera angle. "Listen, I've been seeing her everywhere talking about how you two were high school sweethearts. Which isn't a lie."

One point for her. "That's the only truth she's been spewing."

"Agreed."

I sit up. Is there any way this man I don't recognize could help me out? After what he did back in high school, his track record sucks. Still, he owes me one. Or twenty. "I'm listening."

Curtiss moves around again. "I know she didn't go to the junior prom with you because she went with me to the senior prom, and not due to her self-described money issues."

Gotta give him props. At least he didn't walk away from the truth. "Yes. You asked her out, knowing we were a couple." I can't keep my animus from years ago at bay. "Some best friend you turned out to be."

"I know it was a shitty thing for me to do. She was your girl, but I was the king of the tennis team back then and wanted a beautiful lady on my arm. Lissa was the prettiest one I knew. Even though she was yours, I couldn't help myself. I figured, if she agreed to go with me, you two weren't meant to be."

Can't argue with this logic, considering I just asked Jenna—not Lissa—to be my wife. "Guess that's one way of looking at it." I run my finger around the rim of my glass.

"I tried to call you about it several times, but you never returned my calls."

I scowl. "I wasn't interested in talking." not. "Get on with your story."

"Fine. I went to the senior prom with Lissa. We hung out. She fed me some line about not wanting to have sex until marriage."

At least she told him the same thing as me. "Told you."

"You did. I figured after I graduated, you and I would work things out. But your father—" He trails off.

No need to relive this part of my life. "Yeah."

"And you went underground. I actually drove to the funeral but couldn't bring myself to go inside."

My hand fists. How do I respond to this? "It's all a blur anyway." *Why did I let him off the hook?*

"Then you were working at the amusement park. The next thing I heard, you were dropping out of high school to join a band. I was off to college on a tennis scholarship. Our lives went in different directions."

Enough memory lane shit. "How does Lissa play into this, Curtiss?" I deserve props for not adding a hiss to the end of his name. Or hers.

He pushes his glasses up his nose. "After your father died, Lissa came to me. All weepy. Said she didn't know how to help you. Felt she let you down by going to the prom with me."

My fingers strum on the armrest. When he doesn't continue, I prompt, "And?"

"Well, she needed comfort. So did I. We, we had sex." It's as if Río did a rimshot to punctuate his admission. "Throughout the summer, we were together. When I came home on college break, it continued."

"Bully for you. Hope she was worth it."

"I didn't tell you this for any other reason than context. You know how Lissa was, always concerned about her appearance and stuff. After you took off with the band, she dove in deeper. Adding hair extensions. Going for plastic surgery on her nose."

"I noticed something was different with her face, but I missed the nose job. She must've had some good surgeon."

"Yes, he was good." He takes off his glasses, revealing tiny lines around his eyes. "About this time, she decided she wanted to become an influencer. Untamed Coaster was an unknown, and I think she was trying to show you what you were missing."

I huff. "Just what I needed. Another crazy in my life."

Curtiss doesn't respond to my comment, although he acknowledges it with a nod. "She met with a bunch of modeling agents trying to break into the business. All of them told her she had to drop at least ten pounds."

I frown. For all her faults, Lissa never had an extra ounce of fat on her body. "From where?"

"That's what I told her. She ignored me, though, and started taking diet pills. Laxatives. Anything so she could shed the imaginary pounds."

Ashley comes by and takes my glass. Wordlessly, she asks if I want a second, but I shake my head. I need all my wits about me now. "Go on."

"Well, throughout it all, we continued to have sex during my college breaks. I can't be sure, but I think she also dated other guys in high school."

More to myself than to him, I say, "Lovely."

"Yeah. I was getting ready to break things off with her when she told me she was pregnant."

I sit straight up. She *was* pregnant? "There was a baby? It was yours? The one she's been telling the world was mine?"

"I can't be sure. I believe the baby was mine."

"What happened? Did she also have the miscarriage she's claiming?"

"She did." He pauses. "I'm convinced it was from the diet pills she was taking. Her body was super-thin at this point, and whatever hormones the pills put in her body couldn't have helped."

I take in everything he's telling me. He was the father. Her obsession over her body contributed to her miscarriage. Still, it's his word against hers. Unless. "Do you have any proof of this?"

He looks straight at the camera. "That's what prompted me to reach out to you."

Chapter 10

Jenna

I busy myself making tea while I wait for Ma to wake, my mind on everything I have to do today. First up is the interview with Jeremy Davis. I need to convey to him that I'm all in at At Your Service PT, even though I've been touring with UC for the past months. Downplay the Black Widow bull while extolling our physical therapists. Discuss our upcoming new clinic yet keep Bennett's proposal on the down-low. Easy peasey.

Despite it all, I can't stop dwelling on the fact that Bennett asked me to marry him. Even more amazing was his confession that Ma gave him her blessing. By the time I got home yesterday from preparing with Court, she was already in bed. I need to ask her what changed her mind about him.

I check my texts. He sent me a photo of him blowing me a kiss, saying he can't wait to do this in person again. I sigh. Me neither.

"That's a big sigh." Ma walks into the kitchen, stopping to hold on to the back of the chair.

How is it she seems to deteriorate every twenty-four hour period?

"Here," I leap to my feet. "Let me help you."

She waves. "I'm good. You can pour me some orange juice, though."

"On it." I move to the fridge, keeping an eye on her as she settles into her chair. I place the glass on the table in front of her.

"What's on your agenda for today?"

"We had a reporter reach out. He writes for a magazine in the record industry and wants details about the whole Black Widow thing." I sit next to her.

Ma snorts. "Send him my way. I'll tell him it's all a load of crap."

"We both know that. It's my job today to convince him of it so he can write a good article."

"What does Bennett say about this interview?"

Since when does she ask me about other people's opinions? Whatever my fiancé—I silently scream at his new position in my life —and she discussed must have been huge. "He says it's a reputable magazine. Now tell me, what switched your opinion about him? Last we talked, you preferred Darren to him by a mile." I lean back in my chair.

She picks up her glass and takes a slow sip. She replaces it on the table and looks at me. "I remember what I told you before." She shrugs. "I've changed my mind."

"You don't change your mind. Remember when I was in high school and begged you to buy me a black dress for prom. Even when all my friends were wearing black to the dance, you refused. I wore pink." My arms cross.

Her shoulder lifts again. "You stood out. No use being a lemming."

"Talk to me. What made you give him permission to marry me?"

She gasps. "He told you?"

"He asked me to be his wife," I correct.

"Oh, honey!" She opens her arms, and I move to fall into them. How won't I be receiving her amazing hugs this time next year? I close my eyes as realization sinks in that I'll be missing more than her hugs all too soon. "Tell me all about it."

Needing to share something happy with her, I return to my chair and start from our fight and my snide remark about his mother.

Ma interrupts. "He's not close with her, right?"

"Ma, she's terrible. He told me about their strained relationship, but I didn't believe him. I mean, what mother on earth would blame her only child for killing his twin *in utero*?"

Ma's hand flies in front of her open mouth. "Oh my God. That's awful."

I nod. "They were IVF babies. She was pregnant with twins, but only Bennett survived. Ever since, the woman's claimed the twin was a girl and makes all sorts of comments to him like, 'if your sister were here . . .'"

Her hand falls to her lap. "What about his father? Is he around?"

"He passed when Bennett was seventeen." I pause. "The year he joined the band and left home."

"At least he has his bandmates. I remember Darren telling me they were like brothers to him."

How much should I tell her? I guess if she's focused on Bennett's story, she won't be thinking about her own. "His mother's scars, plus the ones from Lissa way back then—not to mention the ones she's putting on him now—left a lasting mark. He doesn't view the members of UC as anything more than coworkers." It feels so good to discuss this with someone else. Someone who loves him.

"What are you going to do to straighten your boy out?"

"Seems like I have my work cut out for me." I sip my lukewarm tea. "But before we move on to fixing him, I want to know what he said to you that made you give him your blessing?"

"It's not so much what he said," she begins. "It's what he did. When you arrived back here, you told me you ran out on him. There had been a big fight."

"It wasn't so much as a fight. More like a—" I trail off. "Well," I sigh, "I guess it was a doozy of a fight. He wouldn't let me explain and all I wanted to do was get here to be with you."

"As I said. You left him on bad terms." She gives me one of her patented "mother knows best" expressions.

"Fine." I dunk my spoon in the tea.

"And what did he do? Did he continue on tour with UC? Worse, hook up with one of the millions of willing women who surround him?" She drinks her juice. "No. None of that. He flew here, from his concert, to be with you for an *afternoon*. This told me everything I needed to know about him."

A smile grows across my face. "He's pretty wonderful like that."

"He loves you, Sweet Pea. With everything he is, he loves you. Emotions like that don't come around often, and when they do, you have to hold on to them."

I can't help but wonder if she's referring to my father? Did they have a big romance at first, but life twisted it on its head? "Was it like that with you and Daddy?"

She rubs her forehead. "What we had burned bright and fizzled. I loved him, but we didn't want the same things. I wanted a family and to be a mother while he needed to be free." She scowls. "Don't look at me like that. I don't regret spending years with him at all. After all, he gave me you and your sister, my two greatest achievements."

"I don't remember much about him." I was five when they got divorced, but Ma never made me feel as if I was to blame.

"He's a good man." She's speaking in the present. I don't have the opportunity to question her because she continues, "Bennett, however, knows who he is and what he wants. I thought he was cocky at first, but I think he puts it on as a mask to protect himself. Now that you've told me about his upbringing, I can understand where it comes from."

I add, "When you add Lissa to the mix, it does all make sense."

"She's causing quite the ruckus, isn't she?"

"The problem is, Bennett doesn't have anyone from back then in his corner. His mother certainly won't give him any references. His father's gone. The only person he was friends with back then"—I stare at the table. No need to air *all* of Bennett's dirty laundry—"they lost touch years ago."

"Your Bennett will figure it all out. The truth has a way of coming to light in the most unexpected ways." Her voice is steady.

Her conviction rolls over me. "You really do love him, don't you?"

"So long as he's good to you, Sweet Pea, I'll be happy to call him family. If he does something stupid, though, I'll haunt him from the grave." She chortles.

I sit in horror.

"Too soon?"

"You think?"

"We have to face facts. We both know how this is going to end, sooner rather than later."

A lump forms in my throat. "I don't want you to go."

Her hand touches the top of mine. "Sometimes we don't get what we want. But we get what we need."

"Are you seriously quoting the Rolling Stones to me now?" Her words echo those Bennett said to me recently.

"I think their lyrics are slightly different, but you get my gist." She smiles. "I believe Darren sent Bennett into your life to help you through my passing."

I *hate* when she talks like this. I swipe yet another tear off my cheek. "It's a beautiful way of putting things, but stop talking about your death as inevitable."

"Oh honey, everyone leaves this plane sooner or later. But think of it this way. I'm leaving you with Bennett, and your sister with her family. I think I did pretty good with my time here."

When she puts things in this perspective, it does sound like she's had a life well lived. Still. "I wish we had more time. Time so you could see me as a bride on my wedding day. Play with my kids. Cheer on Kara's kids as they make their way into the world."

"Don't you worry. I'll be watching all of this from above. Just because I won't be here, don't think I won't be a heartbeat away."

That does it. I break down and cry, hugging Ma close. She rubs my back as I feel some of her tears fall too. Then something amazing happens. It's as if our talk gave me some catharsis, and for the very first time, I *accept* what the doctors told me.

I'm okay with her diagnosis.

Mostly.

We break apart. "Ma, I think I understand now. Let's fill whatever time you have left with laughs and fun. Get together with Kara and her family to celebrate whatever milestones they have. Hopefully, Bennett will be able to get out here again soon, too."

"Where is his tour taking him?"

"He's in New Orleans now. I think they're making their way across to California next."

"The life of a rock star."

"We'll figure out a way to make it work."

"Of that, Sweet Pea, I have no doubt."

"I think we've covered all my questions," Jeremy says. "Is there anything more you'd like to add?"

We've discussed my being called the Black Widow, the graffiti at the clinics, and Lissa's claims against Bennett. I'm not ready to let the world know about our engagement. Nor do they have a right to find out about Ma's situation. Something about Lissa's latest foray into the media niggles in the back of my mind, though.

"I met Lissa, you know."

Jeremy does a double take, his piercing hazel eyes burning into me. He flicks his head, causing his short blond hair to move across his face. Instead of clinging to muscles upon muscles like with Bennett, though, his clothes simply cover his rather thin body. Still, he's an attractive guy. "Do tell."

"It was here. In Aroostook. She told Bennett she'd been watching his success for years and was grateful for media reports putting him in town for longer than a day or two. Apparently, she was following him for years but never met up with him."

"She's a determined young woman."

Or desperate. "Don't you think if she really miscarried his baby, she would've found a way to reach him before his band became popular? I mean, wouldn't there have been urgent messages when it happened?" *If it happened at all.*

He flips through the pages in his notebook. "In one interview, she said she did try to reach out through Darren, but was unsuccessful."

I yank on my ponytail. "That doesn't ring true to me. If someone contacts your, say, brother, asking for you to get in touch, what do you think would happen?"

"I presume he would text me or something."

"Right. All we have is her side of the story claiming she got in touch with Darren. Bennett doesn't remember Darren ever mentioning Lissa to him."

"Really?"

"Nor do I." He scribbles something in his notebook. I hope he'll run down this line of questioning. However, Darren's no longer here to refute Lissa's story. We're back to the *he said, she said* stalemate.

Jeremy snaps his notebook closed. "I want to be upfront with you, Jenna. I believe you. I don't think this Lissa person is on the up and up. If only Bennett had some real corroboration, I could put the story out there. Without that, though, all I can do is print his denial."

I complete his sentence. "And we all know how much a denial is worth."

"Exactly."

I allow myself to wallow in this mess for a minute, then shake my head. "I promise to contact you if something else comes up."

Jeremy stands. "Thank you for your time. I know the readers of *Record News* are interested in hearing about this web you're caught up in, no pun intended."

I half smile. "Please keep in touch."

After escorting Jeremy to the door, I return to Court's office and open a text from Kara.

> Back from taking Ma to the grocery store, and now she's resting. Please call me if anything changes.

> Will do. Thanks.

Kara and I have become a lot closer since this ordeal with Ma started. We're still not what I would call "close," but we've graduated to texting every few days, with sporadic phone calls in between. I appreciate the fact she took on the brunt of Ma's early diagnosis, but I'm not leaving Aroostook anytime soon. I plan on being here for Ma. Until she won't need me.

Court walks into the office. "How'd it go with the reporter?"

"Jeremy was nice. Pretty thorough. He seemed to understand Lissa is lying, but without any proof, his hands are tied."

"What about the graffiti?"

"On that, we're in total alignment. I'm not a 'Black Widow,' and I'm not trying to break up the band. I told him all about Michelle and how we think she's behind it. Let's see what he publishes about it."

"With any luck, he'll out her and she'll lose her pathetic job."

"Amen." My conscience pings. "If only she would go away and leave me in peace. I didn't set out to hurt her. I don't know why she has her sights set on me."

"Well, maybe because you're a successful businesswoman and she's not. Then there's the fact you're dating a famous rock star who wouldn't give her the time of day."

I rub the naked ring finger on my left hand. I've known Court for years, and I trust her. I need to share my secret with someone who isn't related to me. "We're more than dating."

"What do you mean?" She pulls back, notices my hand movements, and her eyes round. "No way! Are you?"

"I am."

She screams and rushes to me, pulling me up to my feet as she hugs me. "You lucky bitch! I've only glimpsed the man a couple of times in here for therapy, and he is one fine gift to the world."

I giggle at her description of my fiancé. "He sure is."

"When's the big day?"

I hold up my left hand. "Getting ahead of yourself? I need a ring first, don't you think?"

"That can be fixed in an afternoon." She beams at me, and I absorb the happy vibes. They're so far and few between these days.

"Besides," I sigh. "Nothing can happen for a while. I have to spend time with Ma." Despite Bennett saying she could celebrate with us.

Court directs me toward the sofa and we sit. "I'm sure you'll know when the time is right. Oh Jenna, you're either on a high or a low. I'm so sorry things are like this."

"Me, too." I shake my head to clear it. "Enough about all this. How are our numbers doing?"

Court glances out the window. "Still about the same."

"Meaning way too many cancellations. I think we need to do something bigger. After all, Bennett has this massive Lissa problem, and Ma's holding her own for the moment. What do you say we contact UC's PR team and get them on it?"

"I say we can use all the help possible."

"No time like the present." I pull up Luke's text with the contact card. Patting the sofa, I say, "Stay with me. My mind's too scattered. In this case, I'm thinking the more help I can get, the better."

A few minutes later we're talking with Hayden Vaughn, the PR person assigned to help us. We fill her in on the graffiti on the building and the sidewalks. "Are these spiders cartoon-like, or more realistic?"

Court pipes up. "They're pretty lifelike. I'll text you a photo."

"Got it. Wow. Yeah, I'd say this doesn't really fit the mold for regular graffiti. They' re definitely there to taunt you, Jenna. After you repainted, there haven't been any more?"

"So far, so good," Court replies. "After Jenna came up with the contest, they stopped."

"Can you tell me about the contest, Jenna?" I fill her in, and Court gives the stats of the number of entries. "This is a fabulous idea."

I puff up at her praise.

"I think we can do more with it, though. I know you were trying to take control of the narrative surrounding you and Bennett, but it's obviously not breaking through. What do you think if we turn it on its head?"

I reply, "That's what I was trying to do."

"We need to think bigger. A T-shirt slogan is catchy and fun, but we need to find your business a way to corral word-of-mouth advertising. Tell me, when someone mentions At Your Service PT, what does the general public associate with your clinic?"

"Great physical therapy," Court responds.

I nod. "Exactly."

"That's what's expected when you go to a clinic. I'm talking bigger, a more generalized idea. I'm sorry to tell you, right now, when your company is mentioned, people probably say, 'Oh, the place with the Black Widow?'"

Hayden's a "rip the bandage off" type of gal. While I appreciate how blunt she is, I can't say it doesn't sting.

She continues, "I don't say this to make you upset. I'm stating a fact so we know where we are and how we can return the focus to your excellent therapists."

"You're probably not wrong." Why is everything so hard? "If only the damn spiders had hip and knee replacements and we were making them feel better."

Next to me, Court sits taller. "You might be on to something here, Jenna."

"Now I know why you're the brains behind this operation," Hayden concurs. "I love it!"

I stare from my phone to Court. "Uh, happy to make your day, but care to clue me in? What exactly do you love?"

"Give me a second."

Court leans over to me. "We can use your idea to make every spider want to come here. Make it cool." She pauses. "I think."

A text comes in and I open it. Hayden sent a very rough mockup of a spider, with its eight legs, all being worked on by therapists. The slogan underneath reads, "If we can fix a black widow, imagine what we can do for you."

"It's a rough idea," Hayden says.

"It's cute. I love the spider, just not the black widow saying. I hate that term." Even though she can't see me, I shudder.

"Give me a little while. I'll shoot you over some ideas. But do you like the direction this is going?"

I stare at her text once more. "I do. But what if instead of T-shirts, we have bumper stickers printed and give them away everywhere in the Hamptons?"

"Oh, I love that idea," Court agrees. "We can put them out at our tables when we attend various fairs in town. I guess we could also put them on T-shirts too."

Hayden says, "Now we're getting somewhere. If you help an insect with eight legs, imagine what you could do to a person with only four limbs?"

Court joins in, "Exactly!"

Our conversation finishes with Hayden promising to get us something more finished, with a bunch of tag lines, soon. When we disconnect, Court says, "Michelle messed with the wrong clinic."

She sure did. I stand. "I'm going to let this percolate for now. I better get home to Ma. See you tomorrow."

After hugging my bestie, I slide into my car for the return trip to Ma's house. Before I even leave the parking lot, I get another text.

Expecting it to be Hayden with a follow-up, I'm more than delighted to see Bennett's name.

He's only been gone for a few hours, and I miss him like crazy.

His fans at the concert are lucky. They get to see my man in living color.

I rub my bare left hand. Yeah, but I'm the only one who can call him mine. I click to open my text app.

Chapter 11

Bennett

I smile at Jenna's text. Yes, Sweetheart, I miss you more. Not wanting to engage in a text discussion, I FaceTime her. She answers from behind the steering wheel. "Are you driving?"

"I'm going to Ma's."

"I need you safe. Call me from her driveway." I disconnect the call. I better set up some ground rules for future conversations. Number one will be no texting—or FaceTiming—or any calls or texts with whomever—while driving. She has to stay safe.

The plane lands and Ashley passes me my bag. "Thanks. I'm sure I'll be seeing you again real soon." I knock on the cockpit door and give my appreciation to the pilot and co-pilot as well.

A black SUV waits near the flight of steps attached to the jet. With a quick wave to the crew, I hop into the vehicle, surprised to see our head of security himself driving. "Hey, Elias. Looks like I scored the top dog today."

He adjusts his sunglasses. "Good trip?"

I think back on everything that happened on this short jaunt. Faith's medical condition got sorted, although not in the way we'd hoped. She did give me her blessing to ask her daughter to marry me, which promptly led to us getting engaged. "Yeah. I would say so." Curtiss's call was an unexpected bonus.

"That's good. I'm taking you straight to sound check."

"Thanks." As I watch the scenery pass, the sky seems bluer than normal. The trees greener. Even the architecture is more vivid. In my hand, my cell chimes with an incoming FaceTime call. I hold it up. "Gotta take this."

Jenna's sitting in her car, clearly parked. I spot some familiar landscaping. "Good. You're at your mother's."

"Had to practice the 'obey' part of our upcoming vows." She ruins her statement by giggling like a schoolgirl.

"I didn't even imagine the word would be in our vows. But now that you mention it, I do like the sound of it."

"Forget it, Rock Star."

"A guy can dream. I'll loosen you up." I blow her a kiss.

She shakes her head. "Anyway, what was so important that you had to call me before you even landed? And how could you do that? Calls can't be made on airplanes."

I love her naïveté. "That law doesn't apply to private jets. They let us do whatever we want on there." I stick out my tongue and move it up and down. "If you get my drift."

She pretends to be scandalized. I know better. "Settle down, over there. Talk to me."

I do. I tell her about the shocking call with Curtiss and how I can get out from under the vile shit Lissa's spewing. She fills me in about her interview with the *Record News*. "And," she finishes, "I did it. Court and I talked with Hayden."

I do a quick mental rolodex and can't place a Hayden in it. I hope context will help. "Was she helpful?"

"She really was. She had a great idea for how we can do even more with the spider thing. I didn't tell her about Michelle, though. I think if her idea works—and with some tweaks both Court and I think it will—it'll be even better than calling her out by name."

Got it. Hayden's on the UC PR team. I file her name for future use. "I'm glad you got some outside help. Care to share this idea?"

She wiggles in her seat. "No."

I love when she plays the coquette. Hell, I simply love her. I don my best puppy dog eyes. "Not even one little hint?"

"Fine," she fake huffs. "We're going to use the attributes of a spider to our advantage."

All right. I didn't see this coming, and I can't even imagine what would be considered a positive about a spider. "Not sure what on earth that would be, but I trust you. Can't wait to see the campaign."

"Hayden's working up some ideas. I promise to show them to you when they're ready." Her eyes drift toward the house and she squints, leans forward, then rears backward. "I think Ma just fell. I have to go." She unbuckles her seatbelt.

Before she can disconnect the call, I beg, "Text me what's going on."

"I will."

The phone goes dead before I can tell her I love her.

From the driver's seat, Elias says, "I hope everything's all right with Jenna's mother."

Because we still have a ways to go to get to the stadium. Because I'm raw after our conversation. Because I need an outlet and he's always been the face of discretion—being our head of security and all —I admit, "Her mother's been diagnosed with pancreatic cancer. She looked pretty good when I saw her today, but I've noticed a decline in her health since we first met. Doctors say she has maybe a couple of months left."

"Wow. I'm sorry." He turns left. "Please let me know if there's anything I can do. Jenna's a doll. I liked her before," *when she was with Darren* remains unsaid. "She's grown up since then. You two are a good fit."

Two fingers rub over the bridge of my nose. "I love her."

"Great to hear. You'll figure out how to help her mother."

I don't unburden myself on Elias any further. He doesn't need to hear of the multiple doctors who have examined her, only to reach the same prognosis. I simply say, "Or be there for Jenna."

We continue our ride in silence, pulling up to the back of the stadium where a crowd has gathered behind iron gates. His knuckles clench around the steering wheel. "Stick with me, Bennett. I'll get you into the building without any issues."

"Will do." My mind remains in Aroostook. I need to get an update from Jenna about her mother. Why hasn't she called me back yet?

He pulls to a stop as close to the doors as possible. We get out and the mood in the crowd shifts. Like it always does. Although, this time, excitement is interlaced with something else. Hostility?

"Bennett!" Someone screams my name. My head whips to the sound. I let my performance mask fall into place, smile, and raise my hand.

Followed by, "How could you abandon your high school sweetheart when she was pregnant?" My arm lowers.

"How could you be so heartless?" I keep my face trained on the cement.

"Why are you with the Black Widow? She's nothing compared with Lissa Baker!" My stride lengthens.

"I can't wait to see you perform tonight!" This final shout, at least, makes me feel somewhat better.

Elias nods at the security guarding the door, which the burly guy opens. I give him a thumbs up and follow Elias into the stadium. Once the door closes, I lean against the wall. Now I understand why he picked me up at the airstrip. "Christ."

"I was hoping we would've avoided any interactions with the public before I got you inside. Things escalated since Lissa's latest interview."

"I'd say." We resume walking toward backstage. "I might have a lead that will end things. Still working out the details."

"Good to hear."

Elias doesn't ask me if what Lissa's been spouting is true. Guess it doesn't matter to him either way, but I have a need to set him straight. "For the record, she wasn't pregnant by me."

"I believe you."

His trust shocks me, given it's still only a *he said, she said* situation. A couple of steps later, I say, "Thank you."

We turn the corner and Elias opens a door that leads to the stage. This is my domain. Better prepare myself to perform, even if it's only pregame. Before I even can close my eyes to visualize the staging and our performance, Elias puts his hand on my shoulder. "I've got your back."

His heartfelt sentiment lodges in my throat. This man has been like a father to me since I joined UC. For the first time, I wonder what his home life is like. Does he have a wife? Kids? I need to talk with Luke and get the dirt on him. See how I can make his life better. It certainly can't be easy dealing with the five of us on the regular.

My cheeks puff. "I'm forever grateful."

"B, you're back!" Luke walks up to us as Elias melts into the background. Where he always is, ever vigilant. Making sure his charges are safe.

"Hey, Luke. What did I miss?"

"The usual. Ready to run through sound check?"

No mention of the shitstorm swirling around me from outside. Not wanting to cause anymore headaches or discuss my fiancée—I have a fiancée!—I reply with the expected, "Of course." I hop onto the stage and run through the regular ritual.

After the sound check, we enjoy an amazing catered meal from one of New Orleans's famed restaurants in one of the rooms tucked away in the bowels of the stadium. "These people really know how to cook down here," Coop notes.

The rest of the band chimes in with their favorite dishes. The discussion gets heated over gumbo versus jambalaya. I let their talking swirl around me, with our opening act providing the background music. My mind's firmly in the Hamptons, hoping Jenna's mother is all right. She still hasn't texted me.

007 asks, "Which do you prefer, Bennett?"

"Huh?" I glance around the table.

"What are you looking at?"

"I'm waiting for a text from Jenna, if you must know."

Our bassist runs his palm over the table. "Gotcha."

On edge from waiting for Jenna, I can't take his passive-aggressive shit tonight. "What's that supposed to mean?"

007 raises his hands. "No offense, man."

Yeah, right. He's had it out for Jenna since she first set foot back-stage following the movie premiere. I erupt, "You better get used to her. Jenna's my woman. We're getting married."

Five sets of eyes home in on me. Luke is the first to find his voice. "Come again, B?"

I toss my napkin onto the table. "There's a lot of shit going on." I spring up and take longer strides than usual, ignoring the tiny twinges from my pulled muscle.

Luke comes up next to me. "How about we save this for after the show? You guys are on in twenty."

I hang my head. Since when have I been led around by a woman's fingernail before? *Since you fell in love.* I force my body to face the table. "Sorry, guys. Jenna's mom is sick. Like, really sick. Right before sound check, she fell. I'm waiting to hear a status update from Jenna."

The table stills. "Jeez, Bennett, we're sorry to have been busting your balls," Coop, ever the wise peacemaker, says.

My eyes close. "You didn't know." I suck in air. "Let's go and show NOLA what UC can do." Even to my own ears, my pronouncement sounds hollow.

The guys finish their plates. I take a final swig of my tea, which doesn't produce its usual calming effect. Sneaking a final check of my phone, it still shows no new texts. I do something I haven't done since my father died. I issue a prayer that her mother's all right.

Luke gives us a much-needed pep talk. "All right, guys, let's hit the stage and show the crowd how good UC is!"

We return to the greenroom and after Nese gives us her final approval as well as confiscates our phones, we huddle. Knowing I need to get my head into the game, I try to muster my usual performance mask. It doesn't quite fit tonight.

I glance from Coop to Río to 007 to Tris with their fists raised into the air. I yell in a way that's intended to rile all of us up, "Strapped, locked, and loaded, are you ready to roll with Untamed Coaster?" Our usual collective whoop bounces off the cement walls and we make our way to the now black stage.

The show is going well. I hit all my marks and the band, as usual, sounds phenomenal. I take off in a run to cross the catwalk, and a ping from my right thigh reminds me why I haven't done this since the tour started. I pull up short next to Coop.

Sensing I'm off my game, he walks toward the audience, sliding his guitar across his hips. The ladies in the crowd scream their appreciation. I take the opportunity to give everyone my back, trying to get this pain under control while my band takes up the slack.

007 makes his way over to me. "Are you okay?"

"Kicked up my groin pull," I answer through gritted teeth.

"Shit." He circles around me, tilting the neck of his bass toward some women in the front row. "What do you need?"

Jenna. Ice. More Jenna than ice.

"Give me a minute."

"We got you covered." He makes a show of returning to "his" side of the stage while Coop returns to me.

"Turn your back to mine," he whispers.

Taking my time, I offer him my back and pretend to wail on my imaginary guitar while he does for real. I do a tentative slide downward, and my thigh doesn't protest. Good sign.

Río rocks out on the drums next and I turn to face Coop, who leans forward, "We've all got your back."

For the first time, I begin to understand what he means. Could these guys become my first friends since . . . Curtiss?

"Thanks man."

"Take it easy out there," Coop warns as Tris's keys take the spotlight.

The way my bandmates rally around me breaks a notch on my performance mask, which I shore up before retaking my position as the lead singer. Our musical interlude pumped up the crowd unlike I've seen it do before. Perhaps we should schedule something like this in each of our shows?

After our last bow following our encore, our final wave to the audience made, we exit the stage. Coop speaks for the group, "You okay, Bennett?"

I'm back to walking like a normal person. "Yeah. I did something stupid, and my injury yelled. Got it worked out during the song. Thanks for covering for me."

He pats my back. "We've got you."

Now that the performance is over, I need to check my cell to see if Jenna got back to me. She better have. I approach Nese with my palm held out, motioning for her to plant my phone in it.

"Great job, as usual," she says as she drops my cell into my hand.

"Thanks," I reply then turn away to check my messages. Thank fuck there's one from Jenna.

> Ma's all right. She fell and was disoriented. The ambulance came and checked her out but she didn't need to go to the hospital. Kara's here and Ma's stabilized.

Things must be really bad if her sister came all the way out to Aroostook from the City. I rub my forehead on the phone.

Luke approaches, his eyes burning into me. "How's Jenna's mother?"

"Jenna says she's all right. She didn't have to go to the hospital."

"Good news."

"Yeah." However, things aren't going to get better—and they're going downhill fast. Everything swirls in my head. I need someone to hear me out. Jenna's been my sounding board, but she can't help me here. Dare I do as she did in allowing UC's PR team in, and seek some outside help myself? "Hey, Luke." The words pop from my mouth before my brain can reconsider.

"What's up?"

I take a deep breath. Here goes nothing. "What's our schedule over the next few weeks? Before our US tour ends and we get our two week break?" He gives me our dates. Since we're here overnight, I bet I can find a good jewelry store in New Orleans. "What do I have to do to use the jet?"

"Just give me your dates. Go back to your woman as often as you like. Help her mom."

"There's no helping her, Luke. She's dying." My hand swipes over my eyes, then I rub my fingers together over the moisture.

"I didn't realize things were that bad."

Coop appears at my side with an ice pack. "Why don't you take a load off and ice your thigh?"

I try for some humor. "Is this some sort of bad game of *Clue*? A guitarist in the greenroom with an ice pack?"

"Seems like it," Tris quips, passing me a pair of shorts.

"Thanks." Not bothering to seek privacy, I strip out of my black leather pants and don the workout shorts. Coop and Tris start changing as well. Looks like I started a trend.

Shirtless himself, as usual, Río drags over a chair as I'm switching out my own T-shirt. "Have a seat." He pushes down on my shoulders ensuring I follow his instructions. The ice pack goes on top of my thigh.

007 is the last to approach, but he does. He's already in street clothes. I look at each of my coworkers. Colleagues.

Friends?

"Thanks for saving my butt out there. Your jam session gave me the time I needed to get this under control." I point to the ice pack.

"Gotta admit," Río says, banging his hands on his legs. Once a drummer, always a drummer, it doesn't matter that he just finished playing a three-hour concert. "It was nice to change things up a little. Our impromptu jam session was the bomb."

Our manager agrees. "It was. Nice improv out there, guys. What do you think about adding this into our regular shows?"

"Good idea," I answer for the whole band. Around me, their murmured agreement backs me up. Unlike before our gig, my stomach does backflips. I need to share this with them.

"Listen, guys, Jenna's mom isn't going to get better. In fact, she's going downhill. The doctor gave her a few months." I hold up my cell. "But I have an idea."

Chapter 12

Jenna

"We have more flowers in here than a hothouse nursery," Ma remarks, even as she stops to smell the newest delivery—a multicolored vase filled with white roses. Knuckles white against the side of the table, she plucks a bloom and rubs it against her cheek.

"It certainly is a beautiful addition to your home. And mine. And both clinics." I smell a red rose from another day's delivery.

The doorbell rings. "I wonder what your boy sent now?"

I giggle. "Let's find out." I rush to the door where a delivery person hands me a couple of pizza boxes. I scramble for a tip, even though Bennett's told me repeatedly he's handled everything. "Thank you."

"What is it?"

Ma makes her way into the living room and stands beside her chair, her hand reaching for the back of it. She's a fighter. She tires more easily, takes longer and longer naps during the day, but is still relatively mobile. A quad cane rests in the corner for added stability, courtesy of Kara.

I read from the top of the box. "It's pizza from what's billed as

'The Best Pizza Place in Chicago.'" My mouth waters. I love New York pizza but am more than willing to suffer through trying a deep dish all the way from the Windy City.

"Not too boastful, are they?"

"I guess we better try it to decide. You stay here, I'll heat this up." I rush into the kitchen and preheat the oven, while putting two slices from the first pie onto a cookie sheet. They're massive. And saucy. And filled with mushrooms. Yum.

The ring on my left hand catches the light and I stare at it. When Bennett was here last, he put this ring on my finger, and I swear it was made for me. The diamond is a round cut solitaire, so it won't snag when I'm "working with a patient," as he said. The setting isn't too high, either. The fact it's a flawless two carats on a platinum band makes it timeless. Like the man who gave it to me.

I break free from my woolgathering when the temperature alert bings, sliding the cookie sheet into the oven. I place two plates onto the counter and bring napkins and silverware into the living room. Once the makeshift table is set in front of Ma, I repeat the same for myself. Returning to the kitchen, I take out the hot pizza and bring the full plates with me.

"Oh my, this smells divine," Ma places her face closer to the pizza and inhales.

At least she still has her zest for food. I pause in setting my napkin on my lap. I glance over at her, watching her chew. "Good?"

"Oh my God. This is fantastic. Don't get me wrong, I love our pizza out here, but this is different in a really amazing way. What did the note say?"

Bennett always includes a note with his presents. I pick it up and clear my throat. "UC enjoyed this restaurant during our stop in Chicago and I thought of you two. Maybe save me a slice?"

"When's he coming back again?"

"Today." I glance at my watch. "In five hours, twenty minutes, and thirty seconds. But who's counting?"

"Right. Who would do such a crazy thing? How long will he be able to stay this time?"

"Two whole days!"

She smiles around another forkful of pizza. "He was here what? A week ago? How many breaks does UC have anyway?"

"Only these short ones in between gigs. He's coming up on a two-week break soon, though." I'm excited to spend fourteen whole days with him. My engagement ring glimmers with its secrets.

"You'll appreciate that, I bet." Her fork clatters onto her remaining pizza, about one-half of the slice. She did a good job.

"I will. Especially if our PR campaign keeps going as it has." Hayden has done a bang-up job. With Ma's health taking up more of my attention, having her has been a UC godsend. One I now admit was more than needed.

Ma reaches into the pocket of her chair and pulls out the book she's reading, flips it open, and removes the bookmark, which is actually one of the bumper stickers Hayden created. Holding it in the air, she reads the slogan, "We'll Fix All Your Limbs." The At Your Service PT logo is set next to a cartoon depiction of a spider with therapists working on all eight legs.

"This is brilliant. You got back at that Michelle without calling her out by name. As Don Vito Corleone said, 'revenge is a dish that tastes best when it's cold.'"

I lower my fork to my empty plate. "Actually, that was from a deleted scene in Part Two of *The Godfather*."

She smiles. "I stand corrected by my *Godfather* buff."

"If only Bennett would see it your way." Our ongoing *Godfather* debates take up a good part of our texts. The rest are general information about our days, Ma, and, well, sexting. Heat stains my cheeks as I think about some of the racier ones. I check on my phone, which is sitting by my plate. Better not let this out of my sight.

"I'm happy for you, Sweet Pea. Bennett is a good man. He loves you and the feeling is obviously reciprocated."

"Totally."

"I can tell by the way you blush whenever you think about him. And that ring! Bring it over here so I can gawk at it again."

Rising, I take the few steps to her chair and kneel next to her, my left hand outstretched. "The man sure has mighty fine taste."

"He had help. He told me when he was in New Orleans, he and his manager, Luke, scoured the city for the right jewelry store. When they found this one, they knew it was perfect for me."

"He has some good friends."

I sigh, "He does. I think he's starting to realize it, too."

She twists my left hand from side to side. "This is so big; you better be careful. You don't want to poke someone's eye out with it."

"I will be careful, I promise."

She squeezes my hand, and I try not to notice how light her touch is compared with a year ago. Or even last month. "I know you will." She yawns. "I'm a bit tired. I think I'll take a nap. Would you help me into my bedroom?"

"Of course." I pop up and move the tray, then allow her to use my body as her makeshift cane. We get into her bedroom. "I only need to rest for a little bit. Don't eat all the pizza."

I kiss her cheek. "I'll leave you a slice, Ma."

Once her door is closed and the living room is righted, I clean up the kitchen and check the time. Only a couple more hours. Kara said she'd stop by soon so I can surprise Bennett at the airstrip. My two realities hit hard. On one hand, I'm my mother's caretaker. On the other, I'm Bennett's fiancée. I've learned to put these two things into separate buckets and not dwell too much on one when I'm living in the other. It's not easy, but it's my reality.

I'm checking my phone to see if Bennett's sent me another text when Kara breezes into the house. "How many flowers is this man going to send you?" I'd take offense but for the smile across her face. "Lucky duck."

"Feel free to take a vase or two to your place. I'm sure Ma won't miss them."

"She probably can't keep track of all of them."

My shoulders lower. "You're not wrong. She's seeming weaker to me. I just helped her get into bed for a nap after we had pizza."

"From where?"

I smirk. "Chicago."

Her mouth falls open. "Bennett?"

"Don't you know it." I take a step toward the kitchen. "Want me to heat you up a slice? It's deep dish and delicious."

"When you put it that way, how can I say no?" She follows me into the kitchen, and we sit at the counter while it heats. "Other than the sleeping, how is she doing?"

I give her Ma's medical updates, which we discuss while my sister devours her slice. "How long is she napping?"

"It's been getting longer every day. My guess is she's out about an hour or more in the afternoons."

"This is for the best, you know."

Kara pushes her empty plate to the side. Even as kids, when she was finished eating, she'd always move her plate away from her. Ma does it too. I don't remark on her habit, keeping this tidbit inside. Instead, I ask, "What is?"

"Ma making her own decisions about her end-of-life care. She's at home, relatively happy and comfortable." She glances around. "Surrounded by flowers and eating Chicago pizza."

"Two very good things." I fiddle with my ponytail. "In my head, I understand what you're saying. My heart wants her to stay longer, though."

"I hear you." Kara pushes away from the table and brings her dishes to the sink. "Sucks big time. But the best gift we can give her is dignity. Let her choose her own path." She rinses off the dish and I place it into the dishwasher.

Her words make me stand straighter. "Is this from you or your husband?"

"He started it. I've embraced the sentiment and now we're trying to explain to our kids why grammy can't come visit anymore."

"Your munchkins are the best. I know they make Ma happy when they call or you bring them over."

"Thanks, kiddo."

Kara called me *kiddo* when we were young. She hasn't used this nickname for me in decades. She has to be feeling Ma's health issues as deeply as I am, only she has a family to attend to and help her process. Bennett's been awesome, but given our distance and his relationship with his own mother, he hasn't been as available as I would've liked. Hell, with me twenty-four seven might not be enough.

"Before I forget, do you have Ma's medication list for me?"

"Yes, I have it in my bedroom. Come on." Kara's been able to purchase Ma's meds at a discount, but always double-checks the doctor's notes against the prescription.

Together, we go into what is now *my* messy bedroom, with my open suitcase on one bench and clothes scattered on top of all flat surfaces. Kara frowns. "I don't remember you being this disorganized."

I pick up a couple of items and half-heartedly toss them into the suitcase. "I don't make it back to my house too often, grabbing whatever I can before coming back here. Getting this room under control isn't a priority for me right now."

She places her hand on my shoulder. "I'm here for you."

She means it. We may not have been close before Ma's health issues, but we're becoming closer since the diagnosis. "I know you took on the brunt of the doctor visits when I was on tour with UC. I'm only doing my part."

"Hey, we're both doing what we can. We're a team." She gives me a hug.

A team? With my sister? If anything good is coming out of this awful ordeal, it's I'm building a relationship with Kara. She's pretty cool. "Ma made some pretty good humans, huh?"

"She sure did." We break apart. "Now, about Ma's meds?"

"Right." We approach my desk, filled with all sorts of paperwork. Including . . .

"What's this?" Kara snags the official paper.

I purse my lips. This is my sister, who I'm getting to know and trust. Out of everyone on earth, she deserves to know what's going on. I have no doubt she'll keep our secret. "It's something Bennett and I did the last time he was in town."

She stares at the paper. "Is this what I think it is?"

I pluck it from her fingers. "If you're thinking it looks like a marriage license, then yes. You're right."

She stares at me for a moment, her gray eyes darkening. "My baby sister's getting married?"

I nod.

"Oh my God. Come here!"

She folds me into our second embrace of the day, this one filled with excitement and happiness. If only all of them would feel this way. I squeeze her tight.

"Don't tell Ma or anyone about it, all right?" I step back. "We have sixty days from when it was issued to get married. Bennett's trying to get everything set up for tomorrow, but I don't know if even he can pull this off."

"What can I do?"

I haven't told anyone about this development—not Ma, not Court—due to the possible PR fallout. But being able to share my secret with someone feels so right. "You can be my maid of honor."

Her palm flies in front of her face. "Me? Don't you have people you're closer to?"

"None of them are my sister." Yes. This is the right choice.

"I would be very honored." She tosses some clothes from the bed to the floor and pats the newly empty spot next to her. "If you're getting married tomorrow, what do you need? Do you have a dress? Flowers? Someone to marry you?"

"I picked up a white dress off the rack at a nice boutique a couple of towns over. As for flowers, Bennett has an 'in' with the one he's been using, so we're all set there." We both smile. "He's working on connections to get us a minister."

"Music?"

Her last question elicits a chuckle. "My groom has an 'in' with the biggest band on the planet, so I think we got that one covered."

Her head shakes. "I can't believe my brother-in-law is going to be Bennett Hardy. *You're* going to be Jenna Hardy!"

"Shhh," I remind her. "We don't want to wake Ma."

"What do you think she'll say?"

"Well, she did give him permission to marry me." I swoon inside. He asked. She agreed. He suggested we get the license so Ma can attend our ceremony. If only she would be around to see our ten-year anniversary. Hell, I'd be happy with our first.

"You're living a fairytale."

"Complete with the paparazzi calling me Black Widow, a crazy ex of his from high school claiming he's the father of the baby she lost, and a potential media storm about to be set ablaze."

"Aside from all that, it'll be a normal wedding, huh?" She giggles, which sets me off. Who knew Kara could be so funny?

A tenor voice sails through the air. "Can anyone join in this gigglefest?"

"Bennett!" I spring to my feet and leap into his strong arms. "You got here early!" Our mouths fuse as if it's been months rather than days since we last saw each other.

I break away from my fiancé's delicious lips. Getting lost in his green orbs, I ask, "Did you get it?"

"I did." He kisses me again.

My heart beats faster and I squirm away from him. When my feet land on the floor, I announce, "We're getting married tomorrow!"

"That we are," Bennett agrees.

"It's going to be the best celebration ever," Kara vows, tugging my arm away from my gorgeous groom. "But with this deadline, I think we have some things to handle."

My brows pull together, as do Bennett's. "I got everything covered."

"Music and an officiant do not a wedding make, my dear soon-to-be brother-in-law. Why don't you enjoy some Chicago-style pizza from the fridge while I monopolize my sister for an hour. That's all I'll need." Taking in the air swirling with desire, she adds, "I swear." Then she shoos him out of the bedroom.

Retaking our seats to the soundtrack of puttering in the kitchen, Kara says, "I know you got this under control, disaster in this bedroom notwithstanding. Let's run through a quick checklist, and I'll take care of whatever you haven't done." She whips out her phone, clicks on a wedding app, and we go through each item. "Great. I've got my list. The only one on yours is for you and Bennett to tell Ma."

She kisses my cheek and leaves, exchanging happy compliments with my fiancé before the front door closes. She's right. As much as I want to surprise Ma with this news, I don't want to overtax her. As I enter the kitchen, Bennett's inhaled half of the remaining pizza, his cheek now sporting a tomato sauce streak.

I sit in his lap and lick it clean.

Which ends with us kissing like teenagers.

Reality finally makes me break apart from him. "Kara said we should tell Ma. I agree. Don't want to shock her system or anything."

He steals another kiss. "Who do you think recommended our officiant?"

Chapter 13

Bennett

"Thanks, guys, for coming out to Aroostook." I raise my Manhattan to the ceiling, and we all drink. "I really appreciate it."

"Hell, it's not every day one of the members of Untamed Coaster gets hitched," Luke says, sipping his drink.

"Damn straight," Río joins in. "Let Bennett do that shit for all of us. We'll be free agents 'til the end!" He raises his glass. Tris and 007 join him. Coop stays in the background.

I leave the bar area and wander over to our new keyboardist, unsure of what to say or how to say it. So I go for a softball. "Hey. Thanks for coming out here."

He glances around the basement of my new home—I signed the papers for it last week. "This place is amazing. It has a name, right?"

"Secluded Rest."

"I get it."

His gaze travels to the arcade games, where the rest of the band is cheering on Coop. My eyelids lower. The guitarist better not be playing Asteroids Deluxe. Eh, no matter. He'll never beat my score.

Returning my attention to Tris, I rub two fingers over my nose. "If

I didn't say this before—or ever—thanks for taking care of Jenna in Memphis. It means a lot to me that you helped her." *Just don't do it again.* After today, her happiness will be my singular responsibility.

"I didn't do anything except offer her my shirt as a tissue." He pats his torso. "I'm happy things worked out between you two." He pauses, and I let him collect his thoughts, a bit surprised at where he goes. "Of course, I never knew Darren personally. From all accounts he was a great guy. A real joker."

A small smile graces my lips. "Can't argue with you there."

"I understand he was in love with Jenna, and she with him. But I've seen you two together and can't imagine whatever they had would've come close to what you and she share. You're my relation-ship goal."

Thud. My heart skips five beats at Tris's confession. While I wanted to kill the guy for my ill-perceived thought that he and Jenna were hooking up, this is what he was thinking? How do I respond? I choose my truth.

"You'll find your path, Tris. Hell, you found your way to UC. How much harder could it be to find the one woman on earth who understands you? Who encourages you. Who supports you."

He snaps his fingers. "Yeah. Piece of cake." The corners of his eyes crinkle. "Don't think I'm stepping onto your crazy train anytime soon."

"Never say never, my man."

The doorbell rings and Luke's discombobulated voice comes over the intercom demanding I get up to the foyer stat. "Better go see what's up. All good?"

"Definitely."

Surprising myself, I give the guy a hug, then climb the stairs. Luke's in the front hall, surrounded by people bringing in flowers. Having a florist on speed dial to send Jenna flowers every day sure did come in handy today. I direct them to place the arrangements on the tables outside and the boutonnieres on the coffee table in the family room. Thank God for King and Angie, who got us needed rentals of tables and chairs from their staging stash. While not matching, everything looks great. At least in my humble opinion. Guess since I'm the groom, only my opinion counts today. Well, and Jenna's.

Now in the family room, I take in my surroundings. Organized chaos is the best way to describe it, as workers prepare items for our few dozen guests who'll be arriving in about one hour. Luke strides over to me. "Better go make yourself look pretty or your bride will turn around and run down the aisle." His hand clamps on my back.

Ever since my conversation with Curtiss, I've been feeling all sorts of things. With Luke's good-natured comment, another chink inside me cracks. He's always had my back. UC is lucky he's our manager, and I'm grateful to have him in my corner. "You don't think my workout gear will do it?"

"Probably not a good idea. I've already sent the rest of the band upstairs to their rooms. It's your turn."

He leads me toward the stairs. I haven't taken the elevator in ages, and don't plan on starting on the day of my wedding. My groin pull still complains sometimes, but it's less frequent and quieter. Better stay that way throughout the day and night. Especially the night.

With each step, my conviction over this final decision grows. Jenna asked me about it last night, and I know if I don't do it, she won't care. Or will pretend it doesn't bother her. Hell, for the first time in as long as I can remember, I actually *want* to do this.

About halfway up the staircase, I grab the handrail and Luke turns. "Everything all right? Does your muscle pull hurt?"

I shake my head. "No. I feel great. I'd like to ask you a question."

He smirks. "Seems like you asked Jenna the right question already."

"That I did. But I don't want to ask you to marry me, thank you very much. I wanted to ask if you'd be willing—I mean you don't have to—no pressure at all." I rub sweaty palms together. In my ear, I can hear Jenna encouraging me. Here goes nothing. "Would you mind standing up next to me during the ceremony?" I suck in my breath.

Luke's face nearly splits in two, his grin is so wide. His coffee-colored gaze stares right into me. "I'd be honored, B."

My body sags. The next thing I know, I'm opening my arms and pulling him in for a hug. "I couldn't think of anyone else I want to stand up for me." Except Dad. The florist suggested we place a white rose on his empty chair for the ceremony to honor him. Yet, Luke makes a great substitute. Dare I consider him a *friend*? After my recent conversation with Curtiss, the last man to hold the title, I might be willing to try again.

Our bodies move from side to side. The fact we're standing on the main stairs comes rushing back to me when we nearly lose our balance.

"Shit!" I reach for the handrail, which saves both of our sorry asses. Or they would be sorry if we had fallen.

Once we regain our equilibrium, a pink-cheeked Luke says, "Let's not tell anyone about this, all right?"

"Your secret's safe with me." We chuckle and go up the rest of the steps, where we part ways to get dressed.

In the master suite, I take a quick shower and put on my Armani suit. All of the guys have them from a recent awards ceremony, so we decided they would be our best option. *Sans* footwear and tie, of course. I pull out the flip-flops Kara dropped off last night, explaining to me that all of the wedding party has to wear them.

My next stop is my dresser, where I pull our wedding rings from a drawer. Luke helped me pick these out at the same store where I got Jenna's engagement ring in New Orleans. Leaving all of my other rings and bracelets on the top of the dresser, I pat the only other piece of jewelry I'll wear today—my necklace with the UC pendant Jenna gave to us years ago.

In silence, I slip on my new gray Tungsten ring, which matches Jenna's eyes. It's big and chunky and will be seen from the nosebleed seats at every stadium. Perfect. I want everyone to know I'm taken by the most precious woman on earth.

"Almost ready, B?"

I return my wedding band into its box nestled next to hers, and snap it shut. "I think so. Hold these for safekeeping, all right?" I pass him the jewelry box.

He examines the box for a second before putting it into his pocket. "Damn. I can't believe you're the first one to fall. Well, after Coop."

We both shake our heads remembering what happened. I refuse to let his youthful experience sour mine. Luke continues, "Never thought I'd see the day when any of us would take the plunge again."

"When you know, you know." My smile dims. But for Jenna's mother's illness, would we be here today? Maybe. Maybe not. I have no doubt that we would've ended up here sooner rather than later, though.

"I brought your boutonniere, but you better ask someone else to put it on for you." He points to his lapel. "The florist did it for me."

I take the flower. "Is TLR here?"

"Already playing demure music downstairs for the ceremony."

I snort. The Light Rail is many things, but demure is not one of them. While I've crossed paths with the guys throughout the years—even playing with them once—King was instrumental in getting his brother's band to play for us. While UC wants to play a song or two at the reception, I didn't want to make us responsible for the whole thing. And no fucking way was a DJ going to dictate our party!

I'm about to leave when a thought hits me so hard, I almost stumble. I haven't heard from Jenna all day. "Is Jenna here?"

Deadpan, Luke looks at me. "Is she supposed to be?"

Panic surges through my bloodstream.

My manager laughs. "You should see your face, B." He smacks me on the back. "Of course she's here."

I give him a dirty look. "Dude. Maybe I should rethink the whole best man concept."

"Too late." He smacks my back again. "Let's go."

We enter the hallway and the guys surround me. "If I even harbored an idea of getting married, you've set the bar so fucking high, there's no way I could reach it," Río announces. "Seriously. TLR?"

I shrug as if getting this band was no big deal. "My real estate agent is King Hunte. You know, the lead singer's brother." I bump Río's fist.

Glancing from him to Coop to Tris, my gaze finally lands on 007 who, despite his conflicted feelings toward Jenna, appears happy for me. I suck in all the air.

"You guys each have supported my relationship with Jenna in your own ways. It means the world to me to know you will be at our side for today and going forward. Thank you." Not exactly a declaration of lasting friendship, but this is more than I've ever shared with my bandmates.

They seem to recognize this as each one of their fists fling high into the air. Instead of my starting our check in though, Luke steps up. I raise my fist.

Luke clears his throat. "Strapped, locked, and loaded, are you ready to celebrate this wedding?" We all let out large whoops and barrel toward the stairs.

The next hour flies by. Luke and I stand next to the judge. Our guests fill up the chairs. Courtney helps Faith into her seat of honor in the first row. The white rose for my dad is on a chair next to hers. Kara flip-flops down the aisle, beaming at me. Then Tris stands at the end of the aisle, my gorgeous bride in white on his arm.

My heart skips a beat. Maybe two.

The Light Rail plays the wedding march as the pair make their way to me. I didn't realize Jenna asked the new keyboardist to do the honors, but it makes sense. Everything about today does.

We recite our vows—ones we wrote in secret—to each other. Exchange rings. Kiss as the judge pronounces us husband and wife. Maybe our kiss goes on a little too long, as the guests start to snicker and clap and roar. Only when Jenna giggles into my mouth do I release her lips, whispering, "I love you forever."

"And a day."

We turn and face our friends and family, and TLR strikes up their hit, "Let Me Give You A Sweet," as we sashay down the aisle to Faith. I kiss her cheek and accept her hug as she says, "I'm so happy to call you 'son.'"

I may or may not have had to use one of Jenna's tissues.

The caterer serves appetizers, which we devour as if we hadn't eaten in ages. We laugh with our friends. I enjoy dancing with my new sister and her kids. Even enjoy chatting with my new brother, the cosmetic surgeon.

Luke pulls me away from them. "Hey, B, it's time."

With an apologetic glance to my new family—family!—I follow our manager to the stage, mentally reviewing our new song. The one I took the lead in writing, although the rest of the band added their own touches. Jenna's comment about how we, as a band, create our music together rings true. Today it was my idea, but tomorrow Coop or Río or Tris or 007 could take the lead. The fact we've never followed the traditional path in creating songs never hit so hard as it does now. Perhaps we are much more of a unique group than I ever realized? Filled with friends.

Shaking my head to get into the zone, I climb the stairs to the stage. Trent Washington-Hunte hands me the microphone. "Thanks so much for doing this for us," I whisper into his ear.

"Happy to help you out. Besides, my wife Cordelia always roots for true love. She would've handed me my balls if we didn't do this for you." He blows a kiss toward his wife, who's sitting by Court, my wife's—WIFE's—bff. They look thick as thieves.

"You better watch out for those two."

"Don't I know it. We'll be back to take over after you're done. Hit it, man." Trent leaves the stage and I check in with my bandmates, who each give me a thumbs up as they get situated behind The Light Rail's instruments.

I face the audience. No, not audience. Family and . . . friends? Close acquaintances? My eyes close, and as I reopen them. I raise my newly ringed left hand. "My wife and I want to thank you for dropping whatever you were doing to come all the way out here to celebrate our wedding with us. It means more than you can imagine that you're here supporting our new life together."

Everyone claps. Nese even whistles.

"Untamed Coaster wanted to sing this song for you. It's new, so go easy on us. It's called, 'Take The Chance.'"

Río bangs his drumsticks together three times and the guys play the intro. I scan the crowd until my gaze rests on Jenna, who's sitting next to Faith. Both of them beam at me. I blow my wife a kiss, then focus on the lyrics. I sing heartfelt sentiments.

Telling her how she changed my life.

Telling her I'm so lucky she agreed to be my wife.

Telling her I'm ready to take the chance. With her. Only her.

The bridge plays, then I repeat the chorus.

Sweetheart, I'm ready to take the chance
Believe me when I say you make my heart sing
'Cause there's no music when you're not around
I can do anything with you at my side
Let's go and let our love fly high
As we take the chance. Forever.

I speak the last three words. "I love you."

When the last note reverbs from Coop's guitar, our guests jump to their feet, clapping. I don't care about anyone else, my sole focus is on my wife. The beautiful Jenna Hardy. The woman who owns my body and soul, who breathed it back to life. If there ever was any life before her.

Jenna kisses her mother, then races to the stage where I pull her up next to me. With happy tears streaming down her face, she embraces me. "That was beautiful. I'm so blessed because you took the chance on me."

I kiss her, much to the encouragement of our guests. "I got the better end of this deal."

All of my bandmates huddle around us. We don't say anything, simply hold on to each other. I've never felt so much unity, happiness, kinship from my band. Ever.

I'm brought out of my head when Trent steals the mic I forgot I was holding from my fingers. He addresses our guests. "Great new chart-topping song, guys. Let's give it up for Untamed Coaster!" Everyone roars, and we turn the stage back to TLR.

We dance and eat and talk with everyone throughout the early evening. When I take to the dance floor with my new mother-in-law to Cole Manchester's hit, she kisses my cheek and says this is the happiest day she can remember in a long, long time.

There's nothing more that I could've asked for from our wedding.

Jenna and I deliberately planned the day to end around eight because UC has to leave for our next gig in the morning and I wanted to be sure I'd have at least a little bit of alone time with my new wife before that happens. I survey the backyard and find Faith sitting and chatting with a man I don't recognize. She appears animated, but I can discern the strain the day's taken on her.

I dance with my wife. "Think it's time we cut the cake and bow out?"

Jenna's fingers play with the back of my neck. "What do you have in mind? It's still light out."

My grin turns wolfish. "Keeping my wife up and screaming until the sun comes up."

"I like your plan. Your wife's a lucky girl."

I pick her up and slowly drag her body down mine. Into her ear, I agree, "She sure is."

When the song ends, we make our way to the double-tiered cake. The Light Rail strikes up "Speak Softly Love," the theme from *The*

Godfather, which makes Jenna giggle. I could live on this sound for the rest of my life.

After we—politely—feed each other, a delicious concoction of vanilla cake with cannoli icing, we say our goodbyes to everyone. She lingers with Court and Kara plus her niece and nephew. I take my time with Luke, who agrees to make sure Faith is brought home soon.

Then the rest of the band rushes over to give me their last bits of advice. "Make sure she comes first," Río offers.

"And often," Coop clarifies.

Not to be outdone, 007 says, "Shower off the cooties and wash in all the crevices. Then use soap."

Tris grabs my shoulder. "Don't go to sleep until you're back on the plane with us."

This feels like *more* to me. Much more than we've ever shared. Perhaps it's the setting in my new home, or the fact I'm now a husband, but the way these men have rallied around me mean the world to me. "You guys . . ." I can't get out any more than that, but they seem to understand.

Río pronounces, "Group hug!" The six of us smother each other.

Coop's the first to break the group. "You've got all of our advice. Now go consummate this marriage. We're gonna stay and trash your new house."

With these parting words, I join my wife and kiss her hand. Which is cold. I tilt my head. "Ready?"

Jenna's face is frozen as her eyes fix on a man sitting at the back of the gathered crowd. She whispers, "My father is here."

Chapter 14

Jenna

Sound whooshes through my ears. The only reason I recognize him at all is because Ma and I were looking through some old photos and I asked who he was. After all, I was in kindergarten the last time I saw him. Why would my *father* choose today of all days to show up? I squeeze Bennett's hand.

Bennett's voice lowers. "Your father is here?"

I nod, using my chin to point to Ma. And the man next to her.

"Do you want to talk with him?"

"No."

His hands press down on my shoulders. His green gaze sears into my soul. "Then don't let him ruin our perfect day. I married the woman of my dreams. All I want to do is make her scream out in pleasure. The rest will take care of itself."

His sentiment sinks into my very being. Who cares that my father showed up to my wedding? It's *my* wedding day, the one I'm sharing with the love of my life. My so-called father will disappear like he always does, not to be heard of again. Bennett, on the other hand, promised before God and our friends and family to be my husband forever. "I choose you."

"Us," Bennett corrects. "It's us against the whole world."

He lowers his head and kisses my lips. At first, I'm still too caught up in the fact my father showed up for my special day to return his passion. On an empirical level, I feel my husband hardening against my body, but my mind won't release the questions of why *he* chose today to show up. Why *he's* talking with Ma. Why she's talking with *him*—the man who left her decades ago and never looked back.

Bennett's hand goes to the back of my head. He exerts more pressure against my lips, yet I can't give in to his persuasion. When his tongue darts into my mouth, though, my knees react to what my body's been fighting, and I collapse into him. For a second, I'm his puppet, moving to his beat. Power returns to my limbs, and I stand taller, my hands rubbing against his super-sexy stubble. The stubble I want to rub against my thighs.

My husband steps back. "Time to go."

I blink, unable to comprehend. "Go?"

His fingers intertwine with mine. The look he gives me smolders with promise, causing my stomach to leap. Bennett's the only man on earth who can flip my switch from control freak to a compliant woman in love. This issue about my father will be here in the morning. Reality is, UC will not be, due to their tour schedule. Bennett arranged this day so Ma could be here, and I couldn't be prouder of him. We turn and wave at our guests.

He ushers me into the waiting limo. As soon as we're situated inside, glasses of bubbly already filled, I say, "You never told me where we're spending our wedding night."

He beams. "Given our time constraints, I rented us a private villa on the ocean."

My heart sings. While Bennett could've done anything he wanted—fly us into New York City for an over-the-top experience—he chose to stay close to my home. Something he knew I'd love. Placing my glass into the cupholder on the armrest, I link my fingers around his neck. "Have I told you how much I love you?"

His eyes dart back and forth. "Not for the last half hour."

He blinks several times, which causes me to giggle. "Then let me rectify the situation." I climb on top of his lap, swiveling my hips exactly where my body craves his. Our mouths crash together, and I moan when his fingers slide over my boobs. Squeezing. Pinching. Weighing.

The limo pulls to a halt.

After several seconds, we break apart, panting. Bennett's head lands on the headrest. "Are we here?"

"Yes, sir."

My husband's hand slides down to my hips as he moves me onto the seat next to him. "You're going to love this place."

"I don't care so long as it has a bed."

"Oh, it sure does. And a sofa. A kitchen counter. A shower. A—"

My hand clamps around his mouth. "Shut up and take me there."

Bennett glides out of the limo and holds his hand out to me. As soon as my feet touch the pavement, he swoops down and picks me up, bridal style. I giggle. I actually *am* his bride.

He takes purposeful steps toward the front door of the villa, as he called it. It's a gorgeous Tudor, with flowers, in all colors, blooming everywhere. The stone facade looks as if it belongs in a forest somewhere. I glance around at all the trees around us. Simply gorgeous.

Bennett opens the door and we sweep inside the marble foyer, our driver hot on his heels. "Where do you want these?" He holds up our bags.

We swing around. "You can leave them there. Thanks."

With pink cheeks, the driver bows his head for a moment. "Congratulations on your wedding, Mr. and Mrs. Hardy. I'll be back around ten in the morning to take you to the airstrip, Sir. Enjoy your night." He disappears through the front door, which closes behind him.

"Alone at last with my beautiful bride." Still in his arms, Bennett kisses me.

Despite being carried away by his insistent tongue, I want more. I want to feel his skin against mine. I want his hands to roam over my body, and for mine to return the favor. I want our bodies locked together in exquisite pleasure. I wiggle in his arms, forcing him to put me down.

"Let's check the view," I suggest.

"I only need you to look at," he growls.

His sentiment warms my heart. "And I you. Come on." I tug on his hand and we walk through the house until we reach the French doors, which he opens. My mouth drops open. Laid out in front of us is the ocean. Pristine sand beckons us out to the fire pit, and I walk toward it as if in a trance.

After a minute or two, Bennett joins me by the outside bedroom. A massive, king-size bed lounges on the beach, and not merely a hammock. A true bed, facing the waves. He puts down a tray with more champagne and my favorite—pizza. Not deep dish this time, but from someplace local.

I turn to him, accepting the flute. "You're my hero."

He clinks his against mine. "Only the best for my wife."

We make plates of food and sit on the bed to eat the mushroom and cheese pizza. When our slices are consumed, Bennett takes the plates and puts them on the side tables, his eyes devouring my body. The sun is just starting to set—streaks of pinks and purples cast an amazing glow over us.

"You're the most beautiful creature I've ever seen," he fingers one of my blonde locks.

"I appreciate what you're saying, but you forget I've seen some of the women in your orbit. They're gorgeous. But I'm happy to be the woman who makes you sing."

He rests his weight onto his forearm. "No one holds a candle to your honest purity. I love the way you love with your whole heart. How you understand what I've been feeling. How devoted you are to your mother. You don't have any doctor-enhanced anything, which makes you more real than the silicone and Botoxed groupies who are always around UC. So, you, Jenna Hardy, are the real deal. *My* real deal." He kisses my nose.

When he says things like that . . . I can't restrain myself. I tackle him to the bed. His Armani suit jacket is the first thing to go, sailing through the air to land wherever. We both kick off Kara's flip-flops at the same time, and they land on the sand carpet below with a tiny thud.

My fingers open his crisp white shirt and stroke his pecs. Beneath my ministrations, his muscles flex and bow, as his breathing becomes more ragged. His hands shoo mine away, and he pulls his shirttail out of his pants, tossing it onto the beach as well.

I sit up. Seagulls fly overhead, pronouncing their approval of our wedding. The salty air urges me to twist around, offering my husband the back of my white dress. With care, he tugs the zipper down, kissing every square inch of skin as it's exposed. When he reaches the bottom, I slip the material over my hips and leave it in a ball at the foot of the bed.

Waves crash in the near distance, providing the only soundtrack necessary. In only my white lingerie and him in his boxer briefs, we stare into each other's eyes. He swallows. "Whatever I did to deserve you, I want to keep doing it forever."

"Keep on being you, Bennett."

He groans as he removes my bra, then lowers his head to suck my already puckered nipples. He takes his time with one, then moves to the other to repeat the same motions. I hold his head to my boob, awash in sensations.

"It's been too long."

"Hell yes," he agrees. "One hour is too long." He pulls back. "And I'm leaving on tour tomorrow. Come with me."

My body begs me to accept his offer. Fly away from here, and all my problems. If it were only the stupid Black Widow stuff from Michelle, I might be convinced. But Ma's face from today swims into my field of vision. I shake my head. "Ma."

His arms wrap around my body and I snuggle into his warmth, needing it to do away with the coldness I know is soon to come. "I know, Sweetheart." He kisses my neck. "I know."

We remain locked together for a while, until Bennett rests his body weight on his forearm again and his thumb plucks at my bottom lip. "Today was a good day. Your mother enjoyed it. I think she wants you to enjoy tonight too."

Let tomorrow take care of itself.

I allow this mantra to take hold. "You know what?" I maneuver my hips closer to him. "My husband is a real genius. He says the smartest things." I kiss his mouth.

His lips quirk upward. "If you think a high school dropout is smart, I have a house in Aroostook I want you to share with me."

I hate how he judges himself against academic standards. Besides, he did get his GED. And his experiences of traveling the world have opened his heart and mind to more than most people get in college. "I'm excited to share Secluded Rest with you. What's mine is yours, and vice versa." I kiss him again. "For the record, I think you're much more than the sum of your schooling."

"That's a good thing." His eyes dart toward the ocean.

"Hey," I cup his cheek and force his gaze back to mine. "Many guys in your position would have given up on their schooling. But not you. You got your GED. That's a big accomplishment."

"Thanks. Darren was the driver behind that, remember?"

I do recall. "He was a good man." I kiss my husband again. "I'll forever be grateful he brought us together." I rub my boobs against his torso.

Green eyes dart downward, then Bennett rolls us so I'm on top and his hands are at my waist. "You know what I'm forever grateful for?" His fingers loop around the blue garter on my upper thigh that Kara insisted I wear. Good call.

"What?"

"That my sexy wife is about to do a striptease for me." His hands go behind his head and an expectant expression crosses his face.

My eyebrows raise. "Really?"

"Uh, huh." He nods.

I shrug. Why the hell not? We're married. Everything we do from now on is legal. I extend my leg and play with the garter. "Like this?"

"It's a start."

Pulling the garter downward, I tease it around my knee then bring it back up to my thigh. "Think the blue matches the sky?" I glance upward.

"Before the sun set, sure. I prefer my blue in the heavens and not on my wife's leg, though." He tugs the garter all the way down my leg until it pools at my ankle. "Oops."

Giggling, I kick the material off my body. "Which comes next?"

Bennett doesn't answer, simply lifts his hips and tosses his black boxer briefs onto the end of the bed. "Answer your question?"

I sit up and stare at my husband's body. Take in every muscle and dark hair. His pulsing erection, which grows under my scrutiny. Vein protruding, begging for my attention. I lean over and oblige. With his cock in my mouth, I suck hard, causing his eyes to roll back in his head. My tongue swipes the bit of pre-cum that seeps out, and I enjoy the salty tang.

"Damn." His hands pull my hair, not in a suck me posture, but more of a come up here one. I want him to lose control, though. Be at my mercy. So I redouble my efforts, deep-throating him, thrilled when his hips dance.

This time, instead of pulling me away, he tugs me closer to his hardness. My hand slips downward, and I give his balls a soft graze.

His hips bounce off the bed. "Oh my God, Jenna."

Like the rest of my life, whatever control I thought I had, he convinces me otherwise. In a smooth move, he pulls away from me and strips off my panties, then directs my back onto the bed. "You and me," he huffs. "We're coming together for the first time ever as husband and wife. I want us to remember this moment forever. When I'm away on tour. When you're dealing with clinic shit. When good and bad things happen. Remember now. This is what matters. Forever."

His words. My heart flutters. All I can do is mutely shake my head. And open my legs to accept my husband into my body.

He doesn't rush straight into me, like I thought he would do considering how worked up I made him. Well, me too.

No. He prods at my entrance, swiveling his hips to coat himself in my juices. I clamp my thighs around his body, trying to guide him into me, but he remains still.

On trembling arms, he stares into my eyes. "I love you."

"Oh, Bennett. I love you forever."

In this instant he slides into my body with a slow, deliberate movement. Once he's fully seated, he smooths the hair away from my cheeks. "So beautiful. Thank you for taking the chance."

His play on the title of the song he sang to me—with UC—elicits a strangled cry. I force my hips backward, then surge around him. His restraint breaks.

Bennett's hand urges my leg up, which he cups underneath my knee as if it were a microphone stand. Using his newfound leverage, he pumps in a hard beat into me, making me see stars on the horizon that have nothing at all to do with the darkening skies.

A minute later, the orgasm that's been building all day crashes over me, and I clench around him, screaming his name. For his part, he continues to bury himself deep into me. When I return to the land of the living, he's moving his hips, biding his time.

I lift up on my elbow and kiss his sweaty brow. "Your turn."

"Oh no," he replies. "Ours."

He picks up the pace between us once more, grunting his pleasure when I lock my ankles around his hips. His hands drag mine over my head. Sweat drips between us, but neither one of us minds. This union means everything.

Like I knew it would, another orgasm shimmers on the horizon. This time, I want to take him with me to oblivion. I reach around and grab his hard ass, dragging him deeper still.

"Come for me, Sweetheart."

With his order, I fly free, touching the face of the moon emerging from tonight's sunset. My body clamps around his, and his Adam's apple bulges when he strains with his final thrust, then freezes above me. A second later, he roars his completion so everyone within a mile of the beach can hear. I don't care. This man is my everything. And I'm his.

He collapses onto my spent body, gasping for air. Soon, he flips to his side, his hand covering his forehead.

"Oh shit," he murmurs. "Condom."

Chapter 15

Bennett

I've *never* not used a condom. Why did I forget this time—with my *wife*? She's going to want to divorce me before our marriage even starts for being a careless, selfish bastard. Fuck.

Her tiny hand turns my head toward hers. I can't bring myself to look into her gray eyes. I don't deserve such closeness. "Bennett, it's all right."

I continue to berate myself. How did I manage to have sex bareback with the most precious woman on earth? We've never even talked about having kids. Her sister has two, sure, but Jenna isn't Kara. I'm most certainly not daddy material.

"Everything's fine." She shakes my head.

I blink, not registering what she's saying. My wife. "Huh?"

"I said, it's okay. We're married. If we get pregnant, it's no big deal."

I sit up. "No big deal. You were born to be a mother. You're kind and sweet and loving. Me?" I rake my palm up and down my body. "I'm not built to be a father. Look at my role model. Oh wait. You can't because he isn't here." I slam my lips into a thin line.

"Because he passed away a decade ago," she replies in a quiet voice. Her hand taps the center of my chest. "But he was here, Bennett. With you. In you. You placed a rose on the chair to honor him. He lives on through you, can't you see?"

My mouth hangs open. "Dad was a great man. He tried to help me in any way he could." I shake my head. "Not me. I'm not as good as he was. Then there's Mom." My eyes fall to the bedding. "I didn't even tell her I was getting married."

Jenna slides next to me, kissing my jaw. "Your mother isn't capable of supporting you, and you didn't want her negativity at our wedding." She kisses my cheek. "You can still tell her. Maybe you should before the media gets hold of the information and runs with it." Her nose scrunches.

The last thing I want is to worry Jenna about my stupid crap. She has more than enough on her plate. "I'll deal with Mom." Somehow.

Ignoring how my stomach folds on itself, I bring her to my body and reiterate my initial issue. "However, I don't want to put you at risk. Having unprotected sex was risky."

"Do you have any diseases I don't know about?"

"What?" I shake my head. "No. I'm clean. Luke makes us take tests on a monthly basis, just in case he has to do some clean up."

"Oh wow." She shakes her head. "Did any of you ever come up positive?"

I purse my lips. "All I'm going to say is one of us had to take antibiotics for a while. But he's clean now. We all are."

"Who was it?" Her hands tap on my shoulders.

"Not me." I make a zipping motion across my lips. "It's old news, Sweetheart. We had that one scare, and we all learned our collective lesson from it."

"Fine," she pouts.

Coop's story is his alone, so I return to the issue at hand. "Jenna, I forgot to use a condom. What are we going to do?"

Her head tilts and she places her index finger against her lips. "I don't know, Bennett. What do you suggest?"

There's a pill that could take care of any complications, but I can't bring myself to suggest this to the beautiful naked woman in my arms. My wife. "I—"

"This is why I knew Lissa was lying, even before I heard the true story." She hugs her body against mine. "You won't tell me to do anything about a possible baby, and we're *married*. No way would you have abandoned her back in high school."

I frown. How did my wedding night turn into a conversation about my high school girlfriend who's trying to blackmail her way into the spotlight? "Jenna, one thing has nothing to do with the other."

"They both show your character."

Women. Who can follow their logic? "Listen, I'm talking about us right now. You and me. The fact I went bareback."

"Have to admit, it was a very memorable way to consummate our marriage." She grins.

"That's beside the point." I rake my fingers through my hair. "What are we going to do if you're pregnant?"

Her head lands on my shoulder. "Have a baby."

Those three words would have caused my body to convulse before I met Jenna. Even now, I can't wrap my head around this possibility. Yet, her solution seems so easy. "As in you and me plus a baby carriage?"

She giggles. "I want him to have your green eyes and amazing lips. Not to mention your personality."

"Oh no. The only way I'd have a baby with you is if we had a girl with blonde hair and gray eyes. Whip smart, like her mother."

She sits up. "I forgot. Our son will have to be able to sing like his daddy and perform in front of thousands of fans."

I force myself upright next to her. "Our daughter will go to school and get her graduate degree like her mother, and set the world on fire." I cross my arms across my chest.

Jenna laughs, a full-on sound that makes my heart sing. Her face collapses into my lap, where I stroke her long hair. After a bit, she regains her composure and leans against the headboard.

"I love that we just had a fight about whether we're having a son or a daughter." She wipes a stray tear away from her eye.

"It wasn't a fight," I correct. "We were talking about our hopes for the future. Not an immediate problem to be resolved."

"Well." She places her palms onto the bed and sits straight up. "What we did, we did. It was amazing." She leans over to kiss me. "Given where I am in my cycle, it's highly unlikely I could get pregnant. Plus, we're married, so it doesn't really matter at all anyway."

I puff out my chest. "You don't think my super sperm could knock you up, wrong time of the month and all?"

She dissolves into another fit of laughter. "Super sperm?!" Her laugh is contagious. Soon I'm fighting my own chuckles. I bite the inside of my lip, but one still escapes.

Her hands go around my naked waist. "How about this, Mr. Super Sperm?" She laughs again. "We make sure to use condoms from now on and not worry about it. One day, whether in nine months or a few years, we'll have kids. Never fear, you'll be a fantastic father." She crawls on her knees up to me and kisses my mouth.

This time, I don't hesitate. If she thinks I'll be a good father, perhaps I will. Or, more likely, she'll make up for my poor showing by being the best mother ever. My lips meet hers again and we make slow, sweet love under the inky sky.

At three in the morning, we weave into the bedroom and Jenna yawns. "I have a few hours before the limo comes to take me away. Why don't you get some sleep?" We crawl into bed.

Her arms encircle my neck. "I'm the luckiest woman on earth."

I don't respond, simply lie in bed holding my wife. Jenna is so much more than I deserve. I bury my face in her soft locks and breathe in her goodness.

My alarm goes off four hours later, and I blink awake. Next to me,

Jenna stirs. I watch as she turns to her side, my fingers stroking her body. When I tweak her nipple, her eyes pop open.

"I like waking up like this."

"Me too." I kiss her because I can. Under the laws of New York and God, we belong to each other.

After I make her squirm, shatter, and scream, we sit up. "Shower?"

"I don't want to wash you off my body."

When she says something like that, I almost relent. However, it's now after eight, and I'm being picked up in under two hours. "I don't either, Sweetheart. But reality intrudes." I toss the blankets off our cooling bodies.

Taking her hand, we walk into the bathroom where we brush our teeth and hop into the oversized shower. She holds onto the shelf as I pummel her from behind, and she comes all over my cock. I pull out and jerk off onto her back with a loud groan.

Once we're washed and clean, we go to the kitchen, where she makes pancakes while I prepare the coffee. "I'm going to miss you," she admits.

"Not any more than I'm going to miss you. But we have Zoom. And texting. And phones. We can make it through these next couple of weeks, and then I'm off for fourteen days. We can go to Secluded Rest and fuck our way through our entire new house."

She pauses from flipping a pancake. "I still can't believe that's ours." She emphasizes the last word.

"All I have is yours, Sweetheart. Including access to the band's private jet, which I plan on using as often as possible."

She plates a pancake and makes one for herself. "I have to stay here for Ma." Her voice dips.

"I know. I wouldn't have it any other way. Enjoy your two weeks with her. Make her watch our shows on YouTube."

Jenna points the spatula at me. "What are you planning?"

"Guess you'll both have to watch to find out." I pour syrup onto the pancake, wishing I were putting it onto her sexy body. This fantasy will have to wait another two weeks.

She flips her pancake and my cell goes off.

LUKE

Sorry, B, time to go. The limo will be by your wedding night villa in an hour.

I don't bother to respond because Jenna's placing her pancake onto her own dish. Smiling like our time isn't coming to an end. We eat our breakfast, talking in low murmurs. The rest of the world can fuck off.

Still, I want her to be safe when I'm not here. "Promise me you'll reach out to Hayden and let the UC PR team handle anything that comes up. None of this is your fault. Your sole focus should be on your mother."

"Thanks, Bennett. I'll do my best. Looks like Michelle's been pretty well shut down, though. Time will help the clinics get back on their feet."

"I want to be as healthy as you are when I grow up." I drag her into my arms.

"Not sure I'm healthy. Someone called me 'controlling.'" She leans back and gives me a saucy grin.

"Controlling can be a good thing sometimes. Like when we're naked in bed. It can be very good then."

"Yeah, but you always usurp my power there. So not fair."

"Hey," I tip her chin upward. "If you were in control, what would you do?" Can't wait to hear her dirty thoughts.

"I'd—" She bites her lip. "I'd tell you to make me come on your fingers and mouth, then I'd rock your world."

"Oh, baby, you already do that to me." If only we had enough time to do this. "Next time, all right? Next time, you get control." I smile against her neck. "Until I take it back."

She shoves against me. "Jerk!"

We laugh and wrestle and kiss until a knock sounds at the front door. We walk through the foyer, and I grab our overnight bags while she opens the door for our limo driver.

Fun and games are over. We're returning to our real lives. Where I'm on tour with UC halfway across the country and she's here, tending to her mother and her physical therapy clinics. We get into the limo.

"Hey, you haven't mentioned how the two new clinics are coming along."

Gray eyes study my face. "They're doing good. Court's taken the lead and they're in the middle of renovations for the third, while she's scouted a few different locations for the fourth one with Angie."

"Court's a great friend."

"Yes, she is." Her hand drops to my thigh. "And you're a great husband. I'm lucky you picked me. Thank you, Rock Star."

What on earth is she thanking me for? "You got it backward, Sweetheart. You saved me from a shallow life and gave me so much more than I ever thought was possible." The limo pulls to a stop beside UC's jet.

Blood pumping, I pull Jenna into my arms and kiss her like I haven't been doing it all night long. All too soon, Luke opens the vehicle's door. "Sorry, you have to get off the honeymoon train. But you can pick it up in two short weeks, I promise."

My manager's voice is both annoying and soothing. I say, "Can't come soon enough."

"I'll see you when you come back." Jenna kisses me one last time and sits back against the leather seat, offering a wave to Luke—who reciprocates. At least he has the decency to appear embarrassed to end our honeymoon night.

I tamp down threatening tears, which Luke would never let me live down. Fourteen days and we'll be back in each other's arms. I lean over and kiss my *wife* again, then scoot out of the limo before my ass refuses to move.

Luke shuts the door. I sling my overnight bag over my shoulder and follow our manager onto the jet. All the while my thoughts remain on the solitary woman in the backseat of the limo. Who takes the front seat in my life.

When I get onto the jet, all of UC is there, congratulating me on the wedding. "The man of the hour," Río exclaims as I flop into a seat.

"Hey, guys," I reply. "Thanks for yesterday. It was a day I'll never forget."

"We had a blast," Coop interjects. "Your house is the bomb. Arcade in the basement? Way too cool."

"Kicked your ass at pinball," 007 ribs our guitarist.

Tris rubs his hands together. "I did pretty well on pinball myself."

Luke laughs. "Can't say you guys aren't competitive."

I don't know what I missed, and frankly don't care. I was with my wife, which beats every arcade game ever invented, in my book. A different flight attendant is on duty this time, and he offers us all drinks. The jet lifts off and soon we're hurling high above New York State, on our way to the final leg of our U.S. tour, which can't come soon enough. I'll be back in Jenna's arms in no time.

Somewhere above Illinois, Luke's voice rouses me. "All right guys, we need to discuss how we're dealing with this whole Lissa situation."

I prop myself up in the chair, using my palm to cover my massive yawn. "Did you tell them what Curtiss told me?"

"Sure did," our manager replies. "Spoke with our PR team as well. Now that your wedding is over, it's time to focus on making Lissa disappear."

I like the sound of that. "Good."

Río adds, "For what she's done, she deserves more than to disappear." I offer him my fist.

"B, are you sure this Curtiss guy will go on the record with what he told you?"

"Absolutely. He owes me, if nothing else." Besides, it was his kid.

"Great. This is what I'm thinking," Luke dives into great detail about how we're going to bury my ex. I only half listen, my mind firmly on my wife back in Aroostook. I text her:

> Missing you

> Soon. Need to do some clean up over here.

Clean up? What's she talking about?

> What happened?

> Michelle found out we got married. Posted it on all the gossip sites in the Hamptons

"Fuck!" Five sets of eyes bore into me. "Seems like the media found out about my wedding. Jenna's handling the fallout on her own." I give Luke a dirty look.

For his part, our manager scrambles to his phone. "Shit. I'm calling the PR team." He shakes his head and stalks to the back bedroom.

Coop is the first to speak. "You knew this was going to come out in the media. Better get it over with sooner rather than later."

"I know," I grit my teeth. "I was only hoping it would come to the surface when I was back there with her for two weeks. I hate she's having to deal with all of this on her own, not to mention helping her mother."

"She looked pretty good yesterday," Tris offers. "I knew she was sick because you told us, but she seemed in good spirits, man."

I force a sad smile. "Thanks. None of us know how long she has. But yesterday was a good day."

Luke reappears. "Change of plans. We can deal with Lissa later. Right now, we're focusing on your big day, B. Are you sure Jenna can't join us out here?"

"Positive. Remember her mother."

"Gotcha. Well, this is what we're going to do."

Chapter 16

Jenna

Bennett will be back tomorrow. I've managed to get through the paparazzi shitstorm (as Bennett calls it) about our wedding. The moment he stepped foot off the plane in Seattle, he was ambushed by more reporters than I even knew existed. His gray wedding band is the number one trending video on TikTok, with men vowing to purchase one and women demanding their husbands wear one.

All I want is for *my* husband to be at my side.

"The remodel is going according to schedule," Court points to the plans. "I kept them on their toes."

"I couldn't have done this without you," I tell her. "You've made this all possible."

She shakes her head. "I only was following your lead. I'm happy we're on schedule, given all the shit Michelle's been pulling."

There's the second thorn in my side. When her Black Widow graffiti stunt didn't work out the way she thought it would, she continued to refuse to refer patients to my clinics, as witnessed by our patient count. My lunch today with her boss is my last-ditch effort to get her to stand down. I straighten the construction notes.

"Let's hope my lunch goes well."

"You got this." Court gives me a hug, helps me into a blazer over my scrubs, and ushers me out the door. I call Ma on my way to the restaurant.

"Hi, just wanted to remind you I'm going to lunch with Dr. Marlow."

Her voice, less and less reminiscent of herself, replies, "Good luck with him." She laughs, but it ends with coughing.

"Ma, are you sure it's okay if I go out to lunch? I can reschedule."

"No, Sweet Pea. I want you to get on top of this stuff with Michelle. I'll be here when you get back." She pauses. "I promise."

"All right," I agree. Only because this has to stop with Michelle. "I'll see you at home."

I disconnect the line and place another phone call. To Kara. "Hey, just spoke with Ma. She sounds weaker."

"I know. I'm on my way out to her house now."

The fact my sister's coming out to Aroostook is both calming and disturbing. "I'll be back as soon as I can."

A short time later, I pull into the restaurant's parking lot. I'm ready to deal with Michelle once and for all. I don't have time to waste on the likes of her. Not when Ma is fading so fast.

At the table, Dr. Marlow smiles at me. "How's business going?"

I tilt my head. "It's busy, but I've been surprised by the lower numbers coming from your practice." Best to be honest.

He jerks backward. "What do you mean? I'm referring the same number of patients to your clinics. You do an excellent job."

The waiter delivers our sandwiches and I take a bite. "Thanks for the vote of confidence, but someone on your team doesn't agree. I've checked the numbers, and referrals from your office have dropped off by more than half."

"I have no idea why. I do the surgeries and send them to you for rehab."

I sip my lemonade. "I think your receptionist may be sending them to another clinic."

"Why would Michelle do that?"

Because she's hated me since high school. Because I married Bennett Hardy. Because she's a total bitch. "I think this might be a good conversation for you to have with her."

"I will. Don't you worry. Your numbers will soon be where they were."

"Thanks, Dr. Marlow." I take another bite of my sandwich, the churning in my stomach lessening for the first time in a long while.

"If I didn't mention this before, congratulations on your marriage."

I fiddle with my wedding and engagement rings. "Thanks." My phone goes off and I raise my finger to my dining companion. "It's my sister. Excuse me." I step away from the table. "Kara?"

"Ma's not doing well. We're going to the hospital now."

Oh. My. God. My whole body wants to convulse, but all I can think of is keeping it together in public because the media are waiting to pounce. Besides, Ma said she'd be waiting for me tonight to hear about my meeting. I swallow and return to the table.

"Dr. Marlow. Thank you for meeting me for lunch and your kind words. I need to go to the hospital. My mother—"

The doctor stands. "Go. Go. And don't worry about this business between us at all."

I nod and take measured steps out of the restaurant so as not to attract any attention, despite wanting to run and scream and yell. I get into my car and put it in drive, heading for the hospital. I press Bennett's number.

"Hi Sweetheart. How are—"

I interrupt him. "Ma's in the hospital."

"What? No way. She's been doing well."

"I knew she was fading, but Kara went to the house when I was out to lunch with Michelle's boss, who told me not to worry, and she called the ambulance."

"I'm not sure I got all that, but you're driving to the hospital now?"

"Yes. It's right ahead. See you tomorrow." I disconnect the call as I pull into a parking spot.

In a blind daze, I rush into the hospital. At the reception desk, I ask, "Faith Westfield?" and am directed to a private room. Where Kara sits outside a door.

"Kara?"

She leaps to her feet, arms outstretched. "When I got to the house, Ma's color was bad. Her nurse said she'd been that way for about thirty minutes. I didn't wait. I made the decision to come here. The doctor is working on her now. I'm sure she'll be stabilized soon, and we can go home together."

I've never seen Kara like this before. My normally stoic and distant sister approaches a frantic pitch. I place my hands on her shoulders the way Bennett's done to calm me down in the past. It works on her too.

I gaze into her matching gray eyes. "Ma will pull through. She's with the best doctors here, so let's sit and try to send her good vibes, all right?"

She nods and we sit. We don't talk, simply co-exist side by side. After a bit, a woman in a white coat exits Ma's room. Kara and I approach her.

The doctor consults her clipboard. "Ladies, I'm not going to sugarcoat this. Your mother may not last the night. Her numbers are low, her heart rate is erratic, and the cancer has spread. We're doing everything we can to make her comfortable. I suggest you go in there and say what you need to say. I'm very sorry."

After she leaves, Kara and I stare at one another. "No." I shake my head. "We were supposed to have more time with her."

Kara, now back in control of her emotions, replies, "We had her for several weeks. She was at your wedding and had a great time. She got to see both her daughters married. She met two of her grandkids." She breaks off, her eyes closing.

"She didn't meet any through me," I whisper. Either she didn't hear me or didn't acknowledge what I said, but this truth cuts through me like a sword. I remember when Bennett forgot to use a condom on our wedding night. This is the true reason I wasn't upset. I thought I'd have more time with Ma, and would be able to at least tell her I was pregnant. Now this has been robbed from me as well.

"Let's go in to see her."

Kara holds up her phone. "You go. I want to call my husband first."

With a nod, I enter Ma's hospital room. The first thing that hits me is it's so sterile in here, something I strive to avoid at the clinics. Instruments beep. With a stilted gait, I walk to her bed. She lies still. Too still.

I grab her hand, which is warm. A good sign. "Hey, Ma," I begin. "Way to break up a business lunch," I try to joke.

Her gray eyes, now cloudy, open at my voice. She pulls the oxygen mask from her face. "How'd it go?"

The fact she remembers what we were discussing before my lunch has to be a good sign. Maybe the doctor was wrong? Happens all the time. "It went well. Dr. Marlow promised to have a discussion with Michelle and to make sure his patients come to me in the future."

"Good." She whispers. "That's good."

Kara slips inside the room. "How are you feeling, Ma?"

"Been better," she jokes.

Humor has to be a good sign, right? Yes. These doctors don't know what they're talking about.

Then she starts to cough. The coughs come one on top of another, and she can't catch her breath. More doctors enter the room and kick us out to work on her. I stare at my sister. "She cracked a joke. That's a good sign."

"It is. But the coughing is not." She sighs. "My family is coming here tomorrow. At least the kids had a blast with her at your wedding. After you and Bennett left, we enjoyed TLR. UC even took the stage again, with Trent singing lead. We all danced and had a blast. Even Ma danced from her chair."

I relish this story. Even though I wasn't there to witness it, it warms my heart to know she enjoyed the party until the very end. "TLR was amazing, right?"

"Well, not as good as UC," my sister winks at me. "But they were fun. King and Angie too. You have some cool friends, *kiddo*."

"I try." I'm amazed at her candor. It feels like we're beginning to overcome the fact that we grew up a decade apart. I approach a subject that might blow everything up. "Did you see our father at the wedding?"

Kara stills. "I did. He was talking with Ma for a while, then he slipped out. I didn't talk with him. Did you?"

"No. I saw him at a distance with Ma, but then Bennett and I had to leave. Why did he come?"

"I don't know. He showed up to my wedding too. Do you remember that?"

"No." A second ticks by. "Why?"

"I honestly have no idea. I don't want to ask Ma now, in her condition."

"Yeah."

We lapse into silence again, the medical team leaving Ma's room and allowing us to re-enter. This time, she's sleeping. Kara sits on one side of her while I take the other, each of us holding her hands.

We talk in lower tones about my sister's family and their plans for summer vacation. I discuss growing the clinics. Day turns to night. I suggest Kara go home and she does the same for me. Neither one of us takes the other up on the offer.

Kara falls asleep in the chair to the sound of Ma's machines. I try to stay awake, but fail.

Something touches my shoulder, and I bristle awake. "Shhh. I didn't mean to wake you," a dulcet tenor voice whispers in my ear.

I swivel my neck, trying to get some of the kinks out. "Bennett. You came."

"Worst fucking gig of my life. When I couldn't get back in touch with you, I had Elias find out your mother's status from the hospital. I'm sorry."

I squeeze Ma's hand, which is still warm. "She's a fighter."

"Like mother, like daughter." He crowds onto the chair, picks me up, and settles me onto his lap. "Better."

Across the way, Kara stirs. Her hand goes to the back of her shoulder. "Ouch."

Bennett asks, "Want me to give you a massage?"

A pinprick of jealousy races throughout my body that he'd offer such services to another woman. Then I realize he did it for family. He's coming to understand what the term means. I turn and kiss him as Kara declines.

Ma opens her eyes and pulls the oxygen mask off her face. "Kara." She turns her head to me. "Jenna. Bennett. You've made me the happiest woman ever. Continue to change the world. I love you all so much."

"Ma," Kara and I begin.

Then the machines blare. Her hand goes slack. Her gray eyes become unfocused.

No, no, no! This isn't supposed to be happening! I leap into the air to try to hug her, get her to respond, anything, when Bennett pulls me away. "Sweetheart." His lips brush the top of my head as I fight against him.

The medical team rushes in and orders us out of the room. In a daze, Bennett carries me out. Well, I'm in a daze. Kara looks defeated. Bennett looks like someone ran over his dog.

In the hallway, we huddle in a three-way embrace. Send up prayers that Ma will pull through. Bennett's holding both of us when the doctors reappear in the hallway. A different doctor walks over to us.

"I'm sorry. Faith passed ten minutes ago. You may visit with her as long as you wish."

I burst into tears, crumpling. I would have hit the floor but for Bennett, who caught me and kept me upright. Kara's the first to regain some sort of composure and asks if she can go in to see her. All I can do is cry. Bennett tells her we'll go in when she's done.

"Do you want to sit?" I shake my head. "Then hold onto me." I do as he tells me. I've lost all higher faculties. How could this have happened?

"We were supposed to have time."

"I know. This isn't fair."

"I don't know how to go on without her."

"One step at a time. One step," he repeats.

Kara comes out of the room. "I need to talk with the nurses and take care of the paperwork, then I'm going home." She takes a step. "No, home is too far away."

"Why don't you stay at my house?"

Bennett pulls me tighter to his body.

"Oh, thank you." I give my sister the keys to my house, and she goes off to deal with the logistics.

I take a deep breath. "I want to go in."

Bennett nods his head. "All right. Want me to go with you?"

I consider his offer. Do I want this man beside me? "Give me five minutes, then come in, okay?"

"You got it." He kisses me in a sweet, tender, loving way and I force my feet to move forward. I push on the door and it slams behind me. I'm all alone with Ma.

With what used to be Ma.

I approach her. Where she gave us her last loving praise. Tears prick my eyelids. I don't bother to stem their fall.

"Ma," I breathe. "I hope you're happy where you are. You're not in any more pain. Maybe you can see into the future now, and see my children. With Bennett. Our little boy and little girl growing up in Aroostook. Or all over the world."

I'm not making any sense. None of this does. Ma was supposed to be here with us, not her body lying in this bed while her soul floats above us. I want my mother!

"Ma!" I reach out and grab her hand, which is cool to the touch. I recoil as this factoid slips into my consciousness. "You're never coming back, are you? You'll never give me your pep talks about putting Michelle into her place. You'll never again sing Kara's praises, or those of her husband and kids."

I suck in air as realization hits—final and hard—that she's truly gone. Words fly out of my mouth. "I should have forced you to get other opinions. Someone would've done surgery, then you'd still be with me. Bennett talked me out of it, but he was wrong. Wrong! We'd still be laughing and talking and you'd be imparting even more wisdom to me. I listened to him and what has that brought me? You're gone. Dead. It's all his fault. How can I go on without you?"

I bow my head, cover my eyes, and sob.

Strong, masculine hands go around my shoulders. Bennett doesn't say anything, nor does he try to pull me to him. His silent presence, though, is a massive conflict. On one hand, he's the reason we're here now—he convinced me not to pursue more doctors and possible other treatments. On the other, he provides comfort. My tears stop freefalling down my cheeks. My sniffles retreat. I walk over to my mother's body and kiss her cooling cheek. "Fly now. Be free."

Then I turn, and the tears start all over again. In a second, Bennett's holding me, rubbing my back, letting me get it all out. He doesn't try to minimize my pain or backstop it. He merely lets my agony ooze out of me.

I wipe my cheek with the back of my hand. "I need to leave."

"Right behind you, Sweetheart."

I put one foot in front of the other, and reach the doorknob. Something tells me to turn, and what I see nearly brings me to my knees. Bennett has gathered Ma into his arms and is rocking her side to side, like a life-size doll. I can't make out his words, but he kisses her cheek before laying her to rest on the bed once more.

The sight guts me. Then fillets my insides. An all-encompassing need to yell at him for touching *my* mother bubbles, seething like a caged animal. She was *my* mother, not his. *My* responsibility, not his.

How dare he act like he held a piece of her heart—I know the truth that she told me after they first met.

Although she did come around to see him as her son.

And she was so happy at our wedding.

This last piece offers a double-edged balm.

When he turns, I tamp down all the awful emotions roiling through me. A second later, his hand is in mine and we walk out of the hospital room for the final time.

"It's late," Bennett notes. "Do you have your car?"

"Yeah."

"Let me drive us home." He pauses. "To Secluded Rest."

I fiddle with my wedding ring. "Sounds good."

It takes me a while, but I finally remember where I parked and Bennett gets behind the wheel. Given that it's before sunrise, the streets are empty and dark. Mirroring my feelings.

We get into the house and Bennett leads me up to the main suite, asking if I want to eat or drink anything. When I decline, he walks me to the bed and takes off my blazer. The one I wore to meet with Dr. Marlow, what feels like months ago. How could it only be hours?

My scrub top is the next to go, followed by the bottoms. I don't do anything to help Bennett undress me. I raise my arms when prodded. Simple commands are my friends.

"Do you want to take a shower?"

I'm alone. All alone. "Huh?"

Instead of repeating himself, he grabs my hand and leads me into the bathroom, where he shucks his own clothes and walks into the oversized shower enclosure. This time, instead of fun and frivolity, he meets my utilitarian needs. I can't muster anything more and, judging by his own demeanor, I doubt he could either.

Minutes later, the water shuts off and he dries me off, wrapping a towel around my body. I step out of the shower, and he follows me back into the bedroom. When we reach the bed, I toss the towel onto the floor and stand before my husband.

"I love you." I force the words out, knowing he needs to hear them. Maybe I need to hear them too? Or maybe I only need Ma back in my life.

"Even more," he replies, pulling my body into his.

Together, we sink into the bed and close our eyes. Hopefully tomorrow will be a better day.

Chapter 17

Jenna

These past three days have been the worst of my life. Picking out readings and funeral cards and food and flowers and a casket. My body seizes as memories replay. I'm not sure how I made it through the never-ending meeting with the funeral director, yet somehow I did, with Kara. Bennett hovers, trying to be helpful, so I let him. Being useful is a good thing, right? I remember Ma saying something about busy work being good work.

But she's gone now.

I tuck the towel around my chest tighter, ensuring it won't pop open. Today I have to bury Ma. I snag a few more tissues and shove them into my otherwise empty black purse. From across the room, Bennett says, "I think UC's PR team has a good handle on keeping the paparazzi at bay."

"Good." Even more than at our wedding two weeks ago, I don't want the vultures anywhere near today's ceremony.

Despite Dr. Marlow's assurances, Michelle has been ramping it up against me and the clinics. Court's been doing her best to clean up —literally and figuratively—yet it feels like a losing battle. Whatever. Nothing matters anymore.

Bennett's phone rings and he pulls it out, closing his eyes and pursing his lips. *I'm awful, but I wish he'd go away. What's the point now that Ma's gone? No need to make her happy any longer.* "Take the call."

"I don't have to."

Needing quiet, a moment's peace, I insist, "It's fine. I'll be here when you're finished."

His shoulders droop, yet he exits the bedroom as he answers the phone. Solitude. Silence. I crave these two little items like a mermaid needs water. When Darren died, I remember my therapist telling me they aren't healthy for me. *Whatever.*

Here's the reminder why. Things turn accusatory fast.

Why did you run off with a rock band—again—instead of watching over your mother?

How can you help your patients when you couldn't help the only person you loved?

Why did you give into Bennett's demands to let Ma stop meeting with doctors when you knew, YOU KNEW, someone would've been able to keep her with you longer?

These questions and more allegations play on a loop inside my brain. For want of something to do with my hands, I spin my wedding and engagement rings over and over. *How does this get any better?*

From behind me, Bennett asks, "Can I help with anything?"

I startle at his voice, then force a smile to cover up my true feelings. "Let me get my dress. Will you zip me up?"

He puffs out, wiggling his long fingers toward me. "Ready and willing."

Instead of answering him, I go into the closet, taking out a little black dress. Not caring whether he watches me or not, I toss the towel onto the top of the counter and put on my lingerie.

When I reach for the dress, he steps up. In a throaty whisper, he removes the black material from the hanger. "Here. Let me."

Because I don't have it in me to disagree, I turn my back to him and the dress floats over my body. He raises the zipper and closes the hook. His lips brush the back of my neck in a kiss that would've left me in a puddle on the floor.

Before.

Not now.

When I don't react, he asks, "Are you planning on saying a few words today?"

I turn to face him, blinking hard. "I don't think I can. Kara said she was going to do it, and I didn't fight her."

"Makes sense, Sweetheart. Anything you had to say, you already said to your mother. She knows."

A stray tear falls. "Yeah." I stuff even more tissues into my purse. The accusations against him inside my head loop double time. My foot stomps the floor. "This sucks!"

In an instant, he's cradling me as the tears flow free again. "Believe me, this will get easier. Someday. At least you can be thankful for all the great years you two had together. More than most, less than others."

I try to let his words sink in—to accept them—but I cannot. Nothing makes any sense anymore. Instead of lashing out, I remain quiet. It's the least I can do for the man next to me. Who, God forgive me, I wish would disappear. When does he go back out on tour?

A few moments later, he asks, "Are you ready? The limo should be here shortly."

I use this interruption to put on my heels and we take the elevator down to the first level. He suggested the elevator and I didn't put up a fuss. For whatever reason he felt the need to show off his high-end rock star lifestyle. It didn't impress me, but it got us where we needed to go.

At the funeral, Bennett sticks close by me, like a hulking body-guard, as if bodyguards were sought-after prizes. Thankfully, the service goes off without any issues. Kara did a lovely job with her remarks. We're getting ready to leave for the cemetery, my eyes scanning the faces who came to mourn, when I freeze. My mouth drops open.

This cannot be happening. Again. My hands form fists.

Oblivious as usual, Bennett asks, "What do you need?"

Kara appears at my other side. "I see him."

Moments pass.

How dare my father dishonor my mother by coming to her funeral?

"Want me to get rid of him?" Bennett's offer is the only good thing he's said all day. I want to shout *hell yes* and rip the man to shreds. However, decorum dictates we can't toss him out on his ear.

Staring at my sister, I straighten, then so does Kara. Our heads bounce once, then we walk in his direction, both our husbands following behind. We stop in front of *him*.

"Father." The word lands across his jugular like a surgical knife.

"Jenna. Kara. I'm sorry for your loss."

Blood rushes to my head. How can this be happening?

"So are we," Kara says. "We want to know why *you're* here."

"Plus why you show up to all our big events?" I add in a gritty whisper. "I saw you at my wedding not two weeks ago."

His eyes survey the room. "Now's not the time or place. We can talk later."

Hands steal across my shoulders, presumably Bennett's, but I don't sink into them. Across from my father, I stand my ground. The moment lengthens, then the minister invites everyone to the cemetery.

Bennett leans forward and whispers, "He's right, Sweetheart. You need to be with your mother now."

In this moment, I size up my father. So what if he came to some milestones in our lives, he was MIA for all of the smaller moments that make a life. When Ma was with us. He doesn't deserve any more attention. Especially on Ma's day.

Keeping my head high, I sweep away from my father without another word, not caring whether Kara does the same. Bennett grabs my hand and holds it as we file into the limo, which takes us to the cemetery. I leave my hand in his but don't try to talk with him. Nothing needs to be said.

When everyone from the funeral home's assembled in front of the hole in the ground above which Ma's casket is situated, the minister recites a scripture and invites us to say any final words.

Kara already said her piece. Her husband is busy handling their kids. My father is nowhere to be seen. Shocking.

What could I add to the ceremony? How mad I am Ma didn't listen to her body sooner, when treatment could have been an option. I don't think I should scream "why!" to the universe either. I want to lash out at every single person. Ask how they made Ma's life better when she was here. Tears sting my eyes again, but I will them not to fall. The people gathered need to see me as a strong woman, and not the crybaby pushover spider portrayed in the media.

My shoulders square. I hate being the cowering girl in the corner. More accurately, I'm filled with rage about how unfair this life is if Ma's gone and my father's still here. Michelle and Lissa too. They all should take Ma's place.

All the rage and anger over the past days seethes inside me, demanding to be let out. It doesn't matter that Bennett's next to me. Or that his band is here—he doesn't consider them friends anyway. The only saving grace is reporters weren't allowed to enter.

No words fit for polite company form in my brain. I want to extol Ma's love and compassion, but it's impossible when I'm filled with so much fury. Better to keep my mouth shut.

Out of nowhere, a single tenor voice begins to sing. No music, no accompaniment. Nothing. Only a solitary singer performing *Amazing Grace*.

My head swivels and I take in Bennett beside Ma's casket, eyes closed.

I remember all the times I've asked him to sing me a song, and his refusal because he never sings *a capella*.

Yet, here he is, singing for Ma.

In his hauntingly beautiful voice. One featured in so many UC records, but never like this. Now, only singing for Ma.

And for those of us gathered here.

Something breaks inside of me. All my ugly thoughts bleed onto the ground. Tears chase each other down my cheeks, my mouth open to take in much needed air.

Tris comes over and puts his arm around me, and I put my face into his side. Like a big brother, he holds my shaking form while Bennett's last sung words resound throughout the cemetery.

"Thanks," my husband addresses Tris. My body is transferred from one band member to the next, and I suck in a fresh woodsy scent, which I have learned is courtesy of Dior Sauvage. My hands clutch Bennett's shirt, hanging on to remain upright.

Nothing around me registers. Not the people or the sounds or the talking or the shuffling feet. I'm numb. It's only Bennett and me.

"We should go, Sweetheart."

"A minute."

"You got it."

I let his simple phrase sink into my bones, then pull myself free of him. All the other people are walking toward their cars. All except Kara and her family and me. Leaving my husband, I walk to my sister, and we embrace. The ten-year age difference between us evaporates for good.

"Your husband has a good voice," she whispers, her lips quirk.

Not that I've ever heard it quite this way before. "He does."

We move apart. "See you at the restaurant?" Her family approaches and they walk toward the waiting limos.

I turn to stare at Ma's casket, remembering all her shared wisdom, praise, and support. In essence, this is what she was about. Not recriminations. Not mean-spiritedness. Not all the ugly thoughts that have been running through my mind lately. Of course, she wouldn't let a bad person get off without reprisal, either.

Bennett and I got married to make her happy.

She was.

Now she's gone.

A small voice inside screams that we're in love with each other. I've never been happier than on our wedding day.

Grief quickly wrestles such romantic fluff to the ground.

No. I can do this one final act of kindness for Ma. For him. This charade has to end.

Chapter 18

Bennett

Leaning against the wall, I watch my wife walking from person to person. She's talking, accepting hugs and shit, but she's not *here*. There's no life in this version of her. She doesn't search the room for me, nor does she return any of my touches. In fact, she sent me away to get us drinks an hour ago and hasn't questioned why I haven't returned.

Why haven't I?

Like every woman I've ever known, she's leaving me. Step by step. I heard what she said to her mother in the hospital room, about how I'm to blame for her death, but I thought her anger would subside as other stages of grief took over. It hasn't. Now I'm freaking out.

If I call her out on it, how would she react? Would she deny it, and tell me I'm delusional? More likely, she'd ask me to go away and give her space. Now that I've found her, that's the last thing on earth I want to do. I want to be her rock, the one person above all others who gives her comfort. Her grief is messing with her head, though, and I can't figure out a way to break through.

Coop approaches, a plate in his hand, "Hey, these meatballs are the bomb."

"Glad they meet your approval."

He eats in silence for a beat. "Jenna seems like she's doing well."

"Yeah." I shift my weight between my feet. "For a lost soul."

"Hey, it's tough when you lose a parent." He shoves another meatball into his mouth. "As I'm sure you remember. Faith was her only parent, right?"

I scan the crowd for the balding comb-over, but her father's nowhere to be seen. "She has a father, but he hasn't been in her life much." Not going into detail about a story that's not mine to tell.

My bandmate shoves the final meatball into his mouth. "You know this will hit her hard. Be there for her. Jenna's the real deal."

I stare at my feet. "She is. She's hurting right now."

Coop dumps his empty plate onto a tray. "Then take her mind off it. How about whisking her away to a Caribbean island for the next week? We have time before our tour starts up again in Europe."

I consider his idea. Maybe a change of scenery is what the doctor ordered? "That's not a bad idea. Where are you jetting off to?" With over a week free from touring, I remember hearing the guys talking about their plans, but I can't think of one detail. I was going to spend it with Jenna, preferably in our bed. Naked. Given how she's acting, I don't think this will happen.

"I'm leaving with Río for Jamaica in a couple of hours. Looking forward to some sun and sand and beverages."

I nudge his abdomen. "I bet the ladies won't be too bad, either."

"Good bet." He finishes his drink. "Join us?"

I don't waste a second on his offer. "Nah. Jenna needs to stay local and tie up loose ends." My only hope is I can pull her out of the dark pit into which she's descended.

I track my wife as she and her sister make their rounds. Her sister, an anesthesiologist with over a decade more lived experience on Jenna, seems to be handling this better than my wife. Maybe she can get through to her?

Coop's extolling the virtues of his Jamaican hideaway when I straighten. Jenna and Kara are approaching . . . their father. Where was he hiding? No matter, I can't believe he had the guts to show his face here, especially after the funeral.

My hand goes to the guitarist's shoulder. "Gotta run. I think I see a problem brewing and I don't want things to get too out of hand." Perhaps telling her father off is what he deserves, but not here. Later. When Jenna returns to her normal self. Until then, I don't want her to be mortified at her actions today.

I stalk toward the threesome, nodding at Kara's husband and bringing him along with me. As we approach, I hear Kara say, "We said what needed to be said at the funeral. Please leave."

The old dude shoves his hands in his pockets but stands firm. "Faith and I had a complicated relationship." Jenna snorts. "We kept ties until the end."

He faces Kara. "She was so proud when you graduated medical school. She never stopped talking about your life in the City, or your family, or your big fancy job."

Kara's husband and I trade glances, and he wraps his arm around her. I do the same for my wife.

Then her father turns to Jenna, who trembles beneath my hand. "And you, our baby. She thought your becoming a physical therapist was perfect for you. When you got caught up in the Darren mess, she was there to help you, but I was in the background. I never abandoned you."

"You never showed your face," Jenna contradicts in a nasty tone, one I've never heard from her.

"No." Her father moves his foot on the floor. "I didn't want to confuse the issue."

"Then why are you here now?"

Jenna has a good point. What's he trying to prove at this late stage?

"Maybe I'm trying to atone." He lifts his head. "I loved your mother but wasn't man enough for her, and ran when things got difficult. When you were starting kindergarten, Jenna, all I could think of was I couldn't go through all this again, like I did with your sister. The dances and projects and book reports nearly drove me out of my mind the first time, but I did them for Faith. The second time, though, I didn't have it in me. Our love wasn't enough to keep me in the house."

"So you left us," Jenna concludes. "No birthday cards, no holiday gifts, nothing."

His entire being wilts. "I couldn't give you what you needed. I was there with Faith, though. She always kept me updated with your achievements. I celebrated the big ones."

Kara's expression softens. "Like my wedding."

"And graduations. Congrats on being an anesthesiologist. It's a big deal."

As if this dude had any part in her achievements. However, it's not my thoughts that matter. Kara reaches her hand toward him, which he clasps. I track my gaze to Jenna, who shows no such acceptance. After a minute, my wife simply walks away. I make a hasty retreat after her.

"What are you feeling?" I reach for her shoulders, but she keeps moving.

"Nothing." She strides forward. "I don't care if Ma forgave him. If Kara's welcoming him back into her life. I'm not doing any such thing. He had his chance, and he missed it." She approaches the buffet table but makes no move to pick up a plate.

"What can I do for you, Sweetheart?"

Tortured gray eyes meet mine. "Nothing." Her head snaps to one side. "Excuse me, I need to talk with some people." With that, she's gone.

Standing alone, I stare at the food but don't see any of it. What can I do to reach my wife?

I stand by a table filled with photos of Faith throughout her life. My gaze caresses the one of her, Jenna, and me taken during our first dinner together. Who knew such innocence soon would be shattered?

Luke approaches. "How are you doing, B?"

"I hate that question." I turn my back to the table and face our manager. "How am I supposed to be doing at my mother-in-law's funeral?"

"You got me there. Don't have one of them." He shrugs. "Or a wife."

Ever since Faith died, it doesn't feel as if I have one either. "I can tell you it sucks. Faith accepted me into her family, then she died. Jenna's a freaking disaster. Her deadbeat father's here, raising all sorts of issues. So, I'm doing pretty shitty, thanks for asking." My arms cross over my torso.

"Come here," he pulls me into a corner. "Let it out. You shouldn't keep all these emotions locked inside. Rail against God, the world, fate. Whatever. Tell me how you're really feeling."

I open my mouth, prepared to share all my secrets, when I get a text. As does Luke. Around the room, I see the other members of my band pulling out their phones as well. "What the hell?"

Luke's already read the text by the time I fish my phone out of my pocket. "Crap. Why can't these vultures go away for even one day."

Filled with foreboding, I click in my text, which is a link from the PR team. Now the whole world knows about Faith's death, saying the Black Widow struck again. Another link shows Lissa expanding on her lie about me having gotten her pregnant. "For fuck's sake."

"Listen to me. We'll get this under control."

All the negative emotions bubble inside me. "Do it." I leave our manager in search of Jenna. When I find her, I want to go all caveman for a different reason.

Austin is hugging her, and Jenna's hanging onto his body like it's the only important thing in this entire restaurant. Jealously boils inside me and I take three fast strides toward the pair when my groin pull raises it's stupid, little hand. I stop short, breathing labored.

I need to shoulder my way between the pair. To do what? Make my wife feel as if I don't trust her. Which I do. It's the fucker physical therapist who I don't.

After an excruciating period where the two hug like long-lost besties, she steps back. I should take comfort it was she who broke their contact. Plus the fact that if she was hugging PT boy, she doesn't know about how the media's running with this story.

Court approaches me. "She doesn't know yet."

"No." I don't relish being the person to share this awful not-secret.

Jenna's business partner swallows hard. "I'll do it."

She takes one step, but I place my palm on her arm. "No. Don't. It'll be better coming from me. After all, but for me, none of this would be happening."

"Beneath it all, our girl wouldn't be as happy as she is. Remember that."

"Our girl" hasn't been happy with me—or anyone—for days. Not sure how finding out Lissa's spewing more salacious lies about us and her miscarriage, plus the local press making a big deal out of Faith's death, is going to cheer Jenna up.

I approach the pair. Without so much as a hello, I tug on Jenna's arm. In her ear, I whisper, "I need to talk with you." When she doesn't move, I add, "It's important."

She gives Austin a sunny smile, then hauls me off into a different, dark corner. Sans the smile. "What is it?"

Instead of responding, I pass her my phone. She clicks the links, reads the stories, and returns it to me. The only reason I know she read the articles is the rapid rise and fall of her chest.

Not knowing what to say, I settle for, "I'm sorry."

"You're sorry. I'm sorry. Everyone's sorry. The only person who matters, though, is lying in a coffin six feet under."

How can I respond to her? While I dither—something I've never done—she does the unthinkable. She walks away.

I need to reach her somehow. This cannot continue.

Luke reappears at my side. "I spoke with the PR team. They're going to respond to the tabloids as well as put out an affirmative statement about Jenna and her mom."

Without excitement, I reply, "Good."

"Once we get Curtiss's story ironed out, we can do much more."

"Yeah." Jenna hugs an older couple I've never seen before.

He adjusts his tie. "I think we'll be ready to unleash on Lissa before we leave for Europe."

"Fine."

"All right. I know you're a pretty quiet guy, but one-word answers aren't really your thing. Talk to me."

He's so earnest, and I need someone I trust to be my sounding board. How to start? My head drops. "I don't know how to reach Jenna," I admit. "She's so angry. At the world. At me. All I want to do is hug her, but she won't even let me touch her."

"She's in a bad place, B. There's not much you can do, other than let her be. She loves you, man. I was at your wedding, remember?" He taps his chest. "Best man here. She'll snap out of her grief."

"I don't know." This isn't how things work in my world. People don't simply "snap out" of it. No. They die like my father, or they go off the deep end like my mother or Lissa. I need to do something affirmative to keep Jenna with me. "Maybe I should send her flowers?"

"I'm thinking that's a pass. Look at how many flowers she's going to have after the funeral."

"You're right." What else can I get for her? I snap my fingers. "I know, I can buy her another clinic."

Luke cracks his knuckles. "Doesn't Jenna want to earn her clinics on her own? If you give her one, she won't have the same satisfaction."

All the air blows out of my mouth. "Then what can I do? I can't lose her."

"B, you're not going to lose your bride. You two are the real deal. Believe me."

Problem is, I don't.

I spend the rest of the repast circulating through the room, making small talk with people I've never met before but who think they know me. Or at least they know "Bennett Hardy." One older lady even tries to give me her grandson's YouTube channel to scout him for the label. I manage to avoid her for the rest of the evening.

The guys in the band haul me to the bar, ordering me a Manhattan. When they each have their preferred drinks in hand, Río raises his glass to the ceiling. "To Faith Westfield, Jenna's mother. She had to have been an amazing woman to raise such a fabulous daughter. May her soul rest in peace." We all take sips. Including 007.

A while later, I approach our drummer, who's banging on his thigh with his free hand. "Thanks for the nice words."

"Meant them. I didn't know Faith too well, considering we only met at your wedding, but she did a fine job raising your wife. I wish we could have gotten to know her better."

"She was something," I muse. "She had a great outlook on life, and always wanted those she loved to succeed." I sip my drink. "Even me."

Río chortles. "Out of everyone, I think you gave her the least amount of pause. UC's on the top because of you."

"Your drums, too." In a softer tone, I add, "Not to mention Darren."

Did Faith approve of me as a consolation prize since our original keyboardist is no longer here? Is he the man she preferred for Jenna? Like a puppy dog, my gaze skips through the dwindling crowd, until it rests on my wife—who's with her little niece and nephew. Does she really want kids? With a fucked-up guy like me?

Unaware of my inner turmoil, Río continues, "Remember what Luke said before we took the stage for our first concert with Tris? He said Darren sent us our new keyboardist. I bet he also sent Jenna to you, to watch over the people he loved most in the world."

Darren *loved* me? I manage not to roll my eyes. "Yeah, not so sure on that one. He wasn't the sharing type."

Río chuckles. "Not with Jenna, true. A part of me thinks, though, that they were headed for a massive breakup. He was too wild for her.

With you, she's found the perfect balance. Keep on loving your wife and everything will be right in the world."

If only it were as easy as he makes it sound. Two people need to be in a marriage, and right now, I'm getting the vibe she's not with me.

Joining us, 007 mentions he's going to meet us in Europe. "Our boy found a mad rental on the Amalfi Coast of Italy." Río claps our bassist on the back. "That's right," 007 continues. "Tris and I are going to rock some models' worlds while sipping Italian wine and eating our weight in gelato."

"I heard my name." Our new keyboardist joins the conversation.

"Telling them about our rental," 007 explains, his smile wide.

"It's going to be epic," Tris replies. "Hey, think they have cool arcade games like Bennett has at his place? I could get into some pinball action."

"With hot babes lounging across it," 007 adds, rubbing his hands together.

Coop and Luke surround us, and talk veers toward their wicked plans, which include more booze and babes. Luke's even heading up north somewhere for some "peace and quiet," as he describes it. Before Jenna, I would've gone with the rest of the band, running away from any problems I might have. Namely my mother.

Now, however, even her call this morning doesn't register on the meter. My sole focus is on the blonde across the way, who's talking with the restaurant staff. I can tell the second she finds out I paid for the repast because her eyes form slits and her mouth hangs open.

As much as I want to disappear into the fantasy world my band-mates are enjoying, that's not where I need to be at the moment. I must get through to the one woman on the planet who doesn't want anything to do with me. My wife.

When my band finally leaves, I get handshakes and fist bumps, and even a mini pep talk from Luke. Being one of the last people in the restaurant, I know I can't avoid her any longer. I collect my ego off the floor and approach Jenna, who's chatting with Court.

I don a positive expression. "I think everything went as well as it could have."

"I agree," Court replies. She nudges my wife. "Good job."

"Thanks." Jenna's tone is as listless as her demeanor.

Today was a horrible day. The only things Jenna needs from me are love and support, and not my pussy hurt feelings. "Let me know how I can help." I suggest. "Take any of the flowers to the car?"

"Nah. Kara and I decided to donate them to the local women's shelter. I have enough flowers at home anyway." The ghost of a smirk crosses her face.

"Nice." I want to pump my fist in the air at this small victory. My woman is in there somewhere. I only need to coax her out again.

My gaze trips through the room, one I want to leave in the rearview mirror. I need time alone with my wife. "What about the cards and guest book?"

"Kara took them home to log them, so we can send out thank you cards." Her sister and her family left about ten minutes ago.

"Wow. You guys have this all under control." As soon as the last word is out of my mouth, I realize my error. Jenna's all about control. My pointing it out is not a good idea.

She folds into herself. "It's what matters."

I sigh. It's going to be a long night. "I think it's time we head out."

Court echoes my thought. "Yeah. Let's give the restaurant back to the servers."

After many thanks for as nice an afternoon as possible, the three of us make our way to the front door, where our rideshare waits. Jenna hugs her friend, who leaves for her own car. I open the black SUV's door for my wife, who climbs into the vehicle. I slip in behind her, and we begin the trek to Secluded Rest.

"I think your mother would've enjoyed today," I try.

"Yeah."

Silence.

"There were lots of people there."

"Uh-huh."

Silence.

"The UC PR team is in full force against the paparazzi. They'll shut them down."

"I hope so."

Silence.

I reach for something else positive to say. "The minister said some nice things."

"Bennett." Jenna twists to face me. "Let's not. Today sucked so hard. I had to say goodbye to the most important person in the whole world. I don't care who came, or who didn't. It doesn't matter to me that my father showed up, and my sister re-formed some sort of bond with him. I don't want to compliment the chefs or the florists or the limo drivers. None of that matters."

I want to hold my arms out to her and hug her pain away. I want to kiss away her tears and share our love. Something tells me such a gesture might only make things even worse between us.

We reach the security guardhouse in silence and are allowed to proceed. I'm filled with pent-up energy and want to punch something. Or play arcade games. Or walk on the beach. But my preferences don't matter. All that matters is helping my wife.

"Jenna," I say as the car pulls up the driveway.

She waves her hand. "I'm tired, Bennett. Can it wait?"

It's as if she slapped me. I can't form a thought until the driver stops at the front door, and I get out of the SUV. I reach out to help her onto the pavement, and am relieved when she accepts my assistance. At least there's that.

Together, we walk into our new house and she makes a beeline for the stairs. My emotions are running so high that I don't think I should be alone with her right now. Despite wanting to offer her solace, my own needs demand attention.

"Go on up, Sweetheart. I'm going to take a quick walk on the beach and will join you shortly."

"Okay."

I watch her trudge up the steps for a moment, then I turn in the opposite direction and leave the house through the bifold doors, kicking off my shoes in the process. Dumping my blazer and tie onto the outdoor sofa, I roll up my sleeves on my way to the ocean.

When I get to the breakers, I stand facing the horizon, not seeing the waves nor caring that the bottoms of my trousers are getting wet. What can I do to get through to Jenna? In the past, my solutions always involved sex. Yeah, not going to happen.

Shaking my head at its emptiness, I take off down the beach, my mind awhirl with yearning to comfort my wife. I've walked I don't know how long before I turn around, my house not even a speck in the distance.

When my house is on the horizon again, someone yells my name. Great. Just what I need today—to deal with fans. I put on the mask I wear for the public before turning toward the sound.

Michelle marches toward me.

Oh hell no. I go to turn, but decide against it. This bitch needs to be put in her place. My hands land on my hips and I wait.

"I thought that was you!"

"Michelle, you should know I'm in no mood to deal with your shit today. My guess is you know why. I only waited for you because I wanted to tell you to stay away from my wife. Do not have any interactions with her from now on, or you'll be sorry. Do I make myself clear?"

She pulls herself to her full height, which is taller than Jenna's. Makes no difference to me, though, she could be a fucking Amazon and I wouldn't care. My ire needs an outlet and she's made herself pretty damn accessible. Her shit stops now.

"Bennett." She reaches out and touches my sleeve, causing the tendons on my forearm to ripple. "Jenna's been bad luck for as long as I've known her. Hell, you know that, considering what happened to Darren. You're swept up in her, but she doesn't deserve you. Plus, you know she's not a good physical therapist, which is why my doctor doesn't refer patients to her. Her business is failing."

I grab her by her skinny wrist. "I let you spout your lies. Now listen to my truths."

She rushes forward as if I didn't say anything. "The way I see things, you have two choices. One, let Lissa and me wring the precious Jenna Westfield through the mud like she deserves. Or, two, try to counteract what we've told the media and find out what two scorned women can do. Your choice." In a huff, she rushes off the beach.

Great. She and Lissa have combined forces?

What's next?

Chapter 19

Bennett

Sunlight streams onto my face, urging me to greet the day. One eye cracks open, then the other, and I realize it's later than I thought. Crap. I swing my arm across the bed only to realize my wife's side is empty.

I can't let her slip away from me like Mom and Lissa have done. Jenna's my fucking *wife*. Throwing the blankets off my body, I trudge into the bathroom and get ready for the day.

Clad in workout shorts and nothing else, I enter the kitchen and make a pot of tea. My beverage of choice always calms her down, so maybe this will break the ice between us? *Feels like the frozen tundra.*

While the water boils, I wander through the house looking for her. She's not in the basement or family room or dining room. When the kettle whistles, I return to the kitchen and steep bags in two mugs, moving to the sink to rinse out the kettle. That's when I see her sitting in the outdoor living room. My shoulders lower. At least I know where she is.

Preparing a tray with our mugs and some biscuits I find in the kitchen, I bring them outside. All I want to do is wrap my body around hers, yet the chasm between us looms too large. Depositing the tray on the table, I open with, "Made you some herbal tea. Thought you might like it."

Her hand reaches for the mug. "Thanks, Bennett. It's perfect."

Perfect. She said it's perfect. Maybe today's the day I get my wife back?

Picking up my mug, I sit on the sofa next to her. Not touching, but close enough that I can feel her body heat. Well, what little there is of it. "Here, let me." I pick up a throw blanket and tuck it around her lower limbs.

She blows on her tea, jolting a bit. "I didn't realize I was chilly until now." Her head turns toward me. "You must be frozen. You don't even have a shirt on."

Thank God she noticed. "I'm good. You know I run hot."

"That you do." She sips her tea while her gaze scans the ocean in front of us.

"Listen, Jenna, I'm here for you. If you want to talk, feel free. Scream? Have at it. Cry, I'll wipe your tears. Whatever you need." I literally have no idea what else to say to her.

Jenna leans over and puts her mug onto the table. "This has been rougher than I even imagined possible," she begins. "I'm so mad at everyone. I'm afraid I'm not good company."

I place my tea next to hers. "Then we'll be bad company together."

Her body swivels to face me. "Your media is relentless. The only thing in their favor is they spelled Ma's name right."

"Faith Westfield isn't too difficult to spell."

"There is that." She sighs. "Michelle seems to have gone on the offensive again. I thought Dr. Marlow and I had a deal, but I guess not."

It's not so much what she's saying as *how*. Like there's no fight left in her to combat Michelle's lies. She isn't even aware that Michelle and Lissa have teamed up.

I'd pull up my big boy pants—if I were wearing pants.

"The UC PR team is on it. However, I had a run-in with Michelle last night on the beach. She spouted a lot of nonsense, but one thing is clear. Somehow, she and Lissa have combined forces. I don't know what they're up to, but they're definitely working together."

She rubs her thumb and pinky together. "Wonderful. Now the two crazies have become one. Between the two of them, how are we going to get the upper hand? Who are they going to go after first, you or me?"

"We didn't get that far."

"Court and I had Michelle on the ropes. I thought my lunch with Dr. Marlow ended all of Michelle's aspirations against me. I may be wrong about that, but if I'm right it means they're going to hunt you down."

Like an animal. Great. "I guess your theory makes sense. I wonder what lies they'll cook up between the two of them?"

"Well, Lissa already is saying she was pregnant by you. Maybe now Michelle will claim you wanted her to get implants?"

I rear back. "How about a threesome between her, me and Lissa?" Sounds more like me. And, before Jenna, not that far off the mark.

"Yeah. That would work, too."

She picks up her tea again like my suggestion doesn't affect her. I guess it doesn't. Still. "A lie, of course."

"Clearly." She continues to stare into the ocean.

I lean forward. "Look!" I point. "Dolphins!"

Out on the horizon, a pod of dolphins emerges from the water, enjoying their afternoon in the sun. I usually don't get to see them in the wild and excitement buzzes through my body. For her part, though, Jenna barely bats an eyelash.

When she doesn't say anything after a full minute, I ask, "Did you see them?"

"I did."

No inflection. No enthusiasm. Monotone.

I sidle against my wife. "Jenna," I begin.

In response, she stands. "I'm going inside. I'm a bit chilled." Turning her back on the ocean and the dolphins, she walks into the house. Alone.

How am I going to get through to her? If Faith were still here, I'd hit her up for guidance. Kara's in the City, but it's not the same.

As if a gift from above, my phone rings. Maybe this call will be my salvation? When the first strains of "Cleanin' Out My Closet" begin, I realize the *gift* was from a much darker place. Considering I threw her to voicemail yesterday, I guess it's time to pay up. Might as well get all the bad shit out in one afternoon.

Bracing myself, I pick up. "Hi, Mom."

"Hi, Mom," she mimics. "Seriously? I have to read online that my only son married some sort of murderess, who's killed both her ex-boyfriend and now her own mother?"

"I've been busy." I sigh. I should have listened to Jenna when she begged me to call my mother and tell her about our wedding. I was so busy with the band and gigs and putting plans into place about Lissa that I ignored her pleas. This is the result.

"Whatever tabloid you're reading, they've got it all wrong. Jenna had nothing to do with either one of those deaths. Darren, as you know, overdosed. Her mother just died of pancreatic cancer—the funeral was yesterday. My wife is going through a tough time."

"When your father died, I wasn't responsible either."

Wow. A sane thought. I tread lightly. "That's very true." I clamp my lips shut, hoping she doesn't go off the deep end again.

"Tell me, how is it you got married and I didn't know about it?" Her discombobulated voice reeks of pain.

I swallow over a lump. "It was fast because Jenna's mother was dying. We wanted her with us." Oh no. Wrong thing to say. The words hang above my head as if in a bubble with no way for me to retrieve them.

"You wanted *her* with you? Her? Not me, your *own* mother. The woman who gave you life, despite your having killed your sister?" Righteous anger has overtaken whatever pain was there before.

"That's not what I meant. Her mother was sick. Hell, she died two weeks after the ceremony."

"Yet I'm still here and you never bothered to tell me you got married. That I finally have a daughter."

Oh, fuck. She can't have glommed onto Jenna as a replacement for the twin who didn't survive long enough to be born. My fingers squeeze my thigh. With dread, I reply, "Well, I suppose you do now."

With a lethal strike, she pounces, "Who's as much of a killer as you are. Sounds like you two deserve each other."

My gaze searches the sky. "Listen, a lot is going down now with wrapping up after the funeral, as you can imagine. I have to help Jenna."

"Clearly you don't have time for me. You never have time for me."

Out of desperation, I ask, "Is Ramona there?"

"Yes. Where else would she be?"

"May I speak with her?" I wait a beat. "Please?"

She huffs, "Fine."

After a minute, I speak with her nurse, explaining the situation. I heave a sigh of relief when she agrees to calm Mom down and give her my excuses. The woman who birthed me is a raving lunatic. I'm not only talking legally.

I drop the phone onto my thigh. How did it come to this? I'm the lead singer of a world-famous band with thousands of adoring fans. Yet, the one woman on earth who promised—mere weeks ago—to love me, is giving me the cold shoulder. Mom's still living in her own fantasy world. Lissa and Michelle are scheming against me. Where's the off-ramp?

Jenna. She's always provided me excellent advice and guidance. Despite not being qualified, I need to do the same for her. Inside the house, I find her sitting on the sofa staring at the blank television.

I take a seat next to her and put my hand on her thigh. "Jenna, you have to let me in. Talk to me. Tell me what I can do to help you."

She faces me, her big gray eyes luminous. She's never looked so beautiful. So entranced in her, I'm not prepared for what she says next.

"I want a divorce."

Chapter 20

Jenna

I didn't mean to blurt out my request so bluntly. He asked what he could do, and I told him. The truth—we only rushed down the aisle to make Ma happy. Now that she's passed, there's no reason to stay married anymore.

I guess I could've let him down in a more gentle manner, but why? Might as well get the process started now.

"Excuse me?"

I heave a huge sigh. "Bennett, we both knew what was going on. Ma was dying and we wanted to make her last days happy. Our wedding day made her more than happy, she was ecstatic." I picture her smiling face as she hugged us after we walked down the aisle. Pride and bile war within me. "She's gone now, so there's no reason to carry on the sham."

"Sham?" Bennett's world-famous, gorgeous face tips to one side. The one he favors whenever he's thinking about something, I observe dispassionately. He jumps up and paces the room. "How was it a *sham* when we stood before friends and family to profess our love?"

There's so much to unpack here, but I don't have the energy. For him. For us. For anything. "I don't have it in me to fight.

He twirls toward me, hands on his trim hips. "I won't let you leave."

"I'm not your hostage." I rise to my feet. Why can't he see what's plain as day?

"Don't you love me?"

I halt mid-stride. Love? What does it even signify? I loved Ma, and all of my meaningless emotion is buried next to her. Beside my grandmother. Joining Darren. All I feel is rage at not being able to control her situation, at listening to Bennett, and at letting her stop pursuing more doctor's opinions. No room exists inside me for anything else.

My chin rises. Thoughts of my father flit through my mind. "Love is a wasted emotion, Bennett. The only thing that matters is . . ." I trail off. What *does* matter? "Growing your business and amassing more money."

He blinks. Several times. "Jenna."

I turn away from him. I now have my mandate. Build up At Your Service PT to ten—no, twenty clinics. Hire more staff. Make Michelle disappear. Toward that end, I add, "Oh, and getting reporters off my ass so I can go about living my life." I point my feet in the direction of the front door. I'm not staying at his mansion when I have my own fortune to build. My hand reaches the doorknob. "I'll get an attorney on the divorce right away."

The brilliant sunlight is in direct contradiction to my mood, but no matter. I pull out my cell, the only thing of mine I'll take from Secluded Rest, and order a ride service.

I'm about halfway down the driveway when the front door slams. My soon-to-be ex-husband bellows, "I'm not going to let you do this!"

I don't veer from my mission, simply keep walking. He can say whatever he wants, but I'm not going to change my mind. Where's my car?

When I don't respond, Bennett pounds the pavement until he's right behind me. "Jenna. You're grieving. I get it. Let me help you."

This is the final straw. I turn to him. "I don't need your help. I don't need anyone's help. Go live your life as the frontman for UC. Travel the world, bang groupies and fans. Do whatever. But leave. Me. Alone. I'll make sure our divorce is quick and simple since I don't want any of your money. I want to make it on my own, like I was before you barged into my life. I'm retaking it now, and giving yours back to you. Do with it as you will."

I have nothing left to say, so I spin on my heel and continue walking toward the street. From the distance, I see a car making its way toward the house. I speed up to meet it.

But not fast enough.

Bennett grabs my arm and physically turns me to him. "Jenna, I know you didn't mean what you just said. I love you. You love me. We can get through this together." His mouth crashes against mine.

Like always, he molds his lips over mine in what I used to think was the most sensuous manner. A moment of passion overtakes me and I lean into him.

Bennett's arms encircle my waist and he drags my limp form against his hardening body. He still has the same physique that causes women to drop their panties and throw them onstage. Muscles to die for—or drool over. Like I used to, but see where it got me? Burying Ma.

As his embrace continues, he trails kisses down my neck. At my sides, my fingers on my left hand play with the rings there. My wits assemble. I know what I have to do.

Taking a step backward, I manage to free myself from his over-whelming outpouring of misguided sexual desire. I grab the rings, take them off my left finger, and place them on my palm. Hand outstretched, I say, "These are yours. I don't need them anymore." When he doesn't make a move to take them, I stuff them into his pocket.

At the curb, the car arrives.

My gaze scans his form a final time. This beautiful man will find another woman at the drop of a hat. He'll remember me as I think of him, as a brief interlude—a nice way to pass the time while he was healing from a groin pull. I'll always be grateful for the money I earned working with him to open clinic number four.

Without another word between us, I spin on my heel, open the car door, and am driven away from all that represents Bennett Hardy.

Soon, we pull up in front of my house, the place I haven't spent much time in since learning of Ma's cancer. While by no means anywhere remotely in the vicinity of Secluded Rest in terms of size or waterfront views or amenities, it's what I can afford. It's comfortable. I glance at the curtains Ma helped me pick out. At the knickknacks we scored at a craft fair. I enter the kitchen and see the kettle she gifted me for my birthday. This is what matters, this is love. Not throwing around money and fame to get what you want. Like a petulant child.

In my mind, Ma's voice about how she was wrong about Bennett and how much she loved him rings loud. Our vows from our wedding echo. Such sentimentality becomes covered in a black shroud, and I go about getting ready to go to the clinic and taking on Michelle once and for all.

"You're here?" Court greets me with much less enthusiasm than I expected.

"Of course I am," I counter, walking into Court's office. "This is my business, after all."

"I just thought you'd be doing things for your mother's, um, clearing up her estate." She has the grace to look away.

I wave my hand. "That stuff will be there until Kara and I deal with it. My business, however, needs my attention. Have you heard anything more from Michelle?" While I know I need to go on social media again soon, I simply didn't have the balls to face it yet. Better to get a distilled version from Court.

My manager adjusts her glasses. "Well, she kicked up about the Black Widow stuff when your mother passed, but there was a big clapback at her about it, so she stopped. No more graffiti or anything." She pauses. "Michelle's been pretty quiet, which sort of scares me more."

This. Strategy I can dive into headfirst. Sink my teeth into. "Bennett mentioned that she and Lissa might be teaming up, so I think we should consider this more of a regrouping than her giving up."

"Oh." We sit at the table in her office. "So now we're going to take down two women rather than only one? We can do it."

"We sure can. I won't wait for them to come forward, though."

Court asks, "What does Bennett think is going to happen? Can Hayden help us again?"

"I'm thinking we should do this on our own."

Her head bounces backward. "Why? Hayden was a huge help before. I'm sure she will come up with something even better this time. Plus, if Lissa's in the mix, we're going to need UC's help."

Everything Court says is true. However, she's missing one essential ingredient. I shrug. "Bennett and I are getting a divorce. Oh, which attorney do you think I should use?" I search for a piece of paper, finally locating one. Gripping a pen, I scribble some names down and read them to Court. "Think any of these would be good?"

When she doesn't respond, my gaze leaves the paper with five names on it to focus on her face. Which looks like I ruined her favorite medicine ball. "Court," I begin.

"Jenna," she counters. "What do you mean you're getting a divorce?"

I rub my arm. "Exactly what I said. The reason for our rushed wedding is no longer in play."

She shakes her head. "I don't understand. Speak to me as if I were five."

I place the paper onto the table with a sigh. "You and I both know we rushed into marriage in order to make Ma happy. We did it. She was happy. She's gone. No need to keep on pretending."

"Pretending to be happy? Pretending he didn't rock your world?

Pretending you weren't in love with the biggest rock star on the planet?"

I wave my hand. "It was only an act to warm the heart of my dying mother. Now it's over."

"Jenna, I've never heard you talk like this. You sound so . . . callous."

"I'm not being callous. Not at all. Merely realistic. What Bennett and I had was a lovely interlude in an otherwise awful situation. He agrees." I hold up my bare left hand. "He took back his rings and everything. I'm sure he'll be able to return them and get most of his money back." Since I didn't pay for his wedding ring, I didn't have to deal with this minor detail, on top of handling all of Ma's loose ends.

Court grabs my left hand. "Oh my God. You're not lying?"

"Why would I lie? We gave a dying woman her last wish, and now we're getting out of it." I point to the list of attorneys. "Who should I pick?"

Court pulls back. "I don't agree with what you just said. I was there at the beginning, remember? You fell for him, I know it. You were happy at your wedding. Glowing even. So was your mother. Bennett was beside himself with joy. You can't mean this."

I pat her hand. "Believe me, it's the truth. The sooner I can put this whole episode behind me, the better. Did you know my father showed up at the funeral?"

"What?" Her head flips from side to side. "No. Why was he there?"

Our discussion moves away from my misguided marriage to talk about the man who left Ma when I was five. We eventually move on to discussing the clinics' patient load.

"I did have a lunch meeting with Dr. Marlow," I remind Court. No need to mention it being cut short because of the phone call from Kara about Ma. "He promised his office would be sending more of his patients our way. Michelle has to listen to her boss." I lean back, crossing my arms. "Checkmate, Michelle."

Turns out it was more like check.

Two days later, I'm sitting at my dining room table sorting through Ma's accounts. She squirreled some money in one bank, more in another, with another five I still need to check. Rubbing my eyes, I plead for help. No one responds.

My phone chimes with an alert. I finally turned all of my alerts back on last night, thinking the worst would have passed. Over a thousand texts, voicemails, social media messages, and notifications proved otherwise. So I did what any normal person would do, and ignored all but a very select few.

The divorce attorney I selected to represent me.

My sister.

Court.

All the rest can fly off into the ether, for all I care. The Google alert chimes again, and I consider disabling it as well, but it's set for At Your Service PT and I need to know if there are any hits on my business. I click on the alert.

The headline says it all. "At Your Service Gives Happy Endings." I skim the article. "Sources say" my physical therapy clinics are fronts for a massive prostitution ring in the Hamptons. Even Darren's mother is quoted.

I jump to my feet. You have got to be kidding me. Seems like Bennett was correct on this one thing—Michelle couldn't have cooked this up on her own. Lissa had to have helped. Darren's mother simply added fuel to their fire.

I pace through my kitchen, trying to figure out a way to shut this story down before it gains legs. Besides the obvious denials and patient testimonials, I need to clap back. I might have a relatively easy target against Michelle, considering she works for Dr. Marlow, who seemed to be on my side.

The wildcard is Lissa. Bennett's ex. How can I get her to back off? Hell, I'm no longer with Bennett, so what does she want with me anyway?

It hits me. The world doesn't know we've called it off. All I need to do is alert them to our upcoming divorce and everyone will leave me alone. I have an initial meeting with the attorney later today and we can discuss this. More settled than I have been in a while, I return to focusing on Ma's accounts.

At two o'clock, I walk into the legal office and am escorted into a nicely appointed conference room. Important-looking books line the walls with titles like *New York Divorce Law* and *The Statute of Limitations*. Clearly exciting reading.

The attorney, Suzette Pounds, enters the room carrying a notebook and we discuss my short-lived marriage. When we're through most of the details, I say, "Sorry to put a rush on this, but I have a situation that needs to be addressed, and I thought getting my divorce out there would be the best way to handle it."

"What's going on?" I explain to her about Lissa and Michelle's vicious attack on my business. "That certainly puts a spin on things," Suzette notes. "If the divorce is as amicable as you make it sound, as soon as we serve Bennett with the papers, we can go public. The reporters should get off your back."

"I hope so." Lissa and Michelle don't seem the type to back away, but if the media loses interest in me, they won't have any other option. Besides, Lissa's only after me because of Bennett. When she realizes we're through, she'll try another tactic.

"To expedite things, how about asking Bennett where we should serve him," Suzette says. "The documents will be ready to go in the morning. You have a straightforward case."

"I'll reach out to him."

I open the messenger app and, ignoring the long list of unopened texts, search for Bennett. The number seventy-six sits next to his name. He texted me that many times? Frowning, I open the first one:

ROCK STAR

Jenna, I love you so much. Don't do this to us. You need time to process everything that's happened. Call me when you want to talk, day or night.

ROCK STAR

I miss your kiss. I miss your touch. I miss
your smile.

ROCK STAR

Please come back to me.

I stop reading and type him a message:

Looks like you were right about Lissa and
Michelle teaming up. We can shut them
down by letting the world know we're
splitting up. I'm at the attorney's office now.
She wants to know where we can serve you
the divorce papers? Should I have them
sent to Secluded Rest?

"There," I address Suzette. "Sent. I'm sure he'll say the place he
bought, in town, Secluded Rest, so you can put that on the papers for
now."

"Will do."

The alert for a text comes in, and Bennett's name comes through.
I glance at the lawyer. "He's gotten back to me." I open the text:

I'm not accepting them.

Chapter 21

Bennett

In the basement, I punch the bag. Hard. Harder. Again and again. How can this be happening to me?

Sweat rolls off my body when I stop and rip the boxing gloves off my hands with my teeth. I walk over to the bar and grab a bottle of water. In two gulps, it's gone. I take a third.

Jenna didn't answer any of my texts. Or pleading voicemails. All she did is ask where to serve me with divorce papers. *Divorce papers!* I know grief can do crazy things to people, but make newlyweds separate? That has to be a record.

The phone rings and I jump to see if Jenna's mind is working straight and she's finally calling me. Luke's name is on FaceTime.

Fuck.

On the third ring, I answer the call, bottle of water against my temple.

"I would ask how you're doing, B, but a picture is worth a thousand words."

I bring the water to my lips. "What do you want?"

"I need to find out how my lead singer is doing."

"Always protecting the band," I snark. "I'm alive."

"How's Jenna doing?"

Boom.

His question hangs out in the air for a few moments. What should I tell him? That I'm a miserable failure—again—and she left me? I shrug. "She left."

"Oh. That's good right? She's getting out there."

My head shakes. "No. You misunderstand. She left." I inhale. "Me."

His eyes double in size. "What do you mean, she left you? You're not making any sense."

None of this does. Ever since her mother passed away, none of Jenna's actions add up. "What I mean is her last text asked whether I'll accept service of the divorce papers at Secluded Rest." I put the phone on a table so Luke can't see me crumple to the floor, holding onto the gym mats like they were a lifeline.

"Divorce?"

"Yeah." I get myself under control, manage to stand, and return to the screen. I'm sure my tears will combine with the sweat and not make me look like a total pussy.

"B, this can't be right. She loves you."

I let out a miserable chuckle. "Not enough." Or at all.

Then he does the unexpected. Seems to be going around. "Why don't you join me in New Hampshire. It's quiet. No one will bother you here."

I'm about to blow him off when a thought occurs. If Jenna ignores my text and tries to serve the papers here, she could succeed. But not if I'm actually *not* here. "You know what? Sounds like a good idea."

"Great. I'll send the jet to the Hamptons to pick you up shortly. I'll make dinner." He pauses. "Everything will work out, B." Then he disappears from my screen.

All I can think of is Jenna's text to me. Divorce papers? No fucking way. I run up the stairs, only stopping at the top when I realize I'm not in any pain. The groin pull's been bothering me less and less, and now it seems to have disappeared. Much like my physical therapist wife. And every other woman in my life who I told I loved.

With this thought, I enter the bedroom and start throwing random things into my luggage. No way am I giving in to Jenna's unreasonable demands. She's my wife, for fuck's sake. Her mother died happy knowing we were together. She even told me she was thrilled that I'm her son. It's my first maternal score ever. *Jenna can't mean this.*

I chew over this question the entire flight to Luke's. Never come up with an answer. I barely offer a wave to Ashley, the flight attendant, as I exit the jet.

Closing yet another black SUV's door, I sling my bag over my shoulder and take in the house before me. I've been to New Hampshire on tour, but I never saw the rural towns. This place is large, with at least five or six bedrooms. It has a wraparound porch that spans the entire first floor. Two dormers punctuate the roofline. A swing is attached to a massive tree in the front yard. Looks like something out of a Norman Rockwell painting.

As I walk up the path, the front door opens. Luke, relaxed in a pair of workout shorts and T-shirt, welcomes me. "B, glad you're here, man. Come on in. I'll throw some steaks on the grill."

He ushers me inside, and I drop my luggage onto the foyer floor. "Nice place you got. Must've been some find on Airbnb."

"Well, actually," he tugs on the front of his shirt. "It's not a rental. This place has been in my family for generations."

My eyebrows lift and I whistle. "Nice. Good to know one of us came from a good home."

Our manager's head leans to one side. "Have you ever been to Río's parents' house?"

"Can't say I have."

He doesn't say anything more on the topic. "Leave your stuff there. We'll pick it up when we go upstairs later. Want a beer?"

While Manhattans are my drink, a beer with steak does sound good. "Sure." I follow him into a massive kitchen, which was redone within the past couple of years judging by the quartz countertops, huge island, and high-end appliances.

"This place rivals Secluded Rest."

"Nah," he contradicts me. Holding up one finger, he says, "The Hamptons." A second finger slides up. "Oceanfront. I think you win."

"Let's say we both win." I open the fridge and take out a few beers while he puts the finishing touches on the tray with our dinner. Steaks, potato salad, and a variety of other dishes are brought outside. If I were hungry, I'd enjoy this.

I'm not.

As the steaks sizzle on the grill, Luke plunges forward. "Jenna wants a divorce?"

I guzzle a beer. "So she says."

"Do you?"

"What? No fucking way. I love her." The truth nags—she doesn't feel the same.

"So what are you going to do?" He flips the steaks.

"What am I going to do?" I repeat, finishing my beer. "What *can* I do? I told her I wouldn't accept service of the papers. That's about all I can think *to do*."

"Well, that's a start." Coffee-colored eyes hold my gaze. "Are you going to fight for her?"

"I." My brain short-circuits. I pick up a second beer and pop off the cap. "My love isn't good enough." *Story of my life*. No one I ever loved stuck around—not Lissa, not my mother (well, she is physically, I guess), not Dad.

I sip the beer, wondering why I'm sharing all this shit with Luke. I *never* talk about anything remotely close to these truths. With anyone. Except Jenna. Look where that got me.

He takes his time placing the steaks onto a platter, then brings everything over to the table. Out of ingrained manners, I sit and place some food onto my dish. Not that I have an appetite. Or manners.

Luke cuts the steak and savors the morsel. "You know," he begins. "I was there from the beginning. I remember when you did that crazy-ass jump that landed you in need of a physical therapist in the first place. I practically had to beg you to see Jenna for treatment. You were adamant about not going."

I play with the label on my beer bottle. "I remember. The doctor said if I wanted to keep my commitments to UC, I had to get physical therapy, so I had no choice. Jenna was the logical person to help."

"Right." He deposits a forkful of potato salad into his mouth. "Because she dated Darren."

There he is. The ever-present band member who we can't allow to cross over to the other side. "She did." I play with my fork.

"Who was an ass."

His statement hangs like a broken guitar string. "He was the driving force behind UC," I contradict him. "Darren invited me to join the band when I was still in high school. He got our bookings, before we met you. He was many things, but an ass isn't one of them."

Luke puts his silverware down. "His over-the-top lifestyle was getting old before he hurt his wrist. Afterward, he got addicted. He didn't seek out help. He lied to all of us, including Jenna. He was a great keyboardist and contributed to some of UC's greatest hits. But he still was an ass."

I adjust my weight in the chair. "He did do all those things, but it doesn't make him an ass. It makes him an addict, a disease shared with so many other people."

"That's true. But we could've helped him. You want to know why he didn't tell us?" When I don't reply, he answers, "Because he didn't want to come clean. He was fighting his own demons like all of us. His were big but not insurmountable. When he found drugs, he used them to self-medicate and take himself away."

Luke lets this sink into my brain. I consider it from all angles and have to agree with him about Darren's personality. Plus the fact he wanted to relieve his pain. Don't we all?

"Do you know why I'm telling you this, B?"

He picks up his knife and fork and cuts another piece of steak. I touch my silverware and make a tentative cut into mine. A perfect medium rare. My lips close around the first bite of food I've eaten since Jenna slapped me with her announcement. "I'll bite. Why?"

"Because I don't want you to become an ass, too. I can't lose another friend."

Friend.

My silverware clatters onto my plate. I don't do friends. True, I asked him to be my best man—at Jenna's urging, might I add—but that doesn't bestow the title of "friend" on him.

Or does it?

I choose the easy route. "I'm not a drug addict."

"True. Not yet, anyway. But alcohol is an addiction as well."

As he says this, I'm finishing my second beer. I haven't been here more than an hour. "I don't drink to excess. Often."

"So far. Tell me you didn't want to drown your sorrows in a bottle?"

I remember, or don't as the case may be, the past few days. Which I spent alternating between texting and leaving Jenna voicemails, and drinking myself into oblivion. "The past few days excepted, I don't drown my problems."

"That's right." He cracks his knuckles. "You're the resident sex addict."

"What?!" I pop up so fast my chair flies backward. "I am not."

He remains seated, chewing on his dinner. "In the past, when UC's scored number one on the charts, what did you do?"

Pacing, I think back to all of our number one hits. All the women I took into various places—buses, beds, closets—and fucked their brains out to celebrate. I stare at the table. "I had sex."

"And when UC won the Grammy's?"

"Sex."

"How about when the band came up with a new song?"

"Sex."

"Need I go on?"

"No." I right my chair and retake my seat.

"Has it been the same with Jenna?"

Shit. Have I been such a manwhore and didn't even realize it? Not with Jenna. *Because of your groin injury, dumbass.* Perhaps that's what drew me to her so hard? I actually got to know her, as a person, a woman, before we even had our first kiss. She intrigued me talking about *The Godfather* when I first met her before I knew she was dating Darren. The last time we met I didn't want anything to do with her and physical therapy. But she pushed on. And helped me. When we finally kissed, it was electric. Unlike anything I've ever experienced before.

"With her, things were very different. Ass backward even. I got to know her really well before our first kiss."

"She broke your pattern." He takes a triumphant last bite of his steak.

"I guess she did." I stab a piece of steak and deposit it into my mouth. All this isn't to say I didn't want to have sex with Jenna, because I did. It was the best I've ever had, bar none, but not simply for the physical act. It was our connection. She understood me and, I thought, I got her too. Clearly, I was wrong on that account.

"Which brings me back to my original question. How are you going to get your wife back?"

The steak lodges in my throat, but I manage to choke it down. "For one, I'm not letting her serve those divorce papers to me."

"Good start."

What can I do to actually get Jenna to change her mind? For my whole adult life, I've never needed to chase a woman, but I need her to remember she loves me. Buried beneath all of Jenna's emotions about her mother, I know she does. "I heard her, you know. In the hospital when her mother died. She blamed me for not forcing Faith to seek out more doctors who might have had some treatment options."

"Did you?"

"What? No." I reply. "Well, I did convince her this was Faith's decision to make and she couldn't control her mother. Jenna's a real control freak, you know."

Luke smirks. "You don't say."

I take another bite of the potato salad. "She was so angry at me."

"The first stage of grief."

His statement rings true. "I need to help her through her grief over Faith."

"Now we're talking."

I play with my potato salad, making cross marks across the mayo. How? "What else can I do to make her come around?"

"Good question. How'd you do it the first time?"

"She had to give me physical therapy." I whack my thigh. "All good now."

He tosses back his beer. "I don't think she'd believe you had a relapse. What if you do something about Michelle and Lissa? Get them off her clinic's back?"

I pick up my beer, only to find it empty. Replacing it on the table, I say, "That's not a bad idea. UC's PR team's been doing a good job handling Michelle. Jenna told me about Hayden's idea and how well it worked." I grin. The bumper sticker with physical therapists adjusting all the spider legs was genius.

"Probably why Michelle felt the need to come up with something else," Luke remarks. "We've shut her down pretty well on the Black Widow front."

"Until her mother died and reignited the shitstorm." I push away from the table and gather the empty beer bottles. "Want another?"

"Sure."

All the way inside, I ponder Luke's suggestion. How can I get them to back off Jenna? Tossing the empties into the recycle can, I bring a few more cold brews outside.

Clinking the necks, Luke says, "To Operation Jenna."

"Here, here."

For the first time since Jenna left, I enjoy the bubbles sliding down my throat. I even pick up my silverware and eat off my plate. I don't clear it, but make more of a dent than over the past few days.

After we clean up, we return outside and Luke lights a fire pit.

We stare into the flames and drink more beer, keeping all my marital problems at bay for the time being. Tomorrow, we'll tackle them. Tonight's for being with my . . . friend.

I wake to the sun streaming through my window and birds chirping outside. If only my outlook was as positive as nature. I shower, mindlessly watching water droplets wind their way through the dips between my muscles. The same muscles Jenna used to lick. My cock bobs at the memories, but I tamp him down. This time, though, instead of admonishing him he won't get any ever again, I find myself switching up the mantra to "Don't Stop Believin'."

Bounding down the stairs, I find Luke in the kitchen and bacon wafting from the stove. "Smells mighty good in here."

"Thanks, B. Sleep all right?"

I consider his question. "You know, for the first time since, well, I did. Still haven't decided on a course of action to get Jenna back, but it feels like I will. I'm going to win my wife back."

He slaps me on the back. "Glad to hear it."

An idea forms. "Starting right now." I pick up my phone and dial the florist I used when I sent daily flowers to her at her mother's house. Was that only a few weeks ago? When the clerk answers, I put in my order.

"I'd like to send daily flowers to Jenna Westfield, er, Hardy. I want to cycle through your more exotic collection, anything but roses."

"Sure thing, Mr. Hardy. How would you like the cards signed?"

Shit. When I sent them before, I always included a special message. I need to do even better now. "I'd like to have song lyrics from Untamed Coaster songs on all the cards. I have your email address and will send you at least thirty cards' worth when we hang up."

"Sounds good. One final question, where should we send them?"

My mind halts its rolodex of UC's songs at the question. Where should I send the flowers? I go with my gut. "To her house." Not mine. Yet.

"You got it. I'll be on the lookout for your email."

After we hang up, I open a blank email and start tapping out UC lyrics. To our first song. To our first number one. To our most recent number one. To our wedding song.

Luke brings over two plates piled high with breakfast. "Looks like someone's been busy." He sits next to me at the island.

"Yeah. I'm going to start my campaign with flowers, but they're the easy part." I shovel scrambled eggs, hash browns, and bacon into my mouth without thought. What else can I do?

"Sounds like a good start." He chows down on his own breakfast.

"I need to get to Lissa and Michelle. I can't believe they're accusing Jenna of harboring a prostitution ring at her clinics. It's grotesque."

"They sure are. You know how to pick 'em."

I pause mid-forkful. "I only met Michelle because of Jenna. As for Lissa, well, I was in high school, what can I say? She was different back then." I place the food-laden fork into my mouth. "Besides, my hormones were in charge."

He chuckles around a piece of bacon. "We both know that no one should try to get between you and your hormones."

I whack him in the gut. "Back then, I wasn't getting any—other than from my right hand."

He rubs his stomach. "Must've been getting quite the workout."

Squinting at my friend, I finish the food on my plate. "Not as much as yours, I'd wager." I've seen Luke hook up with plenty of women on tour, but never the plasticky ones like Lissa is today. Usually he chooses the more low key, down-home-type chicks. For the first time, I wonder about his love life. "Do you have a special lady you keep hidden from us?"

"Me?"

He looks surprised I asked about his love life and I give myself a swat on the ass. Have I, and the rest of UC, been oblivious to his needs?

When I motion for him to continue, he chews his food then

places his fork down on the plate. "I'm not dating anyone at the moment. It's too hard with all the touring UC does."

"But," I prompt.

"I hope to meet her someday. Finding a partner who loves this life as much as I do, though, is a tall ask. We'll see. Besides, we're here to talk about you." He cracks his knuckles.

"Yeah, well, I think I need to shut Lissa down. Michelle seems like the hanger-on type. I'd bet Lissa concocted this whole story about Jenna's physical therapy clinics as a way to hurt me, and Michelle went along for the ride."

"Sounds about right." He clears the scraps off our plates into the garbage, then rinses them. "Have you heard any more from Curtiss?"

Curtiss. My former best friend who got Lissa pregnant. "We've been keeping in touch, but he hasn't had any luck finding what he's looking for yet." I sigh. If he can't find the proof, it'll be another *he said, she said* situation. "He did say he was going to his parents' house this weekend, though. Proof has to be there."

"Want me to call Hayden?"

"Desperately. But Jenna probably already hit her up. After all, she was the driving force with the Black Widow shit before."

"You're likely right, B."

I place the dishes into the dishwasher. "Mother Hilliard's comments in the article didn't help matters either. I so want to set that woman straight."

Luke closes the dishwasher's door and cracks his knuckles again. "You know what? How about we hit her up? Obviously, our visit to her house before didn't do the trick."

My head tilts. "Think we could change her mind?"

Luke rubs his hands together. "Jet's still here. Let's pay her a visit."

Chapter 22

Jenna

At my kitchen table, I scour Lissa's social media platforms, searching for a connection between her and Michelle. They have to have teamed up against me. Bennett's right—no way would Michelle have thought up this prostitution ring idea by herself.

Of course, simply putting her name, Michelle Kent, into the search bar yields no results. I try to use variations of her middle name, Jasper, which I'll never forget because I had a goldfish named Jasper in elementary school, and teased her about it. Still nothing. She may be dumb, but she's not stupid. Think, Jenna. What alias could she be using?

Back in high school, she stole my boyfriend. What was his name? I snap my fingers. Right. Thaine. Thaine Bell. I search his names together with Michelle's various names. BINGO! A Thaine Jasper is a match on Facebook. Similar searches on Instagram, TikTok and YouTube yield the same results. Plus, Lissa's been interacting with this "avatar" on socials. All use the same profile pix of a stunningly gorgeous man, complete with a six-pack—on display because "he's" only wearing a skimpy bathing suit. ChatGPT must've gotten a workout the day she created the profile.

The fact she's still fixated on the guy would be depressing, if she wasn't so pathetic. We graduated from high school over a decade ago. Get a life, Michelle.

Now that I've pinpointed her pitiful avatar, how am I going to get her and Lissa to break their unholy alliance? As much as I don't want to think about him, Bennett did mention working on an angle with Curtiss to get Lissa off his back, so I should steer clear of his ex. My focus has to be on Michelle. Besides, I've allowed this girl to annoy me for way too long. Time to rip her a new one.

My mind spins over my next step. Clearly, Dr. Marlow was ineffective. I need to attack her somewhere other than her paycheck. Although, one would think the paycheck would be the best option.

I go round and round, not landing on a single viable idea. Since my business isn't under UC protection anymore, I decide to visit Court at the clinic. Maybe between the two of us, we can figure out a viable idea.

After I change into my scrubs, I toss my now lukewarm tea into the sink when the doorbell rings. Who could that be? Dread washes over me. I hope it's not Bennett. With slow steps, I reach my front door and look out through the window, which causes the air to leave my body. Not Bennett.

I swing open the door. "May I help you?"

The guy bends down and picks up a vase of flowers I hadn't noticed. "You Jenna Hardy?"

My mind forces me to remember my new last name. No guesses needed to find out the sender. "Yes." After I sign some paperwork and give him a tip—positive Bennett took care of this but wanting to stand on my own two feet—I close the door behind me and walk over to the coffee table.

A gorgeous arrangement of gerbera daisies brightens the room. My shaky hand reaches out and removes the card, while my traitorous body remembers all the flowers he sent me leading up to the wedding. Ma used to be downright gleeful every time someone rang the doorbell. I can almost hear her begging me to read the card.

Almost.

I rip open the tiny envelope and lyrics from "Crushing Blow" are written on it. They scream of overcoming the pain of unrequited love. Darren wrote this song—his last. The fact Bennett chose to put these words on this card has to mean something.

Perhaps he's thinking I was better off with Darren?

Is he making a statement about his own feelings toward me?

Whatever. The card drops onto the table. I have more important things to do than try to get into the mind of Bennett Hardy.

Shortly, I pull into the nearly empty parking lot at the flagship clinic for At Your Service PT. Given that it's midday, this place should be hopping. Damn Michelle. And Lissa.

Taking the stairs, I sneak into the back of the clinic. No one's in the waiting room and only a couple of patients are with therapists. I need to right this ship. Again.

"Hey, Court," I announce myself. "I'd love to put our heads together and get through this, ah, slump."

"From your mouth," she replies, tossing some paperwork from the sofa onto the floor. "Here, have a seat. Let's talk."

I get comfortable while Court gets us a couple of cups of water from the dispenser. "Should I scale back on the water delivery?"

"No way. This is only a minor setback. Keep the water flowing." She grins.

My head bows. "I really thought we'd be over this hump when we shut Michelle down the first time. I was wrong."

She places her hand over mine. "No one could've anticipated this newest, ah, allegation."

"Still, I need to fix it. At least we have a few patients who didn't abandon us."

"We do." She flips through the appointment book. "A core group refuse to leave."

"That's something," I muse. "Not enough, though. Look, Bennett told me Michelle and Lissa have teamed up. I figured out Michelle's using the fake avatar 'Thaine Jasper' on Lissa's socials."

"Thaine was your boyfriend in high school that she poached, right?"

"Good memory. Michelle evidently put his name together with her middle name, thinking no one would figure it out." I blow on my fingers. "She was wrong."

Court asks the question that's been rolling around my brain all morning. "How are you going to out her to the world?"

"That's the million-dollar question. I'm one hundred percent sure Thaine has no clue what's going on."

"Where is he now?"

I shrug. "Haven't kept in touch with the guy who dumped me for Michelle."

Court pulls out her phone. "Let's see if he's still around. Thaine Bell, right?" She punches a few things into her phone. "Looky here. Mr. High School Ex-Boyfriend lives two towns over." She clicks a few more times. "Divorced with three kids." She turns her phone around to show me.

"He still has all his hair," I remark dispassionately.

Court studies his photo. "He's not a bad looking guy. I mean, he's no Bennett Hardy or anything."

I wave my naked left hand. "He sent me flowers this morning. Gerbera daisies."

Court's mouth drops open. "What did the card say?"

"It had the lyrics from Darren's last big hit on it. 'Crushing Blow.'" I pause. "At least he went out on top."

She pulls me toward her and gives me a hug I didn't know I needed. Releasing me, Court cleans her glasses on her shirt. "What's the best way to put them in their places?" At least she didn't mention Bennett.

In the ensuing silence, my mind races. What would Ma counsel me to do? Probably choose the lowest hanging fruit. Which, in this instance, is a who.

Thaine.

I bet he'd be pissed to hear she's using his name without his permission. He and Michelle broke up before he left for college, never to be seen together again. How can I use this to my advantage?

"I might have something," I venture. Her eyes descend on me, and I swallow. "Michelle's using Thaine Jasper as her avatar. I say I give my ex-boyfriend a little visit and tell him what she's been up to."

"Devious," she nods. "I like it. Want me to come with?"

"No. I think this is something I need to do by myself." I stand. "I'll let you know what happens."

"You better." She gives me another hug for the road, and I set out to correct some of the wrongs Michelle has rained down on me. Doesn't hurt it gives me a purpose besides dwelling on the end of my marriage.

Using Court's newly gathered information, I plug Thaine's work address into the GPS. As I'm driving, I can hear Bennett's voice encouraging me to stick it to Michelle. Not that I need or want his advice, but it's still nice to know I'm on the right track.

I pull into an office park and walk into the oversized facility. Turns out Thaine works in software development.

Straightening my shoulders and pulling out my ponytail holder, I approach the receptionist and ask to see Thaine Bell. *Not weird at all.* I add that my business is looking to develop a customer relationship management program, and heard he could help us. The receptionist buys it, because soon I'm escorted into a conference room and she's getting me a tea.

The teabag dips into the hot water when Thaine walks into the room. "Hello," a much lower-pitched voice says. "I heard you're looking for a new CRM program. You came to the right place."

I rise to my feet. Keeping my composure, I lift my chin. "Thaine." His name sounds odd coming out of my mouth after so many years. "I actually have a good CRM program, but I needed to see you to fill you in on something Michelle Kent's been doing." For the first time, I wonder if he *did* give her permission to use his name. Too late to go back now, though.

His brows come together as his gaze skims over my body. "Oh." He tilts his head. "Jenna? Jenna Westfield, is that you?"

At least he recognized me. "It is."

"Holy sh—" he cuts himself off from cursing. Bennett never had such reservations. "Wow. I haven't seen you for how long? Ten years? More?"

"Something like that."

His head shakes. "Wait. Didn't I read somewhere that you got married not long ago? To that rock star, Bennett Hardy."

My empty left hand fists. No need to go into my private life with him. "I did, but he's not the reason I'm here." Using my right hand, I point to the chairs. "Can we sit?"

"Of course. Where are my manners?" He pulls out a chair for me then sits, mumbling my name. "So you came here why again?"

I launch into an abbreviated version of Michelle's campaign against me, the Black Widow graffiti, and finally her teaming up with Lissa to concoct the prostitution ring scheme.

He whistles. "That's quite the story you have there. But I fail to see how I play into this?"

"Because Michelle's using the name 'Thaine Jasper' on all socials." I let this final revelation hang in the air while I take a sip of my tea.

I see the second a lightbulb goes off in his head. "Whoa. My first name and, if I remember correctly, her middle. That's messed up."

"It is." I place my mug onto the table. "I thought finding out that Michelle's using your name might be an incentive for you to help me stop her."

Thaine leans back in his chair. Dark hair, almost black like Pierce's, is cropped close to his face. Not a millimeter of scruff on his chin. He looks like he could be an insurance broker rather than a software developer.

"Michelle still pops up in my world from time to time. She got her boss to hire us for a new CRM system a couple of years ago." His gaze drops to the table. "I'm sorry for how I ended things with you back in high school, Jenna. It was shitty of me to do, I see that now."

"I have to admit, it hurt at the time. But we've both grown, I hope, and left high school in the rearview mirror."

"You're very kind."

I can leverage his sentiment. Taking another sip of my tea, I ask, "So you'll help me?"

"I guess I owe you one," he says. "What do you have in mind?"

Chapter 23

Bennett

I didn't know what to expect with meeting Darren's mother, but I had hoped for something more than this. "I don't know why you came all the way out here." Her gaze meets my gaze, then Luke's, holding us to our seats in her family room. In the house Darren bought her years ago. Filled with framed photos of Darren playing the keys at various arenas. "My opinion of that trollop hasn't changed. And it won't."

My body tenses. Instead of going off on her like Luke warned me against, I use measured words. "Mother Hilliard, we're not asking you to change your opinion of Jenna. Merely, keep it closer to the vest."

"You went and married her, right from under Darren's nose. Was his body even cold before you two hooked up?"

How does she really feel? The need to defend my wife obliterates everything else. "I hadn't seen Jenna since his funeral until the movie premiere. You know, UC's movie that was *dedicated* to Darren?" I wait for her to acknowledge my comment, but she doesn't. Further annoyed, I add, "At the gig, I got hurt and needed physical therapy. That was how we met. Again."

Luke hops in, clearly trying to smooth over her ruffled feathers.

"Mother Hilliard, I know how much Darren loved Jenna. And she him. I can assure you she and Bennett weren't together for years after his passing. They were very respectful to your son." This is something, coming from the man who called Darren an "ass" last night.

"Pfft." She crosses her arms and looks away from us.

My wife will come around to me. She has to. For her sake, I can't drop this with Mother Hilliard. "I'm not trying to change your opinion of Jenna. Or me, for that matter. I'm only asking that if a reporter contacts you, that you don't give them additional fodder."

"Seems to me they already have enough to grist the mill with her running a prostitution ring out of her physical therapy clinics."

My head meets my hands. Luke cracks his knuckles and gets serious. "You and I both know that's a crock of shit the media created to feed the firestorm raging around these two." He touches my shoulder. "Reporters have it out for Jenna because she's now linked with Bennett, their 'hot' ticket of the moment."

The front door opens and closes, which Luke ignores. "Your gripe with Jenna goes deeper than Bennett, though. I remember Darren was upset because you didn't accept her with him."

Her hand waves. "She wasn't good enough for my boy."

A new voice enters the conversation—Darren's sister Marni. "Just who would've been good enough for Darren, Mother?"

Mother Hilliard's eyes grow round, then narrow. "He had plenty of women to choose from. I didn't want him to make the wrong choice, which Jenna most certainly was. She reminded me of your father. Flighty, into herself, and using him to bootstrap her pitiful business."

I offer a small wave to Marni, absorbed in what her mother said. The Jenna I know isn't unreliable or self-absorbed. Well, as long as you discount the fact she's seeking a divorce from me right now. Moreover, she didn't have one clinic opened when she was with Darren, and now she's working on her fourth, without his help, support, or money.

Somehow, I manage to keep the steam from coming out of my

ears. In a low tone, I say, "You have Jenna pegged all wrong. She's none of those things. She built her business on her own, after Darren's death."

His mother is having none of what I'm selling, even if it is the truth. "Riding on his coattails, no doubt."

"Mother," Marni snaps. "Jenna's really sweet. I remember you telling me she was *too nice* for Darren. That he would eat her up and spit her out."

I'm taken aback. Luke told me basically the same thing yesterday, in more colorful terms. I remember when Darren insisted I join the band, and how he wouldn't take my excuses as a no. Darren was sort of a bulldozer. Yet, Jenna has a spine. I've seen it firsthand. Hell, I'm living it right now. Maybe she didn't have one when she was with him? Maybe she needed to go through his death to find it in herself? My heart aches for all that my wife's been through—and what she's not allowing me to help her with today. The need to get through to her redoubles. Starting with Darren's mother and Lissa.

Something his mother accused Jenna of sticks with me. I do remember Darren saying his mother raised him and his sister by herself since his father took a hike early on. I take a stab in the dark. "Did Darren's and Marni's father somehow use you to get ahead in business?"

Her arms cross her body. "That man was a menace. We met at work, and he romanced me. The next thing I knew, I was knocked up, and then he swooped in to do my job while I was on pregnancy leave. I thought he was being nice and looking out for our family. When I came back to work, he made a big show of giving my job back to me." She takes a breath. "Then I got pregnant again, left for leave, and came back. This time, he didn't bow out. Said he'd made progress at my position, making the department more efficient. He'd managed to turn my coworkers against me. I did get a job in the office, but not *my* job, and for much lower pay. He stuck with us for a little while, until he found another mark at a competitor, and left."

Marni's mouth hangs open. "I didn't know any of this."

I'd wager Darren never did either.

After a few beats, Luke finds his voice. "Bennett isn't using Jenna to take her job, nor she him. They're in love. I truly believe Darren is cheering for them." He pauses. "From heaven."

Mother Hilliard's head turns away from us. What low-life promotes his career ahead of the woman he loves—the mother of his two children? Obviously, a man who wasn't in love.

"He was scum," I begin. "I'm sorry this happened to you. But not all men are like him. At least, I'm not. I would do anything for Jenna, including leave UC if she asked. She never has, and she won't, because she knows the band is important to me. As are her physical therapy clinics to her. We each want the other to soar, supported by love all the way." *If she'll accept mine.*

"Well, I," Darren's mother begins. "Fine. I won't speak with reporters anymore. If they ask, I'll tell them I only want what's best for the band." Her lips clamp shut. "I might even be persuaded that you mean what you're saying. With time. Lots and lots of time."

I couldn't ask for a better outcome. Rubbing my palms over my thighs, I stand. "I appreciate it, more than you know. We'll see ourselves out." I kiss her cheek and head toward the front door.

"Mother Hilliard, Río and I are working hard on setting up the scholarship in Darren's honor." Luke gives her another kiss and joins me at the door. "Please don't forget that my offer still stands. You'll always be a member of UC, and if there's anything I can ever do for you or Marni, I'm only a phone call away."

"Thanks," Marni replies. Her mother remains quiet.

In the car, both of us exhale. "That was," I begin.

Luke finishes, "Like being put through a spin cycle that never ends."

"Definitely."

Our driver asks, "Where to?"

"How about someplace with burgers and a bar?" I reply. "After that meeting, I need both."

"You got it." We pull away from the home Darren bought his

mother, a bit more settled than when we arrived. At least she's going to stop badmouthing Jenna and me. If she hears about the divorce, though, all bets will be off. Which only makes me more determined than ever to waylay my wife's misguided notion to get one.

Five minutes later, I get a text. Pulling my cell out of my pocket, the name Curtiss greets me. "It's from Curtiss," I tell Luke as I open the message.

> I found some things. Can you come to my parents' house? Or where can I meet up with you?

I exchange a look with Luke and instruct the driver to take us to my hometown, not too far from here. Where his parents still live. Maybe today will turn out even better than we hoped?

About an hour later, we pull up in front of my boyhood best friend's house. The siding color's changed, but otherwise it's as I remember it. Same landscaping. Same basketball hoop over the garage. Same mailbox.

"Are you sure you want me with you?"

"I am. If this evidence is as damning as Curtiss believes it is, I'm going to need an unbiased opinion about how best to use it against Lissa. Because make no mistake about it, I want that woman to go down. And take Michelle with her."

"Then let's do it, B."

Tossing fast food wrappers into the bag, we get out of the car. Side by side, we walk up the path to the front door. Before I touch the doorbell, I need his confirmation. "You already know why I want you here with me. Are you sure *you* want to be here? I don't want to make things uncomfortable."

"Believe me, there's nowhere else I'd prefer to be. I want to bring this chick down. No one makes fake accusations against my friend and gets away with it."

Friend. The truth settles over my shoulders and gives me pride, lodging deep in my heart.

"Then let's do it." I push the button. "Friend."

Curtiss answers the door like he did so many times when I was growing up. Only now, full size and without a screen between us, the truth hits me. He's older, balding, and sporting a dad bod. The years haven't been kind to him.

"Bennett," he pushes up his glasses and dons a large smile. The one I do remember from when we were kids—the smile, not the glasses. He extends his hand, and I shake it.

"Hey, Curtiss. This is Luke Allen, UC's manager. I asked him to come with me so we can begin to craft an effective response to Lissa."

Luke extends his hand. "We talked briefly on the phone a while back."

The door opens wider, and Curtiss ushers us in. "My parents are away for the next few hours, so we can speak freely."

When I enter the house, memories blast at me from every corner. Learning how to play checkers on the floor over there. Big Twister games in that corner. Epic Monopoly competitions in the dining room. "Wow."

"Yeah," Curtiss concurs.

He leads us into the kitchen, where he offers us lemonade in addition to beer. Hope springs up. "Is it your mom's famous pink lemonade?"

From the fridge, he pulls a container containing pink liquid. "The one and only."

My salivary glands get a workout. "Yes, please." Curtiss beams back at me.

Luke's head bounces between Curtiss and me. "Seems like I have to have a glass too."

"Three lemonades coming up." He opens the cabinet containing glasses and gets to work.

I slide into the chair that used to be "mine" at his house, my fingers tracing some scratches I made long ago. For a moment, I let my mind wander down the what-if path. What if Curtiss didn't ask Lissa to the prom? What if I didn't join UC? What if Curtiss and I were still best friends? Would I have turned out like him, living a boring adult life without any zing?

He shuffles over and gives us our lemonades. I sip the tart nectar. I'm being unfair. Curtiss could be content with his lot in life, and I could be judging him unfairly.

"So," Luke asks, "What do you do, Curtiss?"

I lean onto my forearms.

"I run a marketing agency in Philly."

"Impressive," my manager replies. "Married? Kids?"

He's asking all my questions. I take another sip of his mother's lemonade.

"Divorced. Two kids."

So he does have a reason to sport his dad bod after all. "Did Lissa break up your marriage?" I almost add in the word, "too," but manage to keep this bit of gossip out of our conversation. Besides, I haven't been served with divorce papers yet. *I never will.*

"No, that honor belongs to my ex-wife. She hooked up with her personal trainer."

"Ouch." Holy shit, that sucks.

"Yeah." He rubs his bald head. "Happened two years ago. I'm moving past it. When I saw what Lissa was trying to do to you, though, I couldn't let another woman screw over one of my," he glances directly into my eyes. "Friends."

There's that word again. It no longer applies to Curtiss and me, but it did once. I lean on those memories. "I appreciate it."

Luke wades into the charged silence. "Bennett said you have proof she's lying?"

"Right." He jumps up from the table, disappears for a minute, then returns carrying some papers and photos, which he lays out in front of us. "Think these will work?"

Luke and I shuffle through the documents. Which turn out to be love notes between Lissa and Curtiss. Words that would have hurt me years ago, but with Jenna in my life now, they're meaningless. Although, they do paint a damning picture of my high school sweetheart.

In the notes, she professes to be in love with Curtiss. Goes on and on about how good he makes her feel. Says she loves him, more than she ever did me.

Okay, those words sting the high school boy living inside of me. Not for the first time, I'm glad I lost my virginity to a groupie rather than to her. Lissa never was in love with me. I was a real dipshit back in high school. Guess I owe Darren an even bigger one for encouraging me to drop out. Coop, Río, and 007, too.

Luke flips through the last of the photos. "These certainly are damning, Curtiss. But I didn't see anything about her being pregnant in any of them."

I flip through the notes again, and my shoulders drop. "Luke's right."

He points to the photos from the Senior Prom. "Those show we were together, though, right?"

"They do," Luke agrees.

But it's not enough. Please let there be something else. "Did she ever send you anything when she got pregnant?" I ask. "Did you go with her to any doctor appointments?"

"She miscarried before her first appointment."

I'm sunk. If he can't prove anything more than they were together, there won't be a way to stop the rumor mill. Noise at the front door captures our attention, and his parents enter the house

carrying bags. Both Curtiss and I rush to help them. Like old times.
Sort of.

As soon as I take the bag, Mrs. Fanone's free hand flies in front of
her face. "Bennett Hardy? Is that you?"

My beef was with her son, never with her. "In the flesh."

Disregarding the fact that I'm holding whatever she purchased,
she hugs me, bag and all. "I can't believe you're here." She squeezes
me again.

Mr. Fanone comes over and shakes my hand, Curtiss now the
proud recipient of the bags. "It's so good to see you again, son."

Son.

My dry mouth swallows gravel. "It's nice to see you, too." As a
unit, we return to the kitchen, where Luke remains seated. I make
introductions.

His father points to the notes and photos strewn across the table.
"So what do you have there?"

Curtiss's cheeks pinken. "I was showing them somethings Lissa
sent me years ago."

"Yeah," Luke says. "We're trying to figure out how to prove she's
been lying about being pregnant with Bennett's baby. These notes
are incriminating, but don't tie Curtiss to the baby."

Both his parents sit and sift through the notes. Then his mother's
eyes take on a weird gleam. She snaps her fingers and rushes out of
the kitchen without a word. The three of us look to his father.

Mr. Fanone shrugs. "I dunno," he answers our unasked question.
"I do know, though, that we've been saddened by how Lissa's been
playing it in the media. She's quite something."

"An accomplished liar," Curtiss adds.

"So, it seems your life has turned out pretty well, Bennett," his
father addresses me. "Congratulations on your wedding."

I don't want to mar his image about Jenna and me, so I simply
give him a head bob. Besides, I refuse to believe we're over. I can't.
Won't.

His mother returns to the kitchen, carrying a small wooden box, which she places in the middle of the table. The lid reads, "She's pregnant!" Mrs. Fanone opens the box to reveal a stick with two pink lines snuggled against some fabric. The lid's interior says, "Lissa and Curtiss." It's dated after I joined UC, a year after I left high school.

Curtiss stares at the box, then clears his throat. "Is that *the* positive pregnancy test?

His mother replies, "It is. I wanted to commemorate the momentous occasion and had it sent out to be preserved. It came back after the miscarriage, so I never showed it to you, honey."

Luke and I exchange a triumphant glance. This is it. The proof we need.

Chapter 24

Jenna

I get into my car and drive away from Thaine's software company, new plan at the ready to take Michelle down once and for all. I press Court's number.

"How'd it go?"

"Better than expected."

"Spill everything."

"Thaine said Michelle got Dr. Marlow to hire his company for CRM help, so she's still in his orbit somewhat."

Court interrupts. "Are they still together?"

"Nope." I get onto the highway. "Turns out, he dumped her after high school, when he didn't want anything to do with the scene anymore. He wasn't the one to pitch her boss for his business either, but wasn't about to turn away a new client. Thaine *was* pissed about Michelle's using his name online."

"I bet."

"So we decided to go to the press. Rather, he's going to reach out to a friend of his who is a legitimate reporter, who will get the 'scoop.'"

"Awesome. Once reporters sniff out this story, they'll dig into how connected the avatar Thaine Jasper is with Lissa Baker. I bet there's much more to their story than what you've already uncovered."

"No doubt. I don't know if the media can get into their DMs or anything, but we bet there's a treasure trove there. The mere fact of her fake avatar smells bad. For both of them."

"I love how devious you can be."

A smile starts to form. "Feels good to be on the offense." My phone beeps with an incoming call from my sister on the other line. "That's my sister. I'll call you back when I get more details."

"You better."

I switch the call. "Hi, Kara."

"Hi. How's your day been?"

"Good. Better than good. I might have uncovered the way Michelle and Lissa have been communicating."

"Really? Wow. Good on you."

"Thanks." I put on my blinker. "What's up on your end?"

"I had some free time today and decided to spend it at Ma's, going through her stuff and making piles. Think you could join me? This is so much fun."

"I can only imagine." I enter the next highway. "I can be to Ma's in twenty minutes."

"Thanks. See you then."

She clicks off and I concentrate on the road. Leave the highway and navigate the smaller roads of the Hamptons. When my thoughts become too loud, I turn on the radio. UC's "Refocused Destiny" plays.

My hands clutch the steering wheel tighter. Bennett's pitch-perfect voice reaches across the airwaves and wraps around my throat, choking me. I shut off the stupid radio as tears stream down my cheeks, which I brush away. I had him in my life for one reason only: to please Ma. Now she's gone, there's no reason to maintain our ruse. Right?

Our time at Graceland flits through my mind. I remember doing physical therapy with him, and how hard he worked. The way he was so professional at sound checks. How he made my blood sing.

My breathing becomes more erratic. I spot a strip mall and turn into the parking lot. In a corner spot, I throw my car into park, raise my palms to my face, and sob.

Weep for the memories we share.

Scream for the vows we exchanged.

Despair over the vast emptiness extending before me.

A knock sounds on my window. I wave my hand in front of my face, urging the bystander to walk away. Another knock. Can't they take a hint?

I suck in air and press the button for my window to roll down. My hand stays in front of my face.

A concerned female voice asks, "Are you okay?"

Never better. "Fine."

"It's . . . I saw you crying."

My hand lands on the steering wheel and I face my inquisitor—a woman in her early twenties. In probably a more forceful voice than needed, I reply, "I'm all right."

She puts a hand over her chest. "I wanted to be sure." Her eyes widen. "I know you. You're that Black Widow, aren't you?"

I lean forward and press the button for the window to go up.

She places her hand on the half-raised window. In a rush, she blurts, "No. I didn't mean it in a bad way. I don't believe what the media has written about you."

I release the button. She's the first person outside my immediate circle to say this. So young to boot. "You don't?"

She shakes her head. "It seems made up to sell tabloids."

I press the button and the window lowers again. I swallow. "It was."

The young woman looks around the parking lot. "I think you're safe from prying eyes here, but I don't think it's a good idea for you to be out in public like this. You can't let them see you sweat."

Her last comment brings a reluctant grin to my face. "I'll keep your advice in mind."

She nods. "You know, you're the reason I'm going to be a physical therapist. My father needed help after his knee replacement and went to your clinic. He raved about the work you did, and I decided I wanted to be like you. Helping people get better."

I was this girl's role model? While I've been wallowing about Ma's death, others have held me up as someone to follow? "This means so much to me. Being a physical therapist is the best job in the world, if you ask me. There's nothing better than working with someone through an operation or injury, and seeing them improve."

She stands a bit straighter. "I even got into your *alma mater*. I start physical therapy classes next year."

I swipe a stray tear away. "I'm sure you're going to do great. Give me your contact information and when the time comes, I'll set you up with an internship with At Your Service."

"Really? Oh my gosh, I didn't mean to hit you up for a job."

"Which is why I'm offering it." As I get my phone out to put her contact info in my phone, I spy the gift card to the arcade Bennett gave me for my birthday—a present I'll never use. "Make sure you keep in touch with me. I want to hear all about your studies." I flip the card in my hand once. "Here's a gift to remind you to always do your best."

Eyes shining, she hugs the gift card to her chest and promises to keep me posted. "Before I leave, I want to be sure you're really okay." She leans forward.

I go for the truth. "I'm not. But I will be." She waves me on, and I get back on the road, hating myself for lying to her. *Nothing will ever be okay again.*

Ten minutes later, I pull up in front of Ma's house. Car in park, I sit in the driveway as more misery washes over me. *Will I ever find lasting happiness?*

The front door opens, and Kara brings a big black trash bag

outside. *No more procrastination*. I'm here. I turn off the ignition and join my sister at the trash container.

"You made it."

I pick up the lid for her. "How's it going?"

She stuffs the bag into it and sighs. "There's so much to do. Selling her house is the right thing to do, but there's so much stuff in here."

How can she appear so resigned to the chore? Another sob begs to be let free, but I refuse. I need to be as strong as Kara and get through this. "I'm here now. Put me to work." I struggle to put the lid back on, which finally falls into place. Too bad my life never will do the same.

We walk inside the house—really, only an empty shell. With lots and lots of things piled everywhere. Kara explains how she's been dividing up all of Ma's stuff, and I'm reminded of the scene with the Ghost from Christmas Yet to Come from *A Christmas Carol,* when the people come to take Ebenezer Scrooge's possessions away. I square my shoulders. I'm not like those unnamed characters. I loved Ma. She was my world.

Kara suggests, "How about we do her office? I've been through her closet and gave most of her clothes to charity."

"Not the silk scarf?" It was my first gift to her after I got a job. She always wore it with pride.

"Of course not. I kept the things with sentimental value attached."

"Thanks."

With dragging feet, I follow my sister into the office. The desk has bills set into an upright calendar system. Kara takes one look at it and asks, "Why didn't Ma do online banking?"

"I tried. She said she didn't trust the banks and wanted to remain in control of her finances. Can't say that I blame her." *Control.* That's a concept I can get behind.

"I'll go through the filing cabinet while you sort through her desk," she suggests.

"Sounds like a plan."

Kara opens a two-drawer filing cabinet and pulls out a file. "Think we need to keep the electric bill from two years ago?"

"I think it's safe to shred," I chuckle. She points out a variety of other memorabilia—if her stuff can be described as such—and throws it into the shredder.

On an inhale, I focus on my assignment. In no time, I have the top of her desk cleared, with most of the papers being shredded except for a few get well cards from her friends. All of whom were at her funeral. I swallow nothing and toss the cards.

My mind settles on Ma's funeral, and a lingering question. "So, Kara, are you letting our father back into your life?"

She turns toward me. "What?" She puts down some paperwork. "Listen, I had ten more years with him than you did. We have more of a history. Truth is, though, he's been out of my life for more years than he was in it. I told him I'd add him to my Christmas card list, but not to expect anything more from me." She comes over and hugs me.

In her arms, I say, "Thank you." We break apart, "I'm not willing to do even that, but I respect your decision."

"You got it, kiddo." Her hand waves toward the rooms. "Back to it?"

"Yeah." My sister and I are building a relationship with each other. She can keep communicating with our father while I don't have to, but it won't affect us. I mull over this truth as I busy myself by opening the right desk drawer, which contains pens, paper clips, post-its, and other assorted office products. While it would be smart to keep this stuff, I only want it to disappear, so I throw it all away. The middle drawer boasts paper products like notepads, her passport, and even some old romance books featuring Fabio on the cover.

I hold up one for Kara to see and giggle. "Ma was a closet romantic."

My sister agrees, and holds up another book, this time with Fabio as a pirate. "Seems like it."

Wearing a smile for the first time, I toss everything but the passport and go into the third, larger drawer. This one is filled with Kara's schooling, from elementary school report cards to high school book reports, college tuition bills, and photos from her graduation from medical school. She also squirreled photos in here from Kara's wedding, the birth of her two kids, and other family photos.

Seeing as this drawer was all about Kara, I glance to the matching drawer on the other side and take a deep breath. If past is prologue, I'm going to be diving into my life's memories. Or the ones she kept through the years.

I open the drawer and, sure enough, I'm transported into the past. She has the same documents for me as she did for my sister, until you get to grad school. Then, she kept the program from my graduation ceremony. Followed by press clippings that followed my progress from physical therapist to clinic owner. Then two clinics.

She also kept the photos I sent her featuring Darren and me. I stop sorting and flip through these memories. There's one of us kissing. Him performing on the keyboard. Me backstage screaming for the band. A sad smile crosses my lips.

The next picture makes me drop the stack. UC is onstage performing at a smaller gig, judging by the setup and how close the fans are to the stage. That's not what has me gasping for air. No. It's the way Darren's playing the keys, with this head thrown backward. Standing next to him, singing into the mic while looking directly at the camera, is Bennett.

Kara's at my side in an instant. "Are you all right? What are you looking at?"

I can do no more than point to the photo. I don't want to shed anymore tears, yet I feel the all too familiar pricking at the back of my eyeballs.

She picks up the picture, letting it drop onto the desk. "Oh, sweetie."

I turn tearful eyes up to my sister. "Why?" Three little letters packed with so much punch. Why did Darren have to overdose?

Why did Bennett barrel into my life? Why did we go through with the farce of our marriage?

Her arms go around me. "You've really had it rough."

"I miss Ma." A tear overflows. "And Darren."

"Bennett's a good man. Where is he? He should be here with you."

I rest my forehead on her shoulder. "We're getting a divorce."

Kara stiffens, then steps back, her hands on my shoulders. "Excuse me?"

I gather myself. "We got married because Ma was dying and we wanted to give her a happy memory. Now she's gone, there's no reason for us to stay together."

"That would be all well and good," my sister replies. "Except for the inconvenient fact that you love each other." When I remain silent, she continues, "Don't forget. I've seen you two together. The way he looks at you, and you at him. How he sang at Ma's graveside. He didn't do that to make her happy. He did it to make *you* happy."

In a feeble voice, I say, "He was playing a part."

"I don't believe you," her head shakes. "You don't believe you."

"I have the divorce papers to prove it."

"Until they're filed, there's still time to come to your senses." She looks down. "What are you going to do with these pictures?"

At least my sister's efficiency is returning. I glance at the photos. "I don't think I can throw them away."

"Then put them in the 'keep' file, and let's get moving." She walks toward the filing cabinet. I stack the photos into an orderly pile with Ma's passport, and return to the desk. There will be plenty of time to cry over them later.

The rest of Ma's desk isn't as heart-wrenching, so I make pretty quick work of the remaining drawers. I open the last one, holding a bunch of random papers, with two fancy envelopes on top. I pick them up. One's addressed to Kara. The other, to me.

"Kara," I whisper.

"Found something?"

I hold up the envelope with her name scrawled across it. "I think Ma left us each a final note."

She crosses the room. We both stare at the envelopes as if they're going to get up and dance. After a moment, I pass hers to her and stare down at mine.

She asks, "Are you going to open yours?"

"I'll read it soon. You?"

"I'm almost done with the filing cabinet. I think I'll finish it and call it a day. I want to be with my husband when I read this."

I nod. Who do I have to hold my hand when I read Ma's final words to me? Not Kara, clearly—although I don't blame her for wanting to be with her family. Court pops into my mind, but I dismiss her. She's had enough to deal with about the whole Black Widow/Prostitution Ring debacle. Bennett's face comes into focus in the picture with Darren, but I dismiss him as well. After all, we're getting a divorce.

"Let's finish up."

An hour later, both the desk and filing cabinet are cleared, with the important documents set aside. Kara brushes her hands. "I think we did a lot today. Thanks for the help."

"We have to stick together. Four hands are better than two."

"Hashtag true. Are you going to be okay alone with Ma's letter?"

"I'll be fine. Go home to your family. We should meet up here to keep going through Ma's house soon."

She stuffs her envelope into her purse. "I'll let you know when I can come back." She kisses my forehead and is gone.

I collect the photos and my letter and wander into the kitchen. I make it as far as the living room, when I collapse into Ma's chair. Here, her presence surrounds me stronger than ever. I flip through the photos one more time, stopping on the one of Darren performing with Bennett. Or the other way around.

I stare at it. Darren looks to be in his element, happy and . . . alive. It's when my gaze turns to Bennett, though, that I'm hit with a punch to my gut. He's younger, clearly, but no less captivating. He's singing into the microphone and looking at me. The camera, I correct myself. My finger traces the muscles on his arms and abs as my brain tries to forget how they felt wrapped around me.

That was before.

Before Ma died and the fairytale came crashing down.

Taking a moment to collect my thoughts, I place the photos, upside down, onto the tray that served as Ma's dinner table. With shaking hands, I pick up the envelope.

I close my eyes and inhale. Then open the envelope and read:

My Dearest Sweet Pea,

By the time you read this, I will no longer be with you. Please know you could not have done anything to stop this disease from taking over my body. Even the miracles of modern science don't extend far enough to stop the roll of cancer. I'm at peace with this truth. I desperately want you to be as well.

My wish for you is to live a great, big, wonderful life. Darren took you out of your head, and for that I'm forever grateful. However, when he died, he took a large piece of you with him. I know you blame yourself for his death, the same way you blame yourself for your grandmother's death all those years ago. If I'm being honest, I fear you may add my passing to this too-long list. Don't. Please don't.

As you know, I didn't like Bennett at first. I thought you were using him as a substitute for Darren. But when I got to know the man, I saw what you saw in him. The goodness. Kindness. How he supports you above all else, even including his own wants and needs. He is a good man. More than that, he's the perfect man for you. He doesn't want you to abandon your profession, in fact he's encouraging you to meet your goal to expand to ten clinics. He's not selfish.

I'm saying a prayer for you and him to create a loving family, despite the crazies in the outside world. I have faith in you (ha! See my pun?!).

A choked huff comes out. Ma always had an awful sense of humor. My small laughter turns into a sob as I reread this paragraph.

Visions of our wedding day flit through my mind. This time, though, all the feels from deep in my soul override the grief-fueled lies I've been telling everyone. The love I felt for the gorgeous man pledging to be at my side forever. Unimaginable joy when our lips met for the first time as husband and wife. Our honeymoon night filled with pure bliss.

I shake my head. It's over. It's all over.

My eyes return to Ma's note, and I force myself to read her final words to me.

Keep on helping people with your physical therapy, in whatever form it may take. Live each and every day out loud, not hampered with the need for the control you always seek. Control is good, but don't let your desire for it overshadow your own happiness. Spontaneity can be just as fulfilling ~ both in moderate doses. I believe in you!

Always remember that I am with you, in your heart. I'm so proud of you and your sister. What is it I always say? Leave footprints on others' souls. Yours and Bennett's will make marks throughout the world, if you let them. Please let them.

If I know you, though, you are going to push everyone away and blame yourself for not watching over me more carefully. Throw yourself into the one thing that saved you when Darren passed away, which is At Your Service PT. I beg of you not to do this. Attend to your business, sure, but don't forget to live. Let others help you, especially your amazing husband. Leave those footprints.

With all my eternal love,

Ma

It takes me several attempts to finish the last of her message, as reading through tears is excruciating.

How can I leave footprints with Bennett when we're getting a divorce?

Chapter 25

Bennett

After catching up with the Fanones—and finishing the pitcher of delicious pink lemonade—I promise to have tickets available for them to come to any UC concert they want. I hug his parents and give Curtiss a handshake. We are nowhere near the best friends of our childhood, but for the first time it doesn't feel like this piece of me is missing. When the chips were down, he came through.

Carrying the precious wooden box and all the notes and photos from ages ago, Luke and I get into the car. He flips the lid on the box, staring at its contents. "With today's science, I think this will effectively take care of Lissa. For good, B. Forever."

I review all of the evidence we have against her. "I think you're right. When we get the DNA results back, we can prove her allegation against me is false. Bet she never thought I'd be teaming up with Curtiss to take her down."

"Don't forget his mother." We chuckle. "There's some form of poetic justice in there somewhere," my friend says. Luke holds up his phone. "Let's call the PR team and fill them in."

I motion for him to place the call. A moment later, the head of PR picks up. We exchange pleasantries, then Luke tells her about the wooden box and the notes.

"Are you kidding me? The hits keep coming."

Luke jumps in. "What else happened today?"

"Thanks to Jenna, a news story broke discussing the details about the way Lissa and Michelle have teamed up."

At hearing my wife's name, I flinch. Then, pride in her surges. "She figured it out, huh?"

"Sure did, Bennett. According to this article, they were hiding in plain sight, so to speak. Michelle adopted a different persona on social media, and you can see Lissa interacting with the fake avatar. While it appears innocuous, once you know who's actually behind the avatar, it takes on a whole new meaning."

My cheeks inflate. Leave it to my ingenious wife to nail Michelle. However. "What do you mean this came out in a news article? Why weren't you guys all over this from a PR perspective?"

"She didn't contact us."

I bolt upright. "Why not?" Luke places his hand over my forearm.

UC's PR head replies, "Jenna figured this out all on her own. She didn't need us."

She didn't need us. She didn't need *me*. Pride mixes with longing. I want to hold my wife and share in her good news. Share mine. Instead, we're in different states, trying to move forward against the media, with divorce papers between us. I squeeze my thigh in order to stop myself from doing something stupid. Like calling her.

Luke glances at me. "Great news. Thanks. I'll take photos of these notes and the box and send them off to you."

"Sounds good." The line disconnects.

My wife figured out how Lissa and Michelle were communicating, which is good. However, the whole lie surrounding the prostitution ring still remains. "Jenna got halfway there."

"I was thinking the same thing, B. We still need to get the

reporters off the whole idea that her clinics serve up more than good results."

I tap my groin. "She saved me."

Luke nods. "And UC with it."

I'm stewing over the meaning of my wife going it alone when we pass a sign for the town where Mom lives. Haven't been here in a while. As a way to change the subject—or at least divert my attention for the moment—I note, "My mother lives here."

Luke whips his head toward me. "I didn't know that. You never talk about her. We have to visit." He motions for the driver to roll down the window divider.

I raise my palm. "Wait. I don't want to see her."

"Why on earth not?"

Because she's miserable. Mean. Mentally unstable. I shake my head. "I just don't."

"Come on, B. I'd love to meet the woman who brought you into this world."

I let out a humorless laugh. "Believe me, you don't."

"Come on, she can't be that bad. We spent time with Darren's mother. Now *she's* bad."

"She's a walk in the park in comparison." He continues to harp on wanting to meet her. Maybe she won't be so bad, in front of a stranger? It has been a couple of years since I last visited in person. Jenna was always after me to reach out to my mother, until she had a conversation with her, that is. My lips purse.

"I've shown you my family home," Luke wheedles.

It's not his voice that convinces me to give our driver the address, however. It's Dad's. He loved my mother until the end, making me promise to look after her. As soon as I agreed, his last words were, "You've always been such a good—" He never finished his thought.

I owe Dad this much.

Shortly, we pull up to the large building with a sign ending with, "Mental Institution." Our car parks in the side parking lot, and we get out. As we walk to the doors, I head off the inevitable questions. "Yes,

I had to put Mom here several years back. She's been diagnosed as mentally ill, with several conditions ending in -isms. She's not a danger to society, but she has a sharp tongue." I leave out the times she's tried to self-harm. Given Darren's overdose, I don't want to delve into this now.

"I didn't know."

"I wanted it that way." I stop. "Look, if you don't want to meet her, I'd understand. I owe it to my father to check in on her, especially since I'm so close."

"I get it, and I want to meet her. But only if it won't stress you out."

"Stress me out? No. Be prepared, though, for a torrent of accusations to stream out of her mouth." I take a step, then stop. "The most common is that I killed my sister."

His hand covers his open mouth.

"I didn't," I explain. "We were conceived through IVF. With that procedure, it's common for multiple embryos to be implanted, with the hope one will stick. I survived, while the other one didn't. She's decided I killed my sister in her womb. She usually includes some snide remark about how, if my sister were still here, she wouldn't do whatever I'm being accused of doing."

His hand lands on my shoulder. "B, I'm so sorry."

The mask I usually only wear when performing starts to descend. "Her words can't hurt me anymore. I keep reminding myself that she's mentally ill."

"I hear you." He cracks his knuckles and stares into my soul. "I'm honored you want to introduce her to me."

"You say that now."

We enter the building and approach the receptionist to sign in. The poor woman recognizes me and fumbles with the paperwork, but manages to do her job. As we walk through the halls, I ask Luke to send some UC merch to the receptionist. He pulls out his phone and taps out a message.

We stop before her room, with a cheerful Mrs. Hardy on the

nameplate. Please let her be lucid and happy today. I knock and wait for the door to be opened.

"How may I help you?" A short, round, middle-aged Latina woman answers.

I'd know her voice anywhere, even though we've never met in person. "Ramona? It's me, Bennett."

She swings the door wider. "Well, I'll be. Come on in. Your mother and I were just about to play a game of parcheesi."

I kiss her cheek and introduce Luke, and we both enter the suite. Mom's sitting in the Florida room in the back, so I can't see her yet.

I lean over to her nurse and whisper, "How is she today?"

"Good," she replies. "She seems content and on an even keel."

Thank God. Here goes nothing. I enter the room where Mom's sitting, which has floor-to-ceiling windows, overlooking a water feature in the courtyard. "Hi, Mom."

She swings around and stares at me, her mouth agape. She tilts her head from side to side for a moment, then surges to her feet. "Bennett?"

Nodding as I cross the room to her, I pull her in for a quick hug. The doctors warned me against excessive touching, as it might trigger an outburst. "We were in the area, so I thought it would be nice to stop by and visit in person rather than over the phone."

"I can't believe it's you." She reaches to her tiptoes, and touches my cheek. "You've grown up to look so much like your father."

"I'll take that as a compliment." Remembering we have an audience, I introduce Luke. "Mom, I want you to meet Untamed Coaster's manager, my friend Luke Allen."

She extends her hand, which he shakes. If I hadn't spent my entire life with this woman, I would think she was normal. The truth lurks right below the surface. Best not to let this visit go too long.

Ramona asks, "Mind if these nice gentlemen sit with you for a while?"

"I always have time for Bennett and his friend. Can you get us some refreshments, Ramona?"

At least she remembered her nurse's name. Another good sign. Luke and I join Mom at the table and he says, "You have a nice view here. Do you ever go into the courtyard?"

"Oh yes," Mom replies. "We go to the nearby mall as well. Ramona cooks for me, and there's a nice restaurant we visit quite often."

Luke's eyebrows pull together. I clarify for him. "The dining hall was quite a selling feature."

Ramona comes in and gives each one of us a glass of iced tea. Not quite as good as Mrs. Fanone's pink lemonade, but still tasty. Luke raises his glass to her in thanks, and I follow suit. Mom doesn't, simply sipping from her glass. I can hear her brain working, which makes me nervous. Things could go south fast.

I'm about to suggest we cut our visit short, when Mom springs up. "Hey. Where's your wife?"

"She wanted me to let you know she was sorry she couldn't be here," I respond smoothly, urging her to return to her seat. "She was, um, busy taking care of her mother's estate. Remember, she recently passed away."

Mom takes in this information with a nod and retakes her seat. "Then shouldn't you be helping her deal with her mother's death?" She leans over and smacks my shoulder. I don't move. "I thought I raised you better than that."

"Luke and I had some business we had to deal with that couldn't be put off. We're flying back out to the Hamptons later, so I can continue helping her." The lie sounds convincing to my ears. I glance at Luke, who does a slow blink of support.

"I hope you bring my daughter to me soon."

Thinking we avoided the worst, I agree, "I know she wants to meet you."

"Of course she does. I'm her only living mother now."

Luke steps in, "Mrs. Hardy, where—"

Mom cuts him off. "Only when she comes, we won't serve her any iced tea. Or I guess we could," she muses, "So long as we made it.

I don't trust that Black Widow. First she killed Darren and now her mother."

"Mom, I explained this before. You're wrong. Darren overdosed and her mother had cancer."

Mom waves her hand. "You're fine with her, seeing as you already killed your sister. Like finds like, they always say."

Here we go. Do not engage. Step away from the nuisance. I get to my feet and check my watch. "Look at the time. We have to get going before we miss our flight, right Luke?"

Luke's watching us like we're playing at Wimbledon. "What?"

I tilt my chin, urging him to stand, all the blood rushing through my body in triple speed.

He finally picks up my clue. "Oh, right. We are on a tight schedule."

"Schedule, smedule," Mom says. "If your sister were here, she'd find herself a nice guy and settle down in a house, with a mother-daughter suite so I could live with her. But not you. You dumped me here and never visit. No, you—"

Her tirade continues as I usher Luke out of the Florida room. As soon as we're away from her, my eyes close. I exhale through my mouth.

"I'm sorry," Ramona says. "She was in a good mood earlier."

"It's not your fault," I answer her. "Have to admit, she went off the rails quicker this time, but it might be because I was physically here."

"Perhaps. Do you want to visit her doctor? I can see if he's in."

"Thanks, Ramona, but I get updates from him regularly. I don't think it's important to interrupt his day." Although, he may need to know I stopped by and set her back a little. "If you don't mind, please tell him I was here before Mom's next appointment."

"I understand," Mom's nurse replies. "Can I get you anything for the road?"

Luke shakes his head. "No, we're good."

Heartfelt words pour out of my mouth. "I want to thank you for taking such good care of Mom. I know she can be a challenge, to put it mildly."

Ramona replies, "Honestly, she either thinks of me as her maid or as her friend. Either way, I've learned how to handle her nasty. She seems to reserve her worst for you, though."

"Happy to be her trigger point," I mumble. I give Mom's nurse a kiss goodbye.

Luke and I exit her room and walk through the calming hallway, trying to regain my equilibrium. "Wow. B, I'm sorry you've had to live with this. How often do you two speak?"

"Maybe once a week or so. Less if I can help it." We wave to the receptionist and go outside into the warm, cleansing air. "It's always best when the call ends."

He wraps his arm around my shoulder. This tiny bit of kindness is my undoing.

Possibly it's Jenna's seeking a divorce.

Perhaps it's my frayed nerves over Lissa.

There's always Dad's death lurking.

Or maybe it's the encounter I just endured.

For whatever reason, my protective walls come tumbling down in this moment. Out here on the sidewalk, I turn into the arms of my manager—my friend—and sob.

Chapter 26

Jenna

I read Suzette's text again. Where can he be? According to her, he hasn't been seen at Secluded Rest—or anywhere in Aroostook or the Hamptons—for the past week.

My phone pings again. I glance at the screen, where a Google alert notifies me that all of UC is in Europe, preparing for the next part of their tour. There's a photo of the entire band in front of a sign saying Nice, France. At least now I know where he is.

As if the man of the hour knew I was thinking about him, Bennett's name comes up on my messages.

ROCK STAR

Turn on the television.

That man won't quit! Why won't he just accept service of the damn papers and leave me alone? Numb, I walk into the clinic's break room —the only spot with a television—and turn it on. Francis and Logan greet me once more. Interviewing Lissa again. *Joy*. Why is Bennett telling me to watch them? And what's on the table between them? Some sort of box?

Francis passes Lissa some pieces of paper. "Is this your handwriting, Ms. Baker?"

The woman of the hour tosses her long blonde hair over her shoulder, takes the papers, and glances at them, her fake eyelashes batting. "Where did you get these?" She flips through the little notes.

What's going on? I have no one to ask, yet my confusion permeates the room.

Francis replies, "So you did send these?" When Lissa remains silent, the screen cuts to a graphic of the papers, so the viewers can see what Lissa's seeing. My head flies backward. These are some steamy love notes. The one on the screen clearly shows the name Curtiss as the person with whom she was corresponding.

Bennett's ex-best friend.

My heart beats faster.

The cameras return to the studio, where Lissa's shoulder raises. "Curtiss and I dated after high school. After I was with Bennett. I can't believe Curtiss kept these, but then again, he always was sort of a loser."

Lissa's foot taps an uneven beat. I lean forward as Logan picks up the box. He continues, "In those notes, you paint a pretty explicit picture of what you two were up to. We didn't put up the most graphic ones, out of deference to our viewers."

My pulse increases. Despite our impending divorce, Bennett doesn't deserve this.

Logan continues, "The note Francis is now holding explicitly states you're pregnant. And we have proof." He opens the box's lid, to reveal a positive pregnancy test. On the inside of the lid, it says, "Curtiss and Lissa, and a date." The year *after* Bennett left to join UC. My hand flies over my stomach. To no one, I whisper, "He did it. He got the proof."

On-screen, Lissa jumps to her feet. "This is ridiculous. That's not my pregnancy test!"

Logan points to her name engraved on the inside of the box. "How do you explain this?"

"It's a lie!"

Lissa opens her mouth to spew more, when a balding, yet attractive guy walks onto the stage. "Hi, Lissa. Wow. You're even bonier than I remember." He sits next to her on a chair that magically appeared.

Curtiss?

"You're bald and fat, Curtiss," she snarks.

He rubs the top of his shiny head. "Be that as it may, at least I'm not a liar."

Lissa gasps. Francis jumps into the void. "Ladies and gentlemen, may I introduce you to Curtiss Fanone, Lissa's one-time boyfriend. Apparently, also, the father of the baby she lost. Not the rock star Bennett Hardy." Francis holds up a DNA test confirming the test was from Lissa and Curtiss. "We tested it."

"No!" Lissa leaps to her feet. "That's not true."

Gotta hand it to Lissa. She's not going down easy.

Curtiss looks up at her, something approaching pity in his eyes. "It *is* true. My mother—sentimental soul that she is—preserved the pregnancy test you brought to the house when you found out you were pregnant. After you miscarried, due to, I believe, taking diet pills because you didn't want to get 'fat,' she never gave us this keepsake. You not only lost your baby, Lissa, you lost her first grandchild."

Lissa lowers herself to the chair.

When she doesn't reply, Francis states, "I think you owe Bennett Hardy an apology."

Wild-eyed, Lissa looks around the studio as if expecting Bennett to walk onto the stage. He doesn't.

Curtiss chuckles. "He's not here. Why would he be? He's the lead singer of Untamed Coaster, flying well above your petty drama."

Cornered, with nowhere to run, Lissa lashes out. "None of my fans would believe I was with you. Not after being with *him*."

Curtiss looks between the two hosts. Logan says, "In addition to your notes, Curtiss also provided us with some photos of you two from back in the day. Take a look."

Sure enough, pictures of them appear. They show Lissa as a late teenager with slightly different features than she has now and a younger, more fit Curtiss, many with him holding a tennis racket. They made a striking couple.

Logan doesn't wait for her to respond, simply barrels forward. "If I'm not mistaken, you've recently gotten to know a Thaine Jasper online. We've seen several interactions between you two on social media." Screenshots of their comments are posted.

Oh my God. My hand flies in front of my face. Are they going to link her to Michelle too?

"So? Is meeting people online now a crime too?" Lissa hisses.

"Only when you conspire with them," Francis alleges. "Newspaper reports out in the Hamptons have surfaced that you and Michelle Kent communicated online using this fake avatar to slander Bennett's wife. Do you deny this?"

Go Thaine! My mind barely keeps up with this fire hose of news.

"What? Who?" Lissa shrieks.

Court comes into the break room. "There you are. The construction manager for your next clinic wants to meet with you at the building. Can I tell him you'll be there in an hour?"

I shush my bestie and point to the screen. On it, Logan says, "We've done some digging and have obtained your DMs."

"No way!" Lissa sputters. "That's illegal!"

Court doesn't say a word, simply sinks into a chair next to me.

Francis is in the middle of saying, ". . . not when they're willingly turned over by one of the parties. Ms. Kent shared them with us." The host turns into the camera. "And we turned them over to the proper authorities. Seems like you two attacked Jenna Westfield Hardy's business as a way to run her out of Bennett's life. We spoke with Ms. Kent, and she said it was all your idea to call Mrs. Hardy's physical therapy clinics a front for a prostitution ring."

They got them! Although Michelle's trying to pin it all on Lissa. Whatever. They can duke it out between themselves. On-screen, Lissa's head looks as if it wants to explode.

"It was her idea! I didn't care about that mousy thing on his arm." She motions toward her body and throws her head backward. "Not when he could have this!"

Logan doesn't hesitate. "So you confirm that you and Ms. Kent were behind the prostitution ring allegation?"

"I only wanted to get Bennett's attention. Michelle's aim was to run that worthless Jenna out of town. You would've thought having Darren was enough for her, but no. After he died, Jenna moved on to Bennett. *My* Bennett."

The cameras cut to the talking heads, while my heart races uncontrollably. Francis looks at Logan, wearing the same stupefied expression as Court. "Well, you heard it here first, folks. Ms. Baker wasn't pregnant with Bennett Hardy's baby. Plus, she and Ms. Kent conspired against Mrs. Hardy's business in order to ruin her professional life and gain Mr. Hardy's attention."

"It's over." Court stands. "It's all over."

My breath hitches. "I can't believe it. How did Curtiss orchestrate this?"

"Girlie, if you believe he was behind this takedown, I got a bridge in Brooklyn to sell you." She turns off the television and sits next to me. "It had Bennett written all over it."

"Bennett." My husband's name falls from my lips, then my head shakes from side to side. "No. No way. Hayden, maybe."

Court levels me with a hard stare. "Even though I missed the beginning of the interview, I can tell Bennett's fingerprints were all over this takedown."

Could he actually have orchestrated this? I simply cannot process everything right now. Why did Court come in here in the first place? Renovations. I fall back into the comfort of work. "When do I have to meet the construction manager at the building?"

It takes my manager a second to process the topic change. "One hour."

"Fine."

"Jenna, what can I do for you? Now that both Michelle and Lissa were exposed on national TV, and the clinics are cleared, you still look miserable."

Because my husband is in France, yet he cleared my name. *His too.* Maybe I was collateral "un"damage? My head hurts. "Ma just died." I snap. "I think I'm entitled."

My bestie sighs. "Are you still getting flowers with song lyrics from Bennett?"

What is she getting at? "Yes. Although now he's switched things up and is including lines from *The Godfather*." A small smile plays around my lips, as I remember his snarky comment about today's line coming from Part 2, "the second best movie ever made."

"Do you still want to divorce him?"

I don't answer, simply show her the text from Suzette.

"Good." She returns my phone to me. "He's good for you, Jenna. I've never seen a man look at a woman with such love brimming from his entire being. He made Lissa look like a fool on national television *and* probably got her sent behind bars in the process. If I ever find a man who acts like him, I'm never letting go."

"You can have Bennett."

"Really?" She crosses her arms. "You'd be fine if Bennett stopped sending you flowers and started sending them to me? How about if he sang a song to me in front of everyone, would that bother you? I know, what if he kissed me the way he kissed you at your wedding? You'd be okay with that?"

I explode to my feet. "No. You can't have him."

"Why not? You just told me I could."

"Because he's mine."

Mine.

I collapse onto the chair. "Mine," I whisper. I try to catch my breath.

"Then what are you going to do about it?"

"I," I stutter. "I don't know." I reach for my ponytail holder and tighten it to my head.

Court touches my palm. "How about you start by calling off your divorce attack dog?"

"We only got married to make Ma happy."

Her eyebrow raises. "Really? I was there. Seemed to me you got married to make yourselves happy. Your mother's happiness was a wonderful by-product."

My head rolls from one side of the chair to the other.

"Honey, did you also agree to seek out each other for their opinions? Kiss without being prompted? How about those vows? Who wrote them?"

Her every question echoes the sentiments Kara expressed—and those contained in Ma's last letter to me. Where she almost begged me to relinquish some control in exchange for happiness. With Bennett. The man who barreled into my life and dared me to live again.

Who taught me about joy and happiness.

Also, God help me, love.

Something breaks inside of me.

I swallow. In a small voice, I reply, "We did. Because we were made for each other."

"Finally!" Court exclaims. She stands. "Now what are you going to do about it?"

If only it were so easy. "I can't. I have responsibilities here. I have to meet with our construction manager in an hour—you just set up the meeting. There are tons more things to do for the third clinic. As well as the fourth one." I pause. "Assuming I still get paid by UC, considering I cut out before Bennett completed his physical therapy.

If not, I'll get another loan." I rub my arm. "Besides, he's in the South of France."

"None of the work stuff matters when your husband is halfway across the world."

"He's not that far away. Barely nine hours."

Her eyebrows raise. "Seriously? You're correcting my geography?"

My head goes into my palms. "I can't do this right now." I pull myself together and rise. "I have a meeting to attend. I'll let you know how it goes."

"Jenna!"

"I can't!" Ignoring Court's pleas, I toss off these stupid emotions, gather my stuff, and leave the clinic. A short fifteen minutes later, I'm walking into clinic number three. "Hi," I call out to the construction manager. He meets me and starts to go over necessary changes. Even if my mind isn't in the Hamptons.

A few hours later, all the details about the clinic sorted, my head slumps against the headrest in my car. My business will remain afloat, especially since Lissa and Michelle aren't threats any longer. Kara and I will sell Ma's house. I've overcome the Black Widow nickname and the prostitution ring allegations.

I turn on my car but don't have the strength to drive away, so I hit the power button for the radio. Hoping not to hear a UC song . . . or maybe I long for it too much?

After a commercial, the DJ says, "I have a treat for you, ladies and gents. I'm holding a brand-new song right here in the palm of my hand. I've listened to it already, and I can guarantee you're going to love it. Here's the deal, though. I'm not telling you who created this song. I'm going to play it for you, call me when you figure out the artist. First caller wins a signed copy of their brand-new album, which will include this song. Have a listen."

With such a buildup, the song better be fire.

I stare at the radio as music plays the introduction. Without a singer, I can't tell exactly which band it is. The drums beat a hard rhythm. I can discern the guitar too. Oh, there's keys. Who could it be?

All the music cuts out, and the singer begins.

It's a male. Tenor.

My hand flies in front of my face. "No way."

Bennett's voice, *a capella,* comes over the radio. Stripped bare, he sings:

> **I held you in my arms**
> **Kept your demons at bay**
> **Believed our love was enough**
> **Tell me I'm wrong, wrong**
>
> **Sent in a surprise attack**
> **Promised to take them down**
> **And removed the final barrier**
> **Please accept my display and come back**
>   **to me**
>
> **I need you with me now and forever**
> **Prove our vows were meant to be**
> **You make me a better man**
> **All I want to be is yours. Yours**

Instruments re-enter the song, loud and powerful. I can't breathe. I can't see for all the tears clouding my vision, memories of Bennett telling me he never sings alone, yet he's done it—twice—with me. For me.

His voice is beautiful. The lyrics haunt me.

I finally get myself in gear and drive back to my house, which smells of flowers. I pull out Ma's final note together with all of the cards that accompanied the flowers he's sent.

Court's advice replays.

I wander into my bedroom and open my jewelry box, intent on putting away my earrings, when a necklace I haven't seen in a long time catches my eyes. It has a UC pendant attached. Darren was wearing this the night he died.

A sob catches in my throat.

How can I stay here when the love of my life is so far away?

Chapter 27

Bennett

The guys and I are on the beach in front of the mansion Luke rented for us here on the French Riviera. Tomorrow night, we kick off the European leg of our tour at the Théâtre *de Verdure*, an open-air amphitheater. A Frisbee is thrown, and Río acts crazy as usual, diving headfirst into the sand, breaking his fall at the last second. After a while, Coop and 007 take off at full tilt toward the ocean, diving into the warm water and splashing each other. Tris invites Luke and me to go snorkeling, but I beg off. Now's the time a confirmation email from the florist in Aroostook will come in about my delivery to Jenna back in the States. I can't miss it.

"You go ahead. I'm waiting for an email."

Luke collects snorkeling gear from the chair next to mine. "Join us when you can, B." He takes off.

I refresh the screen on my cell, waiting to receive the florist's confirmation. Somehow, opening these emails as soon as they arrive makes me feel closer to Jenna. I tap my cell on my thigh, waiting for the message. Did she hear our new song yet? Did she watch the news, like I told her to? Does she know the threats from both Lissa and Michelle are over? She hasn't responded to my texts.

The florist's email finally arrives. My heart sinks at the first line. *"I'm sorry, Mr. Hardy. Mrs. Hardy wasn't at home today, so I was unable to complete the delivery at its usual time. I promise to try again in a few hours."*

She wasn't there. Or, more likely, she refused to open the door and accept delivery, knowing it was more flowers from me. Today's card had the iconic *The Godfather* line, "I'm going to make him an offer he can't refuse." I need to make her see reason, that we're meant for each other. I didn't propose to make her mother happy. We love each other, dammit.

Luke returns to the chairs, dripping. "Let's get you into the water."

"Nah. Not in the mood—Jenna wasn't home to get my flowers today."

"She must've been out." Picking up a towel, he rubs it over his body, ending by wringing out his shoulder-length hair.

"I guess." I toss my cell onto the foot of the chair.

"She'll come around. Maybe she didn't hear your song yet."

My stomach constricts. Singing our new song almost undid me, but Luke encouraged me to sing those stanzas *a capella*. I was raw. Bared my soul for her. While it's been radio silence from Jenna, her divorce attorney is still on my tail. Or at least she was when I was in the States. I'm too well protected to be served over here, thankfully.

Soon, Tris joins us, followed by the rest of the band. Over the past few days, I've done the unthinkable and let them in more than ever before. 007 plops down next to me, bumping his shoulder against mine. We're still navigating rocky waters over how he treated Jenna, but he's been solid for me over here.

These guys truly are my friends. They've rallied around me, especially once Luke shared all the details about Lissa and Michelle's illegal plots. They've also commiserated with me over the state of my so-called marriage. Urged me to hold on. I'm trying.

Tris's chin points toward Luke. "How's our new song doing in the charts?"

"We're climbing. Sitting at number three right now. Considering it only dropped two days ago, I'd say you have another hit on your hands."

If only Jenna would hear it.

The guys cheer. Río returns to our huddle, directing a few women carrying bottles over to us. "I asked these lovely ladies to join us, considering they have nice beverages and nowhere to go with them."

The guys grab the beers and snag the chicks. I do neither. Doesn't stop a few bikini-clad ladies from coming over to me, plying me with drinks. Remembering Luke's assessment of me as using alcohol or sex to soothe my hurts, I decline both. The latter because none of them are my wife. The former because I don't want any of them to start looking like her. Not that they ever could.

Coop leaves two possible companions and comes over to my chair. "Dude. She's going to come around. Give her time."

"All I can do." I check out his two ladies. Just because I'm not interested, doesn't mean he shouldn't partake. "Go on, enjoy yourself. I'll be fine here."

"Are you sure? I can send them packing and we can play some volleyball on the beach."

I smile at his generosity, especially after his history. "No. You go ahead and have fun for both of us. They look like they'll give you a run for your money."

He chuckles. "We'll see about that. Talk later." Our fists bump.

Music soon filters from the pool area, which overlooks the beach, where everyone's paired off in twos, threes, or more. Across the way, Luke's gaze catches mine. He raises his hands as if to ask if I want to join them, I shake my head, and his head tilts. I raise my palm. He gets the hint that I don't want to join them, simply enjoy the sun. Standing, I pick up a bottle of water plus my towel and walk down to the beach.

At least no uninvited guests can get past our security here. I drink and walk the shoreline, calmed by the waves while picking up shells and tossing them into the water. When I'm far enough away from the bacchanalia at the mansion, I lay my towel onto the sand, sit, and stare out at the waves.

Where is Jenna?

Why did she refuse today's delivery?

How much longer can I derail her plan to get a divorce?

These questions play on a loop.

From behind me, a woman says, "It's beautiful out here."

I must be imagining things—the voice sounds just like my wife's. I check the bottle to confirm I'm only drinking water. Without moving a muscle, I reply, "It is."

"But not as gorgeous as you."

It's her. Dropping my water, I leap to my feet and spin around. Jenna stands on the beach about ten feet away, wearing a dress blowing in the breeze and holding her sandals. Her loose hair blows free. I've never seen a more unbelievable sight.

"Jenna?" My eyes dart to confirm she isn't flanked by a process server, and that her hands are devoid of any papers. Nope, only her sandals. Elias stands behind her several feet, awaiting instructions from me.

"Hi, Bennett." Her cheeks pinken. Her throat moves as if she's trying to swallow.

I cross my arms across my naked chest and widen my stance. I nod at Elias to give us some space. My gaze shifts above him, to where the entire band watches what's happening on the beach. They've let her come to me but are watching to make sure I'm okay with it. I revel in their solidarity.

"How did you find me?"

She tucks some flyaway hair behind her ear. "I, well, after I found out the band's in Nice, I used Google translate to find out where you were staying. The locals are very excited that UC is here."

With a hint of disgust at the lax security, which could've welcomed her process server, I say, "Guess we should make sure our whereabouts are more locked down."

"I'm glad I found you. My backup plan was to scalp tickets to the concert tomorrow."

Does she mean this? Why is she here? *I want to wrap her in my arms so bad.* "How are you doing?"

"I've been better. You know, Ma passed away, my clinics were accused of being a front for prostitution, and I picked a massive fight with my husband."

My arms drop my sides and I will them to remain motionless, even though they're itching to hold her. "I heard he exposed the people behind the accusations and they're going to jail."

She takes a few steps closer to me. "Yeah, he's pretty awesome that way."

I lick my lips, aching to taste her again. "I also heard your husband has a new song on the radio he wrote for you. Even sang a part of it *a capella.*"

She inches closer. "It was breathtaking."

"I also heard he sends you flowers every day."

"Because that's the type of man he is. Even if he can't be nearby, he always wants me to know he loves me."

At my sides, my hands fist. "Yet, you're divorcing him."

"Actually, that's why I flew halfway across the globe." Her head tilts. "No, not that far. Nine hours." She shakes her head. "Listen, Bennett, I was wrong. Ma's passing left me so very angry. At God. At the doctors. At nature. I took it all out on you." She swipes her cheeks.

She's saying the words I've needed to hear ever since Faith died. I want to tell her I forgive her. My mouth drops open, yet the words don't come. I loved her with my whole heart, and it still wasn't good enough to keep her at my side and let me comfort her. I close my mouth.

Jenna either doesn't see my indecision or refuses to believe we're over. In any event, she takes a couple more steps toward me, then stops. "I was wrong. I wanted Ma to live and railed at the universe for taking her away. And by 'universe,' I mean you. I blamed you. Shut you out. Pushed you away. You didn't deserve this, especially when you were being nothing but amazing. You were being you, Bennett."

She runs the final distance to me, landing with a thud against my chest. I long to wrap her in my arms, yet my limbs remain lifeless at my sides.

"I'm not going through with it, Bennett. I called off my attorney. When I went to her initially, I was out of my mind with grief. Still am. But you make everything easier. Truth is, I want you in my life, as my husband, forever."

I need more. "Because I got rid of the women saying your clinics are a prostitution front?"

"No." She takes a step backward, easy since I never hugged her. "Well, thank you for that, but that's not it."

"Then why?" I'm not sure what I need her to say, but I haven't heard it yet. Despite what my body begs me to do.

She tucks her loose hair behind her ear, but it springs free again. "Why?" She swallows. "Because you sang that song to me *a capella*, and only I know what that truly means. Because you're the last person I want to speak with at night and the very first one I want to hear in the morning." She offers a wan smile. "Whether it's true morning or rock star morning." She continues, "I want to be a buffer between you and your mother because you never deserved the way she treats you. You're such a good man, Bennett. I'm sorry I kicked you out of my life. I never want to be the cause of you being abandoned again."

I grasp everything she's said. However, my arms remain motionless. "Thank you."

She looks all around the beach and blurts, "Because I love you with my whole heart. And more."

This. This is what I needed to hear. "Thank fuck."

All resistance drains out of my body, and I drag my wife to me, savoring how she fits like a missing puzzle piece. Against my chest, her entire being shakes. I kiss the top of her head, then look down the beach to see Elias walking away. Tipping my head backward, I look up to the pool area. All of my friends give me their thumbs up, and return to partying. Luke's the last one to turn, lifting his beer high in the air.

My attention zeroes in on my wife. I bring my fingers under her chin and lift her head to mine. Gray eyes, reminiscent of Faith's, are filled with tears. "Hey, don't cry. I'm right here, and I'm not going anywhere."

Her pink tongue darts out. "I was awful to you. I don't deserve you."

"Sweetheart," I step back because I want her to hear me. My hands lift to her shoulders and press down, needing her to be calm and hear what I'm saying. "I love you with everything I am. I've been miserable without you, hoping in vain to see you around corners, and not sleeping. I know grief drove you to do this horrible thing, but it can be undone."

"The divorce papers aren't being filed, Bennett. Never." She takes a deep breath. "I burned them."

Her words give me the last push I needed. "It's just you and me against the world from now on. Faith raised a fantastic daughter, and now I have the opportunity to be at your side since she can't. I'm here, holding you, because you make my world sing." I smile. "You fixed my groin pull, but you did much more than that. You gave me love, excitement, and friends."

"Friends?"

"Luke. The band. You made me realize they are not simply my coworkers, but my *friends*. I've let them in, and it's awesome. But I wasn't complete, because you weren't here."

"I'm here now," she breathes.

I don't know which one of us makes the first move. Whether I pull her body to mine, or she presses against me, it doesn't matter. The next thing I know we're kissing as if our lives depend on it. Which they sort of do. Without her, I cannot function. Without me, I pray she's learned she can't either. Together, though, the whole world sings the most amazing song ever created.

My hands roam up and down her body, ending on her ass and tugging her tighter against my already rock-hard body. I trail kisses down her neck, which she extends. A groan starts low in my belly.

"I want to make love to you for hours," I whisper.

"I want that too." Her hand skims across my bare chest, her fingers following the ridges of my muscles, and ending at my bathing suit's waistband.

I take a moment to glance around, to figure out where I can lay her down and have my way with her. All I see is the beach. I bring my lips to her ear. "While I don't care about getting naked with you right here, right now, I don't want to have sand between me and those leather pants Nese has me wearing onstage."

"Huh?" She looks up at me. Her eyes are filled with trust. Love. And desire—so much desire.

My fingers clutch her delightful ass. "Unless you want sand in every single one of your unmentionables, I think we should take this to my room."

Recognition blooms. "Oh. Can I have one more kiss before we make that long trek?"

"Sweetheart, you can have as many as you can handle, and then some." I close the distance between us and score her lips with my tongue.

Her arms encircle my neck as she returns my ardent kisses. Bending down, I lift her off her feet. "Wrap those gorgeous legs around my waist." As soon as she complies, I abandon my solitary spot on the beach and stride toward the house.

She breaks our kiss, but I don't break my stride. "Your groin pull?"

"I'm over it. I promise to show you just how much."

Jenna's smile can be seen from space. "I can't wait."

Me neither. As I cross the lawn, I hear clapping. Both of our heads swivel to the side, where everyone claps. Well, all the guys do. Some of the groupies appear pissed, but I don't care. My friends know what this reunion means to me.

Jenna faceplants into my chest, which causes me to laugh. I buss her cheek. "It's been too long, I need to fuck you so bad. The guys can wait." In response, her forehead bounces against me. I wink at my friends and continue toward the door, their catcalls and cheers our soundtrack.

In what feels like hours, although was merely minutes, we're inside the house and I'm climbing the stairs to my room. Using my foot, I kick the door shut. "I finally have my *wife* alone." She slides down my body.

"You do. And you're not even out of breath. I'm impressed."

"Believe me, Sweetheart, we're both going to be panting in no time. Strip."

Her sandals hit the tiled floor. She turns her back to me. "Can you unzip me?"

My already hard cock begs to be released from my bathing suit. "With more pleasure than you'll ever know."

A slow and steady zip rings throughout the bedroom. I kiss the crook between her neck and shoulder as the dress falls to the floor. Before she can even take a breath, I unclasp her light blue bra and toss it aside.

Standing before me in only light blue panties, she turns to face me once more. "I love you, Bennett. I'm sorry for what I put you through. How can I make it up to you?"

"Tell me you love me every day for the rest of our lives." My left hand, complete with the chunky wedding ring that I've never taken off, grasps one side of her panties. "Fill my world with happiness." My right hand does the same on the opposite side. "Give me babies one day." I haul them down her legs.

"Yes, Bennett. Yes to all those things." Her fingers touch the top of my waistband. When I don't move, she pulls them down and licks her lips.

I can tell she wants to give me a blow job, but that's not what we need in this moment. "No."

Her hand flies in front of her face. "No?"

I shake my head. "Well, yes, but later. This time, I want to make love with you like a husband does with his wife. You can take care of him later." I push her locks behind her ears. "But there's one thing I have to do before then."

"What on earth?"

I walk away and open the top drawer of my dresser, pulling out my most prized possession. I return to her and drop to my knee. Her hand covers her mouth. "Jenna. Wife. My biggest fan. I asked you this before when I didn't have a ring. Then we got married before our families and friends." I flip open the ring box, holding her engagement and wedding rings. "Now, I want to put these on you and make love with you wearing only them. I love you. Will you be mine, forever?"

With a slight tremor, she extends her left hand. "Yes! A thousand times yes!"

I slide the rings back on her finger where they belong. I kiss the diamond as I rise to my full height. "Now, I want to bury myself inside you so deep you'll never forget these vows."

"Never."

She brings her head to mine, and we kiss and lick and stroke and caress and nibble and thrust and climax. And, like I promised her earlier, pant.

So much panting.

Epilogue - Jenna

"Yes!" I scream my completion as my husband throws his head back and roars his. My body ripples with pleasure streaming through every cell and welcomes Bennett's weight as he collapses on top of me. My hand runs down his sweat-slicked back. How could I ever have thought to walk away from this wonderful man?

He kisses my cheek as he rolls onto his side, taking my limp body with his. "Each time, it gets better." He pushes my wet hair off my face. "How is it possible?"

With a slow blink, I reply, "I honestly have no idea. At this rate, can you imagine our ten-year anniversary?"

He dons a wolfish smile. "I can't wait." His luscious lips cover mine, molding them to his will. "Or twenty. Or thirty." He pulls back and looks deeply into my eyes. "Sixty won't be enough. It'll never be enough for me."

I believe every word he says, because I feel the same way about him.

Church bells outside our hotel room peel. "I never imagined visiting Rome. Ma always dreamed of coming here. She told me we'd visit the Trevi Fountain and the Vatican, get blessed by the Pope, see the ruins, eat all the food, and gorge on gelato." I smooth a sheet over our sweat-slicked bodies. "I'm glad to be able to do this in her honor."

He pulls me into his embrace. "I'm sorry the Pope is away, but somehow I'm not sure how he'd take to giving me a blessing." Bennett chuckles. "Wouldn't want to get struck down by lightning in a fancy church."

I stretch like a cat, entwining my fingers behind his head and pulling him down to me. When we break apart, I tease, "Then you'd be immortalized as a statue and people would pray to you."

"I'd be sure to grant them all their dirty fantasies." He pulls back. "People pray for them, don't they?"

My head shakes. "I honestly don't know. But if you were the one reviewing their prayers, I'd bet they would." I rest my head on his chest. Melancholy, my perennial friend, rears her ugly head. If only I could've taken Ma here. She would've loved it.

My husband's palm rests on the middle of my back, as if he knows I'm going into a dark place. "You know," he begins. "She's here with you, experiencing everything. You carry Faith in here." He moves his palm over my heart. Which, convenient for him, is right above my boob.

"I hope so." I smile as his thumb caresses the flesh under his palm. "I think you said that because you wanted to cop a feel."

He smirks. "Guilty." He skims over my nipple, then settles me next to his body. "Right now, though, I want to offer you strength. And you're lucky . . ."

When he doesn't continue, I prompt, "How?"

"Your mother loved you. She even wrote you a last note with all of her wisdom. She was super proud of you, with your physical therapy clinics. She told me so."

"She really was my biggest cheerleader." His comment brings me to yet another conundrum. My return flight is scheduled for tomorrow, and I don't want to leave my husband. However, my business requires my attention. How can I be so happy, so miserable, and so torn all at once? I need to return to Aroostook and focus on my clinics. Which only ushers in more depression.

"At the risk of ruining our perfect moment—"

"Don't." His lips kiss my nose. "We'll figure it out."

I can't help myself. "My flight back is scheduled for tomorrow."

He rubs two fingers over his nose, a tic I've come to understand he does when he's thinking. "You can stay with me. UC has a plane and there's plenty of room. Let your seat on commercial go."

It sounds so easy when the suggestion pops out of his mouth. But he doesn't have a business that depends on him in the Hamptons. He's not in the process of building a third clinic and scouting out a fourth location, not to mention running two others. Although Court's been doing an amazing job while I've been here, in Europe, reconnecting with my husband.

"I can meet up with you in a couple of weeks. Where will you be then?"

A frown mars his gorgeous face. "I don't know where, but I can tell you I'll be miserable. The guys will try to cheer me up but won't be able to. All our fans will see my sorry ass performing without my heart. It'll be awful."

"Oh, come on. So long as you're rocking those black leather pants that Nese got for you. I doubt any of your *female* fans will even notice."

My teasing falls flat. "I'll know. What can I do to convince you to stay with me?"

"I have to focus on my business, the same way you have to tour with UC. It's what you do—and it's what I do."

"I guess so. But if I only have today, I better make sure you don't forget your husband while you're away." His lip ticks upward.

"I'll try to be as productive as possible and get back to you ASAP. Now that you got rid of both Lissa and Michelle, my job is a lot easier."

He kisses me with blatant sexual desire, which rouses what I thought was my dormant libido. I mean, he did give me three orgasms already. It's never enough with Bennett. Before we can get started, my phone pings with a text.

He breaks away from my lips long enough to order me, "Ignore it."

"What if it's Court?" I murmur between kisses, and roll over to grab my cell.

LUKE

Got a proposition for you.

I stare from the text to my husband. These two have been thicker than thieves lately, as Ma would say. What have they cooked up? "It's Luke."

One eyebrow shoots up. "Really? What does he have to say?"

I read the text. "What proposition, Bennett? What's going on?"

Both hands shoot upward. "Me? Why would I know anything?" He shoves the sheets down to our feet and sits up. "We better get moving. Don't want to make UC's manager wait."

I cross one foot over my ankle. "He didn't say he wanted to meet me."

His cheeks flush. I *knew* they were in on this—whatever *this* is—together. "Really? I thought he did."

He's so cute when he tries to lie. Thankfully, he's bad at it. "Rock Star, what is going on?"

In all his naked glory, he stands and drags me down the bed by my ankles, causing me to laugh. Over his shoulder, he asks, "Why don't you text him back and ask him where to meet?"

What are these two up to? I shake my head, text Luke, and join Bennett in the shower. An hour later, we meet up with the band's manager in the hotel's café.

"You both are glowing," Luke remarks.

"That's what marriage will do to you, friend," Bennett replies, followed by a wink. If I weren't sure I was the root cause of this scheming, I'd be proud of my husband for calling his manager "friend."

Luke and Bennett dive into a discussion about the Oscars, and the fact *Refocused Destiny* officially has been nominated for best song in a movie. I allow their conversation to go on around me. After the server delivers our cappuccinos, complete with artistic milk decorations on top, though, I dive into the heart of the matter. "All right Luke. What's this big proposition you two conceived without my input?"

Bennett snort laughs.

"Now, don't get so touchy," Luke jumps in. "I'm UC's manager, you know. When something bothers one of the band members, it's my job to make sure it gets resolved in such a way as to make everyone happy."

"By everyone, you really mean Bennett, Coop, Río, Pierce, and Tristan, right?"

"That's cute," Bennett pipes up. "Isn't it cute how she still calls 007 'Pierce'?"

My eyes slant toward my husband. I blow on my hot beverage and take a sip, allowing its delicious warmth to spread through my limbs. When neither speak up again, I address the manager. "Please continue. What's bothering UC that you think I can help with?"

Luke replaces his cup onto the saucer. "Actually, I was going to correct your initial statement. UC is more than only the performers. As you know, we have roadies, lighting, sound and music techs, security, stylists—"

My hand lands over Luke's. "I get it. Spill."

"Feisty." Bennett sits taller.

"Fine. I remember what you did for Jeb and the rest of the roadies when they were complaining about back pain."

"I gave them some exercises to do to strengthen their muscles."

"Right. But did you know that they now meet daily to run through your exercises?"

"I didn't know. That's great."

"It is. And it got me to thinking. I reached out to a few of my friends who are with other bands. Hunte, Cole Manchester, The Light Rail, you know, big names like these. Want to know what they all have in common?"

I have no idea. Great music? "What?"

As the moment of silence extends, my husband blurts, "Touring physical therapists!"

Both Luke and I turn to Bennett. Luke looks annoyed. Me? I'm shocked. Slowly, I respond, "I've heard of this for Broadway shows. Cirque du Soleil. Those sorts of physical performances."

"Hey," Bennett crosses his arms. "I'm very physical onstage." He leans closer to me. "Off stage, too. Right, Sweetheart?"

I don't have the bandwidth to deal with him right now, no matter how sexy he's being, so I address my comment to UC's manager. "What exactly are you saying?"

Luke cracks his knuckles and stares into my eyes. "I'm making you an offer, to be perfectly clear. How would you like to become UC's traveling physical therapist? You'd be responsible for the band, sure, but also for all the crew and roadies. We have a lot of those." He bumps fists with Bennett.

"A traveling—" I take a deep breath. "UC's traveling physical therapist?" *Could this work?*

Bennett lifts my hand to his lips. After pressing a gentle kiss in its center, he says, "You're already doing the job. You got me back to one hundred percent, but it looks as if Jeb and the roadies could use your services. Who knows what might happen next? Coop could hurt his fingers on a broken guitar string. Río," he pauses. "Who knows what our drummer could get himself into next? He's a wild card."

"You're not. Anymore," I address my husband. Despite the appeal of his offer, one truth wins. "However, I don't do therapy anymore."

Bennett points to himself. "Excuse me. What am I, chopped liver?"

I shrug. "You were a one-off."

"Did you hear that?" Bennett addresses Luke. "Sounded to me like I was her pity fuck. Did I hear her right?"

Luke bangs on his ear. "I swear I heard something like that, but I must be mistaken."

Four eyes glare at me. My husband breaks the silence. "You were a fantastic therapist to me. I *know* Jeb says the same thing. You even told me when we were working together how much you missed working with patients. This job could give you the best of both worlds. You'll know your patients and see their healing progress, like you did with me."

My heart screams for me to take this position, yet my persistent brain tramples my hope. "I have two clinics back home and another two on the way. I can't leave them."

Luke replies this time. "If you were back in Aroostook, would you visit both clinics daily while overseeing the renovations of the third and preparing the fourth?"

"What? No way. I can't do all that."

"Exactly. You have contractors and employees to do all that for you, right?"

"Well, Court looks out for all my businesses while I'm away."

"She does," Bennett agrees. "She's doing a great job. Seems to me that she handles the day-to-day while you do the bigger things, like dealing with the whole Black Widow bullshit."

"Hayden helped me out." UC's PR team was invaluable. "And Court."

"It takes a village," the manager notes. "Like the band. I couldn't do this without fantastic help."

If I take this job, I can stay with Bennett on the road. When he has a break from touring, we could go home, allowing me time to handle things in person. Ma's note flits through my mind, begging me to let go of some control in order to live my best life. Is this what she meant? Would she support this change?

Bennett doesn't let me stew for too long before sweetening the pot, so to speak. "Imagine it, Sweetheart. We can be together all the time. Visit new cities. Experience places like Graceland." His eyebrows waggle. "Make love on balconies."

I swat his broad chest. "Bennett!"

"What? I toned it down for our manager's virgin ears."

My forehead rests in my hand. Can I really do this? Leave my life behind and join a world-famous band—one that so happens to have my husband as its front man? Hell yes! Only if Court agrees, though. I stand. "I need to call Court. If she's on board with your crazy idea, then I am too."

Before I can take another step, Bennett leaps to his feet and kisses me as if we weren't surrounded by people. Against my ear, he whispers, "You've made me so happy. I love you, Jenna Hardy."

I kiss him once more. "Love you back." I rush out of the café and into our room. This call needs my full attention, and whenever I'm around Bennett, that's not possible.

I organize my scrambled thoughts, FaceTime Court, and explain the situation to her. "I don't know, Jenna." Her head tilts. "I can't figure out why on earth you want to spend all your time with the man of your dreams, traveling the world, and not be here in boring Aroostook fighting tooth and nail to build your physical therapy empire. What could be the draw?"

My smile widens. "Are you sure? Do you really want to become the general manager of all the clinics? Deal with those headaches?" I take a breath. "You'll get a raise, you know."

"Honey, I've been dealing with a lot of this ever since Bennett swept you off your feet. If I'm honest, I truly enjoy handling the challenges with the clinics and therapists. Besides, it's not like you're going to be off the grid, we'll only have to deal with time zones. Promise me you'll check in once a week, and I say it's a done deal."

I squeal. "Really? You'd be willing to do this for me?"

"And for me. Not to mention I'm not one to deny true love."

True love. This foreign concept does apply to me and Bennett. I know his flaws and he certainly knows mine, but together we click.

"Court, I owe you everything. Whatever you want, it's yours."

She giggles. "How about the hunky contractor doing the renovations on the new clinic?"

My head bobs and I blink. "If I have anything to say about it, he's yours."

Court peers into the camera. "All I ever wanted is for you to be happy. I can see you're radiating happiness. Don't worry about the business, we'll figure it all out. To be honest, I got a lead on a fifth clinic, if you're interested. I'll send you the details later. But for now, go and become the best touring physical therapist ever."

I reach my arms forward. "This is me hugging you." I blow her a kiss as I disconnect the call.

Wrapped in an exciting blanket of love and possibilities, I text Kara to tell her my news. Her response is filled with heart emojis.

How can this be my next chapter?!

I return to the café, where Bennett and Luke appear deep in conversation and not filled with upbeat optimism like me. "I'm back." I smile to lighten the mood.

Four rather worried eyes are directed at me. Luke asks, "What's the verdict?"

I look between the two men. One standing a stocky six feet with shoulder-length light brown hair, while the other is two inches taller, sporting a trendy hairstyle a couple of shades lighter, a man who woman everywhere worship. Yet only I get to share his bed every night—along with a love for the ages.

I smile. "Yes. A thousand times yes!"

Bennett wraps me in his arms, swaying from side to side. "You've made me the happiest man on earth, Sweetheart." He sits and tugs me onto his lap, as if any distance between us is unacceptable.

"Her answer makes up for your missed call." Luke's eyes dart to the table, where Bennett's cell rests.

At my perplexed look, my husband picks up his phone, which shows "Mom" as his last missed call. More like declined.

"Oh." What more can I say?

Luke says, "I met her, Jenna. Believe me when I say however Bennett's described her doesn't do her justice. I'm grateful she gave birth to B, but she isn't someone you want in your lives. Especially as you carve out your niche as a newly married couple."

Not knowing what else to do, I give my husband a hug. Someday, maybe, I'll be able to bring them together, but if what Luke describes is accurate—and given what my own limited interaction with her tells me—perhaps not. My Bennett's had a rough start. At this moment, I again resolve to be the best wife and family to the amazing man in my arms. Who is surrounded by friends—a true found family—on and off the stage. I rest my head against my husband's shoulder.

Luke's phone rings. "Geez," he remarks. "Haven't we had enough calls today? Excuse me." Grinning, he answers the phone. "Hey, Hayden."

I wave to UC's PR guru, even though she can't see me. She really helped me with At Your Service PT. She's fantastic.

My husband kisses me and I forget all about the PR team. Until Luke raises his voice. "Wait, what?"

Bennett and I exchange glances.

"Río is *where?*"

At the drummer's name, Bennett's smirks. "Leave it to Río to cause a ruckus."

"I'll be right there." He drops the phone onto the table. In a dejected voice, Luke asks, "Are we all good here?"

Bennett squeezes me. "We're more than good."

"Great. Because now I have to bail Río out of jail."

Want to experience Bennett and Jenna's first meeting? Download this

FREE Bonus Epilogue today at https://BookHip.com/MKNJAAS ~ and enjoy!!

I bet you can guess which band member is up next in the Untamed Coaster series?! Keep your eyes peeled for Animal Beats, about the always "entertaining" drummer, Río!

And stay up-to-date with me by joining my newsletter, https://geni. us/UCNewsletter!

A Note from Arell

Dear Fabulous Reader,

Thank you so much for reading MIC DROP, the final installment in the Passionate Beats trilogy, part of the Untamed Coaster series!

Words cannot express how I feel about the Passionate Beats trilogy coming to a close. I hope you laughed and cried and screamed and are left brimming with love for Bennett and Jenna. These two ripped out my heart and then mended it in their own perfect way. I feel so honored to share their epic love story with you!

As usual, some of my own life experiences appear in MIC DROP ~

- Nice, France. I've been lucky enough to visit there twice, and spent an idyllic week near there post-graduation. If you ever have the chance to visit, I have one word for you: GO!
- Unfortunately, I've had to clean out more than my share of houses after a loved one passed. No one ever left a

message like Faith did to Jenna, but I'm loving the idea.
That way I'd get the last word!

- I do have a confession to make. I've never seen *The Godfather* movies! Big Mike, though, made writing these references very easy!

Please stay in touch! Subscribe to my newsletter at https://geni.us/UCNewsletter **or join Arell's Angels, my reader group on Facebook at** http://www.facebook.com/groups/arellsangels **~ or both!!**

If you have any questions, feel free to email me at http://Arell@ArellRivers.com. I love chatting with readers!

Thanks for devoting your precious time to Mᴵᴄ Dʀᴏᴘ ~ and the entire Passionate Beats trilogy. I hope you enjoyed the Untamed Coaster ride that is Bennett and Jenna!

All my love,
Arell

Gratitude

Mɪᴄ Dʀᴏᴘ couldn't have happened without so many awesome people! First and foremost, this book is dedicated to Taylor Delong, my author bestie! She graciously agreed to beta read the entire Passionate Beats trilogy and gave so many helpful comments. If you haven't already, please pick up one of her books!

As usual, big thanks to my at-home support system ~ my husband, Big Mike (plus our two cats Luna and Loki, with their unique brand of support!), and my Mom. They're small in number but off-the-charts in cheerleading abilities!

Mɪᴄ Dʀᴏᴘ wouldn't be what it is without the fantastic group of editors I've assembled on my team. My plot coach, Theresa Leigh of The Fairy Plot Mother, developmental editor Trenda Lundin of It's Your Story Content Editing, editor Nancy Smay of Evident Ink, and proofreader Roxanne Blouin, all really helped bring this story to life. In addition, Dar Albert of Wicked Smart Designs sealed the deal with this truly delicious cover! Yum!!

I would like to give a shout out to Shauna and Becca of The Author Agency. They have provided so much guidance in how to best package this trilogy ~ I couldn't have done this without them!

To my fantastic alpha reader Taylor Delong - you rock! Thanks for all your comments that truly helped Jenna and Bennett soar.

Big love to my ARC Team!! Each one of you warms my heart with how much enthusiasm you have for all of my projects, including this new band, Untamed Coaster. Thank you for taking the time to read, review, and share EXTENDED BRIDGE!!!

My Facebook reader's group, Arell's Angels, is my go-to place to hang out, check out hot photos, and simply just vent! Shout out to "Arell's Insiders" who post daily and keep the group rockin' with your wit and devotion. To all the Angels who participate in our Hotties of the Month, daily games, my crazy Facebook Lives, sneak peeks, collaborative stories, and author takeover Sundays ∼ you make this journey so worthwhile! And there's always room for more angels!

I'm so lucky to have met, in person and virtually, so many wonderful authors who are so giving of their advice, support, and friendship. To my fellow Kissed by Romance Authors, Taylor Delong, Libby Waterford, Mary E. Montgomery, and Nicole Locke, you are the reason! 🖤 Thanks, too, for all the support from Claire Marti, Darby Fox, Sophia Henry, Anne Lange, and Lilly Wilde!

To everyone who picks up this book, I hope you're "Strapped, locked, and loaded!" If you enjoyed MIC DROP and the entire Passionate Beats trilogy, please share it with your friends and write a review on Amazon, https://geni.us/UntamedCoaster3, and/or Good-Reads, https://geni.us/UC3GR. The next band member to get his own book is the drummer ∼ you'll be seeing Río in ANIMAL BEATS!

Blessings,
Arell

About the Author

For as long as Arell Rivers can remember, she has been lost in a book. During her senior year in college, she picked up a romance novel ... and instantly was hooked!

Arell started writing her first book because the characters were screaming at her to do so. The story came out in her dreams and attacked her in the shower, so she took to the computer to shut them up. But they kept talking.

Born and raised in New Jersey, Arell has what some may call a "checkered past." Prior to discovering her passion for writing romance, she practiced law, was a wedding and event planner and even dabbled in marketing. Arell lives with two adorable cats and a very supportive husband who doesn't care that the bed isn't made or dinner isn't on the table. When not in her writing cave, Arell is found cooking in the InstantPot, working out with Shaun T, or hitting the beach.

Want to keep up to date with Arell? Sign up for her newsletter at https://geni.us/SinsNewsletter. All new subscribers receive a special gift!

Also by Arell Rivers

Untamed Coaster

A found family/he falls first series following the rock band of the same name

Sinful Beats, http://geni.us/UntamedCoaster1 (Quinn and Callum) (crossover from Sins of the Fathers)

Opening Strains, https://geni.us/UntamedCoaster2, Passionate Beats trilogy (Bennett and Jenna, book 1)

Extended Bridge, Passionate Beats trilogy (Bennett and Jenna, book 2)

Mic Drop, http://geni.us/UntamedCoaster4, Passionate Beats trilogy (Bennett and Jenna, book 3)

Animal Beats (Río and Hayden) - up next!

Sins of the Fathers

A billionaire series about the children of 3 notorious businessmen

Vice, http://geni.us/Sins1 (short story, originally published as "Tinsel Bomb" in the 2021 anthology Tinsel and Tatas)

Anger, http://geni.us/Sins2 (Theo and Amelia)

Pride, http://geni.us/Sins3 (Xander and Madison)

Idle, https://geni.us//Sins4 (Paige and Jesse)

The Hunte Family Series

An enemies-to-lovers series about the dynasty created by rocker Braxon Hunte

Out of the Red, https://geni.us/OOTR (Brax and Sara, set in the mid 90s)

Out of the Shadow, https://geni.us/hunte2 (King and Angie)

Out of the Gold, https://geni.us/OOTR (Melody and Chase)

Out of the Blue, http://geni.us/Hunte4 (Trent and Cordelia)

Out of the Box, http://geni.us/OutoftheBox (box set of books 1-4 plus a bonus novella)

The Hold Series

A second chances series about rock star Cole Manchester, his publicist Rose Morgan, and their friends

Hold On, https://geni.us/HoldOn (prequel novella for Cole and Rose)

No One to Hold, https://geni.us/NOTH (Cole and Rose trilogy, book 1)

Hard to Hold, https://geni.us/HtoH (Cole and Rose trilogy, book 2)

To Have and to Hold, https://geni.us/THTH (Cole and Rose trilogy, book 3)

Take Hold of Me, https://geni.us/THOM (Wills and Emilie)

Hold Still, https://geni.us/GDwdlls (Ozzy and McKenna)

Hold Me, http://geni.us/HoldMeBoxSet (box set of books 1-3, 6, plus a bonus novella)

Kissed by Romance collections

Anthologies written by the Kissed by Romance authors: Taylor Delong, Nicole Locke, M.E. Montgomery, Libby Waterford ~ and me!

Steamy Shorts, https://books2read.com/SteamyShorts (4 quick reads guaranteed to bring the heat / my story is OUT OF THE SAND in the Hunte Family series world)

A Kiss at Midnight, https://books2read.com/AKAM (5 interconnected novellas about New Year's Eve at the Grandview Lodge / my story is OUT OF THE JADE in the Hunte Family series world)

Connect with Arell

- Subscribe to Arell's newsletter at https://geni.us/UCNewsletter
- Join Arell's Facebook Group, "Arell's Angels" at http://www.facebook.com/groups/ArellsAngels
- Like Arell's Facebook Page, http://www.Facebook.com/ArellRivers
- Follow Arell on Instagram, http://www.Instagram.com/AuthorArell
- Hang out with Arell on Amazon at https://geni.us/ArellRivers
- Check out Arell on Goodreads, https://geni.us/ARGoodReads
- Follow Arell on BookBub, https://geni.us/BookBubFollow
- Head over to Arell's website at http://www.ArellRivers.com
- Email Arell at http://Arell@ArellRivers.com

Sinful Beats

Want all the tea about the rockumentary that showcased Untamed Coaster's return to the top? Read about the band, as experienced through the eyes of the movie's producer and one of their biggest fans from Scotland!

Enjoy the first chapter of SINFUL BEATS, Book #1 in the Untamed Coaster series!

The line between secrets and sins can be razor thin...

Quinn

I want to make movies that document drama. But in my personal life? I have zero tolerance for it.

So, I intend to keep my gnarly family history to myself. Forever.

Besides, my dream job—making a rockumentary about Untamed Coaster—just fell into my lap and nothing is going to distract me.

Not even my alarmingly sexy Scottish neighbor...

Callum

Gold diggers are everywhere. I learned this lesson the hard way and now keep my family's fortunes hidden.

So, love and romance aren't for me. Not anymore.

My brand and upcoming launch party are what matter now. I can't let anything ruin them.

Not even my very inconvenient (and damn near overwhelming) attraction to the girl next door.

As our relationship intensifies and the launch approaches, I have to divulge my truths. But it's never the right time. When the beats leading up to discovery run out, our pasts collide in a shocking way.

Chapter 1 - Quinn

River "Río" Sullivan points his drumstick at Pierce DeLuca. "You missed your intro, 007."

The normally reticent bassist grumbles, "I was waiting for Coop's riff."

"Well, the keys should've been playing before me." The guitarist, whose given name is Cooper O'Shea, turns toward the newest member of the band, Tristan Lambert. The keyboardist lifts his hands as if in surrender.

I slam my eyes shut. How on earth will I ever complete my documentary in thirty days if these guys can't get it together? This gig will make or break them. My eyes fling open. *Gig?* I've been hanging with Untamed Coaster for too long.

They need a reset, and I need some usable footage. Abandoning my role as director, I ask, "Why don't you try something different?"

My question brings ten eyes to me, causing me to stand straighter. I tuck my hair behind my ear and continue, "How about pretending like you're about to take the stage at the Moray Distillery launch party. How does that go?"

The wall of rockers standing before me are members of one of the most famous bands on earth, but they've lost their mojo. Rather, their keyboardist, may he rest in peace. Hence the reason for my being with them over the past five months. At least we relocated from LA to my adopted hometown for this last month in order to better prepare for the party. That's what Luke Allen, their manager, told them. He wasn't about to say he hoped the change of scenery would inspire them. Or at least turn them into a functioning band again.

"I guess we could try it," Bennett Hardy replies, the group's lead singer and from what I've learned over the past months of shooting, its alpha. "Can't be any worse than the shit we've been playing."

Men. They have some way of communicating with each other. One by one, the band places their instruments onto their stands— River pockets his sticks and Tristan steps away from the keyboard, sinking his hands into his pockets. He's the one to whom my heart reaches out the most. The newcomer. The very talented musician who was tapped to take Darren Hilliard's place following his sudden death.

Poor guy. He's super talented and is trying to fit into the band, but it's hard given they've been playing together for a decade and were friends for many more years before then. *I can sympathize.* I spent my entire life longing to be part of the Hansen family and now they've begrudgingly acknowledged me as one of them, it's awkward to say the least. I met everyone—except Daddy's other wife—at Paige and Jesse's wedding reception, yet felt like an outsider. Of course, the couple of the hour were amazing to me, like usual. The rest seemed nice enough, but I wasn't welcomed with open arms. Or at all. Like Tristan, here with the band.

I snap myself out of my own family's drama when the guys congregate off to one side. Ensuring the cameras are capturing this moment, I direct, "Go on. Do the pre-show ritual you do before heading out to the stage." I have no idea what this ritual could be, but all bands have one. Or so my research indicates.

The four original members of Untamed Coaster glance among themselves. Shrugging, Bennett says, "Sure. Why not." His tenor voice is pure gold, making women faint. Other women, that is. Not me. Although I work in the industry, I have zero desire ever to be linked with such a high-profile guy. Spent my life forced to the sidelines of the spotlight cast by my top-secret father, thank you very much.

All the guys raise their fists into the air, with Tristan last to the party. The lead singer locks his gaze with each of them. "Strapped, locked, and loaded, are you ready to roll with Untamed Coaster?" A collective whoop goes up from the four original band members. They nod at each other and walk toward their instruments. Tristan appears dumbfounded, then takes a step toward his keyboard.

I clear my throat. "Guys, that was cool." The band stops and turns toward me. I can play this in one of two ways, either calling them out on Tristan's behalf or pleading ignorance. I decide to go with the latter. "Where did you get the saying?"

Río taps his drumsticks on his thigh. "When we were working at the theme park, Bennett said it before every ride was sent off."

It's well known that the original members of the band met when they worked at an amusement park, on a rollercoaster called Untamed Coaster. Hence their name—UC for short. "And the raised fist beforehand?"

"A raised fist was our signal to Bennett that everyone was safely in their seats," their guitarist replies.

I study Tristan, who absorbs their responses and does a mini-fist bump into the air. At least he now knows this ritual and the reason behind it. "I love it. And I bet your fans will appreciate this inside scoop. Would you mind doing it again, and this time I promise not to ruin the shot by keeping my mouth shut." I offer a grin.

The guys return to the pretend backstage area, and I count them off. Bennett takes a deep breath and glances at every person in the group, Tristan included. One by one, their fists go into the air. With the first genuine smile I've seen on Bennett's face, he yells, "Strapped, locked, and loaded, are you ready to roll with Untamed Coaster?" This time, the whoop is louder, followed by something new —clapping.

They approach their instruments, followed by the sound of strumming and pounding and hitting the keys. Bennett runs a couple of scales to warm up his voice again. 007 strums his bass and suggests, "Let's play 'Crushing Blow.'"

Tension fills the room as all other discordant noises cease. They haven't played this song since I've been with them. It's the band's last number one before they lost Darren who, I've learned, wrote almost all of its lyrics and melody.

Bennett's fingers tighten around the microphone to the point they turn white. I hold my breath, waiting for the group's response. After a minute, the singer pulls the microphone off its stand. "Good idea. We need to practice this one." He takes a big breath. "Let's do it."

I sag as air enters my body again. They're professionals. They know they have to get it together. Plus, I'm getting this all down on film for the rockumentary, which will provide great footage. My first film ever. I went to school to make documentaries, and I'm finally getting to do one. My time as a director over at *Renovation TV* was fun, but reality shows aren't my passion. Too much drama. Lies. Secrets. Putting together a coherent film about a slice of life jazzes me. It's what I was born to do.

The music starts and I pause from taking notes, instead enjoying how these guys play together. If I wasn't looking at them, I would swear someone was playing their song off the radio, it sounds so good. Tristan's fingers play like Darren's did. It doesn't seem to matter the band hasn't played this song in a year.

Not that I'm an Untamed Coaster fan. But I did my homework and listened to way too many hours of their tracks so I would be familiar with my subjects. Have to admit, I've come to enjoy many of their songs, but "Crushing Blow" is my favorite.

When Barrett joins the song with his signature sound, I stop examining every single nuance. I'm transformed into a fan, honored to get a private performance of a song that's been dormant while the band found their new footing. My head bobs in time with the beat being kept by Río on the drums when an unusual couple of notes are added into the familiar music. On keys, Tristan's fingers introduce a quick riff, adding a special something to the song. I smile.

None of the others do.

Forward momentum ceases as the band stops playing and stares at Tristan with open hostility. Pausing for a moment, he steps back from the keyboard.

"What was that?" Coop's question is more of an accusation.

Tristan looks down as if his keys played by themselves. I want to jump in and . . . say what? His new riff sounded good with the song, but it definitely wasn't how Darren played it. If there's one thing I've learned over the past months, it's Untamed Coaster is having a hard time moving on from his death. "Hard time" is an understatement. As the director of their documentary, though, I'm here to record and not influence. I bite the inside of my cheeks.

Río's sticks slam the cymbals. "Dude. That's *not* how it goes."

Tristan runs his palm over his five o'clock shadow, even though it's not even two. Without meeting the gaze of his new bandmates, he says, "I know. But I've always thought the song was missing a little something."

007 doesn't let this statement hang for a half-second. "It's missing Darren."

My body tenses. The new keyboardist is playing with fire, but I believe he's coming from a good place. He honestly wants to improve upon the song, even if it stayed at number one for three months straight. More pressing, though, is he's messing with Darren's finger-prints on their last masterpiece. And Darren's gone.

Silence. Tension ricochets throughout the room. Without moving my head, I confirm the cameras are capturing every second. This moment belongs to Untamed Coaster. As reimagined.

The lead singer exhales with an audible sound. "This is fucking hard. Coop, Río, 007, why don't you take a break? I want to talk with Tristan."

The other two nicknames I understood right away. Took me longer to figure out Pierce's—he was nicknamed 007 because Pierce Brosnan was playing James Bond when he was born. Without responding, they simply abandon their instruments and stalk out of the room.

Bennett catches my eye and sighs. He shakes his head and walks over to the new keyboardist. Stopping a few feet away from Tristan, the singer begins, "Buddy. I appreciate what you're trying to do by putting your stamp on the song. Feel free to add to anything else in our playlist. But 'Crushing Blow' is sacred. It's all Darren." He pauses. "007's best friend."

I suck in my breath as the puzzle pieces fall into place. Tristan continues, albeit in a lower tone. "I wasn't trying to—"

Bennett raises his hand. "I get it. It's tough coming into an already formed band. UC's been on top of the charts for the better part of a decade. We need to get back to playing our songs the way our fans know them. You can add notes to our new stuff." He gives a sideways glance toward the camera. "Once we have new material."

Tristan's shoulders deflate. "I get it. But if you would only listen to the slight change I was making—"

"No." The leader singer's interruption is forceful and final.

"'Crushing Blow' can't be changed. We haven't been able to play it until now, and we're only doing it for the fans who will expect to hear our last number one. Play it the way it was written. How Darren intended."

The keyboardist stares at the black and white keys. "I can do that."

"Good."

Tristan takes a step closer to the lead singer. Extends his hand. After a moment's pause, Bennett offers his and they shake. Then the vocalist leaves the room to retrieve the rest of the band. The keyboardist focuses his attention on sheet music.

I release my pent-up breath. Not an overwhelming truce, but a truce nonetheless. I make eye contact with the lead cameraman, who gives me a thumbs up. This will make for a great interlude in the documentary, so long as Untamed Coaster can get it together. The jury's still out on that.

As I'm looking over my notes, the door swings open again. The original four band members re-enter the room, slapping each other on the back. Tristan plays "charge" on the keyboard, and the band laughs. Perhaps this was a turning point?

Bennett takes his place behind the microphone. "Let's play 'Crushing Blow' again. Make Darren proud." River starts with the bass drum and soon the song is back in full force. Tristan doesn't deviate from the original this time.

When they finish the song, the music hangs in the air for a while. Their first full performance of their last number one was technically great, but something was missing. I think it was heart. How will they be able to recapture the magic? *Not my job.* I'm here to document how the band is taking strides to return to the stage following the death of one of their own. Not offer advice. Besides, what do I know about their craft anyway?

I'm wrung out and want this rehearsal to end, yet it continues. No wonder they used to be known as one of the most hard-working bands in the industry. They play 'Crushing Blow' at least two dozen more times, until the pain surrounding it isn't so, well, crushing.

At five o'clock, 007 takes off his bass and places it on the stand. "Guys. I'm done. If I have to strum another C major, I'm gonna puke."

Coop plucks the strap of his electric guitar. "I could be persuaded to go out for a beer."

Río jumps in. "Or ten." He performs a drum roll, ending with his sticks flipping around his fingers and pointing at the lead singer.

From the mic, Bennett laughs. "Sounds good." He cranes his neck toward Tristan. "You in?"

"You had me at beer." Looking pleased to have been invited, he shuts down the electric keyboard.

With an upbeat "See you tomorrow!" the five men plus their manager leave me and the camera crew in their quest to quench their thirst.

Today was the best day of filming we've had. Perhaps they'll actually be ready for the party in a month? Guess it doesn't matter either way. We've been hired to capture their progress, not to pass judgment.

I collect my notes while the crew stashes their equipment in the corner. Following our goodnights, I do the one thing I've been avoiding all day. Turn on my phone and check my texts. Mom. Jackie. Paige. Gary. Ignoring the rest, I click on his.

Glad you're back on this coast. Check in after you wrap today. I'll be waiting.

Gary took me under his wing and showed me the ropes before I headed out for the West Coast. Given my body's still on California time, I have enough energy to catch up with him tonight. I send him a quick thumbs up emoji.

Once we're all packed up, the crew and I exit the rehearsal building. Turning away from them, I walk the ten blocks to DocuStudios' offices. Wanting to be prepared for meeting my boss, I stop in my office and dump my notebooks onto the desk. I'm nothing but meticulous, as I'm often reminded by the crew. My notes have notes.

I review everything I've jotted down over the months, from our initial meeting to today's session where they finally were able to play their biggest hit. For their fans' sake, I hope they're able to get it together. Not to mention for Moray Distillery, which hired them to headline their launch party. No pressure, right? No wonder they snapped today.

Ready for the meeting, I enter Gary's office and walk toward a chair facing his desk, which is covered with piles and piles of papers. He's been in the industry for longer than I've been alive. He has great insights and offers even more amazing advice.

The grey-haired man stands. "Let's sit over there." He points toward an empty round table at the windows. Off to the side, his television plays an entertainment channel. Once we've settled in, he asks, "How's it going with Untamed Coaster?"

Softball. I open a red notebook, which is reserved for his wisdom. "Today was a breakthrough of sorts. They actually managed to play their last hit, the one Darren wrote."

He rolls a Mont Blanc pen on the top of the table. "That's good. Only took them five months. Other bands might never recover." His wise blue eyes study me. "How did it sound?"

"Good." I push my hair off my face as I relate the first time they tried. "They got better the more times they practiced it. The first time, though." I shake my head. "I'm glad our cameras captured it. I think this will be a pivotal point in the documentary."

"They mess up?"

"Not really. The new keyboardist added a few extra notes that caught everyone off guard." I remember Tristan's change. "It was only a couple of additions but stopped practice dead."

Gary leans forward, abandoning his pen on the table. "Did they fight?"

"Nothing so dramatic. His riff didn't land well, but they talked it out. Rather, Bennett and Tristan did, while the rest took a walk."

He presses back against his chair, stroking his mustache. "So Bennett is the true ringleader, as I suspected. The others fell in line once he hashed it out with Tristan, I take it?"

"Yeah."

He nods. "You've been working with them for months. What slant do you want to take with the rockumentary?"

This is the question I feared the most. I have no idea where I'm going with this, other than wanting to present the real Untamed Coaster. "I'm not sure yet. I certainly can show footage of them working together and getting used to the new dynamics." Remembering how Tristan tried to put his own slant on today's song, I wonder how long his full integration will truly take. A lot longer than the remaining month I'm filming, I fear.

"Give it a little more time, and I bet a theme will appear. Although, if things continue this way, it may be more of a crash and burn." His fingers play over his mustache. "Might play better in theaters."

I've had enough of explosions to last a lifetime. I don't want this group to be another casualty, even if they implode from within rather than from external forces. "I'm rooting for them."

Our conversation veers into lighting and blocking and locations as I pull up today's dailies sent to me by the camera crew. "I see what you mean about missing a spark. The music's there, just not the 'it' factor." He rolls his pen again. "I know you're there to document rather than direct, but what do you think about suggesting a slight change? The band's been rehearsing alone for months. Maybe things would loosen up if they got in front of a crowd? At a small venue?"

I consider his proposal. "Perhaps. While they sound pretty good,

I can tell they're not in the same groove as before. And if I can discern that, true fans will notice too." I shrug. "I'll suggest it to their manager tomorrow."

"Sounds good."

I close my red notebook. "We flew in late last night and I crashed for six hours before we met up today. My bed's calling me." On tired feet, I stand. "I'll keep in touch about the filming."

He chuckles. "Welcome to the life of a documentary director. You got this."

His faith in me settles in my bones. Never having a dependable father figure in my life, I eat up his approval. With a cheery wave, I scoot out of his office, gather my things, and hit the New York City streets. I inhale, soaking up the walking culture so anathema in LA. On my way home, I stop by my favorite Thai place and pick up some Pad Thai. Tonight, it's me, the TV, and takeout.

After collecting my mail, I walk into my apartment. Leaving my shoes at the door, I put my bag onto the dining room table and go into my bedroom to change into some leggings and a long tunic top. Wearing my pink bunny slippers, I return to the kitchen and retrieve a plate on which I pile a mess of the noodle dish. Using the chopsticks not as utensils but rather to secure my hair in a messy bun, I walk over to the sofa and plop down. What a day. Week. Month. Months, plural.

If only I had someone here as company. Ha! When has adding a man to the mix ever worked out for me or my family? Look at Ma. She and Daddy claimed to be in love, and even appeared to be that way when I was growing up. Sort of. When he showed up. He always chose to stay with his *other* family. Never stepped up and claimed us as his own too. It's a miracle I ever became friends with my sister Paige. Well, half-sister.

A smile plays around my lips as I remember attending her wedding before heading out to LA. I saw something between her and Jesse right from the start of "New York Views," even before they did. The world will never know of their more intimate moments caught by the "hidden" cameras during the taping. Even when they turned us down to take over the winner's show on *Renovation TV*, I never regretted deleting the sexy footage. It showed them happy and intimate and free, scenes not for strangers' eyes.

Ah, to be able to live a life so open like Paige and Jesse's, unfettered from lies surrounding me from day one. I learned from the start about the weight of misdirections, having been hidden from Daddy's other family until recently. From the world, however, is a different story. On this I agree with Daddy—unlike Ma, who fought with him over this topic constantly—I never saw an upside in bringing my connection to the Hansens public. Daddy told me not to tell others because if they knew, they'd look at me differently. Given his incarceration, I couldn't agree more.

I shovel some Pad Thai into my mouth, my gaze skimming to my plants. Since my "plant sitter" last came a week ago, they're droopy. *I get it.* Getting to my feet, I empty the contents of my water bottle into them and toss the empty into the recycle bin. Eating another few bites of my meal, I save the rest for later. Time for some R&R. I click into my digital library and select a wonderful movie by my absolute favorite director, Alfred Hitchcock. Don't care if the movie's in black and white. His stories carry the day.

Before I turn it on, I pour myself a glass of red zinfandel and take a sip, allowing the tingles to soothe my soul. In the living room, I hit play and *Rear Window* fills the screen. Soon I'm absorbed in Grace Kelly's performance. Before she became a princess, she was a fantastic actor.

All of a sudden, my sofa shakes. Bounces is more like it. As if a hurricane pulsates through its springs. Assuming sofas have springs. And I know exactly what is playing since I heard it over a dozen times today—"Crushing Blow." What the hell?

I stare at the floor, from where the offending noise emanates. Pausing the movie, I go into the closet and pick up a broom and bang it with three satisfying thuds. The music continues as loud as ever. In frustration, I groan and stomp. Considering I'm in my slippers, this makes no difference either.

Oblivious to my torment, Untamed Coaster continues wailing their massive hit. In my ear, I hear Tristan's added flourish, thinking he's right and it does add to the song. But whatever. Not my fight. However, this music madness *is*.

Not bothering to put on my shoes, I march down the stairs and stop outside the apartment below mine. Never been here before, but I don't care so long as the band at the center of my work life continues to blare.

I curl my hand into a fist and bang on the offending door—which I, myself, can barely hear over Bennett's voice, dammit.

I pound again and receive the same no response. Should I go down and buzz the intercom? If steam could billow out my ears, it would.

Deciding to give it one final try, I beat on the door for all my worth. I wait a minute and am rewarded when the door handle turns. Finally.

The music intensifies as the door opens. Standing before me is a ginger-headed man with a trimmed beard, wearing nothing but a towel around his waist. Water droplets run from his wet head down his chiseled chest. Bright blue eyes skim me from head to toe. With a deep Scottish accent, he holds up his wallet. "Where's my pizza?"

Great. Not only do I have to deal with Untamed Coaster literally moving me off my sofa, now I have a wet Jamie Frasier living beneath me. Where's my stone to time travel out of here?

Read the rest of Quinn and Callum's story on Amazon at https://geni.us/UntamedCoaster1!

www.ingramcontent.com/pod-product-compliance
Lightning Source LLC
Chambersburg PA
CBHW031559240626
47153CB00002B/570